YOU DON'T KNOW MY NAME

KRISTEN ORLANDO

SQUARE
FISH

Swoon Reads | NEW YORK

An imprint of Macmillan Publishing Group, LLC
175 Fifth Avenue, New York, NY 10010
fiercereads.com
swoonreads.com

Square Fish and the Square Fish logo are trademarks of Macmillan and
are used by Swoon Reads under license from Macmillan.

Our books may be purchased in bulk for promotional, educational, or business use.
Please contact your local bookseller or the Macmillan Corporate and Premium
Sales Department at (800) 221-7945 ext. 5442 or by e-mail at
MacmillanSpecialMarkets@macmillan.com.

Library of Congress Cataloging-in-Publication Data

Names: Orlando, Kristen, author.
Title: You don't know my name / Kristen Orlando.
Other titles: You do not know my name
Description: New York : Swoon Reads, [2016] | Summary:
Sixteen-year-old Reagan, raised to be an elite spy, is torn between honoring
her family's legacy and living a normal life with the boy she loves.
Identifiers: LCCN 2015050178 (print) | LCCN 2016024397 (ebook) | ISBN
978-1-250-14846-9 (paperback) | ISBN 9781250084125 (Ebook)
Subjects: | CYAC: Espionage—Fiction. | Family life—Fiction. | Love—Fiction. |
Rescues—Fiction. | Adventure and adventurers—Fiction.
Classification: LCC PZ7.1.O73 You 2016 (print) | LCC PZ7.1.O73 (ebook)
| DDC [Fi]c—dc23
LC record available at https://lccn.loc.gov/2015050178

Originally published in the United States by Swoon Reads
First Square Fish edition, 2018
Book designed by Vikki Sheatsley
Square Fish logo designed by Filomena Tuosto

1   3   5   7   9   10   8   6   4   2

LEXILE: 750L

To Michael:
My love, my life, my everything.

PROLOGUE

THE NUMBERS ON MY PHONE STARE BACK AT ME.
Thirty more minutes of target practice before I can start my homework. I take a breath and run the back of my hand across my forehead. It's still damp with sweat from my run and the hour of Krav Maga with Mom. I shake out my arms. The exhilarating buzz that comes from fighting is starting its slow leak from my veins as I stand alone in the silent shooting range.

My Glock 22 pistol feels heavy in my hands tonight. My muscles must be more tired than my brain is registering. I aim my gun at the dummy target and squeeze the trigger.

Bang. Bang. Bang. Two shots to the heart, one shot to the head.

"Reagan. Reagan." I hear my father's muffled voice. I remove my bulky black earphones.

"Yeah?" I call back.

"Get in the panic room," he screams. I open my mouth to ask if this is another one of his many drills but before the words can escape my lips, the secret door that leads to our basement slams shut so hard, I jump. My parents' heavy footsteps bounding down the hardwood stairs tell me this is not a joke. This is not a fake break-in or drill. They don't have to say another word. I feel my stomach drop. My body moves without me telling it what to do. I tuck the gun into the back of my pants as I sprint into the weapons room, tear open a metal cupboard, and grab two assault rifles off the shelf.

Just in case.

"Get in," Mom calls from the doorway of the panic room.

"Hang on, I'm just grabbing some—"

"Reagan, there's no time!" There is a tightness and urgency in her voice I'm not used to hearing. She's normally the picture of calm. Grace, even. The flash of fear in her eyes makes my knees momentarily weak. I slam the metal cupboard and the crushing sound of metal on metal echoes off the walls. I tuck the guns under my arms and run into the small panic room. As soon as I step inside, Dad slams the heavy steel door shut. My eyes widen as he frantically punches in a six-digit code. The weighty click of the steel beams locking into place makes my heart race.

"Mom, what's going on?" I ask and slide the guns onto the concrete floor.

I wait for her answer but she's too focused on switching on all the security camera monitors built into the steel and concrete. I lean my back against the wall. My exposed skin bristles against the cold concrete and the gun I tucked in my pants digs into my spine. Ouch. I reach around my body and pull it from my waistband. I hold the warm steel in my cold hands, still waiting for an explanation.

"What's happening?" I ask again. We never use this panic room. Ever. It was built for those code-blue-emergency moments that we've practiced many times but never had. Until now. I search their faces for an answer, for anything, really. They are stone-faced, staring up at the monitors, their bodies frozen. I follow their eyes. And then I see him. Air catches in my lungs as a man, dressed all in black, walks across my dimly lit family room.

"Oh my God," I whisper. I stare up at the security cameras as the stranger with long dark hair and high cheekbones walks down the hallway and into the kitchen, his arms outstretched, a pistol in his hand, his finger on the trigger.

"It's him. I know it's one of his guys," Mom says.

"It's who?" I ask. My voice is sharp and high.

"Not now, Reagan," Dad answers.

I open my mouth to protest, then close it. I lay my pistol at my feet and dig my fingers into my hip bones. I know I'm not supposed to ask questions, but the worried lines on their faces are making me sick. I should be used to being kept in the dark by now but I still hate it. "For your own good," they always say. "For your safety." But I've never been safe. Being their daughter makes me a target. I know their lives are dangerous. The work they do is dangerous. Their enemies would gun me down and kill me in broad daylight without giving it a second thought.

Mom and Dad do their best to ease my mind but I don't know of too many other sixteen-year-olds who have weapons stashed in hiding spots outside of school. Who sleep with knives taped to their headboards or know ten different ways to break someone's neck. Looking over my shoulder will be my life and I guess I'm okay with that. I just wish they'd stop leaving me in the dark; stop pretending like no one can hurt me.

3

The satellite phone rings, cutting the tense silence inside the cramped bunker. Dad picks it up.

"Hello?" he says. I hear a man's voice on the other end. "Yes, he's in. I heard glass break before we got inside the garage. It looks like he's alone." My father pauses. I take half a step closer to him, straining to hear the man on the other end. I can only make out a few words. Gun. Team. Kidnap. Threat. Execute. I step back, close my eyes, and lean against the icy wall. My fingers feel for the double-heart charm that hangs off my bracelet. I take the cool metal into my hand and press it between my thumb and index fingers, trying to find my breath. For years, my parents have been training me to deal with situations just like this. I know what I'm supposed to do. The trained fighter in me wants to run out of the panic room and blow this guy's head off. But a fraction of me—the terrified, anxious girl I push away—she's hoping this is all just a bad dream.

"Okay. All right," my father says into the phone, his voice sharp.

"Who's on the phone?" I whisper to Mom.

"Someone at CORE," she whispers back, never taking her eyes off the security cameras as the hitman makes his way through the second floor, searching for us in bedroom after bedroom.

"They said stand by," Dad says, hanging up the satellite phone. "Backup is on the way. They're monitoring the situation from headquarters."

"How are they going to help all the way in DC?" I ask, anxiety gripping my vocal cords and altering the sound of my voice.

"It's going to be okay, Reagan," Mom says, turning around and looking at me for the first time since Dad locked the panic room door. She puts a hand on my shoulder. Her green eyes are fierce and focused, but her warm touch softens me somehow. It's like she can feel the traces of fear I'm struggling to contain radiate from my body. I reach up and grab her hand. She takes my fingers in her cold palm, squeezes them, and for a moment, I forget about the panic room and the loaded guns and the hitman that's roaming our house. For just one second, I feel safe.

"They're here," Dad says. I look up at the exterior security cameras. A black SUV pulls down our street, turning off its headlights as it creeps closer to our house.

"Who's here?" I ask, my voice dropping to a near whisper.

"Our Black Angel watchers," Mom answers and turns her attention back to the security cameras. A man and woman climb out of the car, dressed all in black. As the woman moves closer to the garage, I recognize her walk. Aunt Samantha. The Black Angel watcher who's protected me my entire life. When Mom and Dad would disappear on missions, Aunt Samantha was there to take care of me. When I was younger, I thought she was just my nanny. But now I know she's an intel specialist for CORE, was awarded the Medal of Valor by the president during her years in the army, and can shoot like no one I've ever seen.

"I'm going after him," Mom says, pulling off her red sweater, revealing a black tank top underneath. Her arms are chiseled and her stomach is perfectly flat, the result of five hundred push-ups a day for the last twenty years.

"No, I'll go," my father replies.

"No. You stay here with Reagan."

"I want to go too," I say, adrenaline pumping through my veins.

"Absolutely not, Reagan," Mom replies. "Both of you stay here."

"Elizabeth, honestly, it could be—"

"Jonathan, this is not up for debate," Mom snaps and spins around, looking back up at the ten different security cameras. "Where did he go?" she asks just as the stranger's boots pound on the floor above our heads, sending our eyes to the ceiling. We stare up until the sound of his feet fade away. We turn back to the security cameras in time to see the hitman open the garage door, bound down the steps, and stand in front of our large tool chest. But it's not really a tool chest. It's the secret door to our basement. I feel Dad's body tense as the hitman pulls on the large steel handles, but the door is locked tight, only accessible by a six-digit code that changes every month.

My mouth drops but before I can say another word, Dad picks up the phone and pushes a few buttons. Before the voice on the other end even says hello, Dad is yelling. "He's at the basement door, Thomas—how the hell does he know about that? Only someone on the inside could possibly know that type of high-security detail." A voice says something on the other end of the phone. "Well, you better figure out how he got that intel and then you put the bastard who gave it to him behind bars for life, you understand me?"

Dad slams down the phone before Thomas can answer.

Mom turns around and holds out her palm. "Reagan, give me your gun." Her eyes are sharp and every muscle in her face is tight. I've watched my parents shoot and practice Krav Maga, jujitsu, and Muay Thai for years. But I've never actually seen them use their skills. I lean down and slowly pick my favorite pistol off the floor. I place the gun in her open hand.

"Please be careful," I say, the words barely escaping my tight throat. She leans in and kisses me on my cheek.

"I'll be fine," she says, giving me a small smile. As she turns and reaches for the door, a million pins prick my skin and I can't feel my hands or my feet or my legs. I drop my head as she punches in the six-digit code. The steel beams unlock and I look up to capture what I'm afraid could be my final image of her.

I've been doing that my entire life. Before they go off on missions, I try to take in every piece of them. The way my dad's strong hands curve around his favorite coffee cup. The way my mom carefully brushes stray pieces of her blond hair out of her eyes. The feeling she leaves on my cheek when she kisses me or the tightness of Dad's hugs. I freeze that moment, hold it tight and file it away. But this time, she's already gone.

Dad slams the panic room door and punches in the code again. The steel beams lock back into place. I watch the security cameras as Mom walks across the martial arts room, then slips out the escape route in the corner of the shooting range, softly closing the metal door behind her. Dad picks up the satellite phone and punches in another number. I hear a female voice pick up on the other side.

"Sam, stand by," Dad barks. "Elizabeth is on her way out. She's on her own so watch her back."

He slams down the phone without waiting for a reply. I look up at him. His jaw is clenched. He's trying to look calm, but his wide, wild eyes give him away. He's almost as panicked as I am. He frantically searches the security cameras for my mother. I look back at the screens in time to see Mom slip out the secret side door of the house and run to meet the Black Angels standing in our driveway, my gun glistening in her hand.

Dad and I watch in deafening silence as the hitman pulls and pulls on the steel doors. He flips open the keypad, typing in numbers with his middle finger. I lower my head for a moment and beg. *Please, God, please don't let him have the right number.* I look back up and search the security cameras for Mom. She's gone inside the house while the other Black Angels creep to the side garage door near the backyard. My heart is beating so loud, it's the only thing I hear as I watch Mom reach the mudroom, pull her gun up to her chest, and pause at the garage door. My body starts to tingle again as I watch the team outside rip open the side door and point their guns straight at the hitman's head.

"Get down on the ground," a deep voice calls out on the security camera. The hitman turns around, points his weapon at the two Black Angel watchers, and fires. *Bang. Bang. Bang. Bang.* Aunt Sam dives behind one of our SUVs as the hitman reaches in his pocket to reload. But before he can shove the magazine into his pistol, Mom has snuck out the garage door and is sprinting up behind him.

"Mom," I scream and step toward the security cameras. Dad pulls at my shoulders as Mom grabs the hitman's arm and slams it into her knee, knocking the gun and ammunition out of his hand. Dad's grip tightens as she tucks her leg beneath his. I know that move. Mom taught me that move. Using all her strength, she flips him flat on his back. I hear the crack of his skull on the cold, hard cement and his breath knock from his chest. He desperately gasps for new air as Mom pushes the barrel of my gun into his forehead.

"Who sent you?" I hear her ask. The hitman says nothing, just grunts in pain. "Who sent you?" she says again, her voice rising. She digs the gun into his right temple. He slowly lifts his head off the garage floor and looks up at my mother. He says nothing as they stare into each other's eyes. Just when I think he's about to give up the puppeteer pulling his strings, he spits in her face. Air pulls from my lungs. My eyes widen as Mom raises the gun into the air. Dad's hand tightens on my shoulders again. Halfway up, she stops. She glances up at the security camera, remembers I'm watching, and returns the barrel of the gun to his temple.

"You're not even worth it," she hisses. Aunt Sam and the other Black Angel watcher search his body for weapons as my mother holds him down, her knee in the center of his chest. A murderous tool kit of pistols, knives, ammunition, and ropes are taken out of his pockets and thrown to the ground.

The satellite phone rings again.

"They got him," Dad says. I can hear Thomas on the other end. "No. No. We need him alive. Tell them to take him back to Langley. We need to find out what he knows. How he found us."

I look back up at the security cameras. Mom is gone. Aunt Sam is tying the hitman up with zip ties. They yank him to his feet. His cracked skull is bleeding. Trickles of blood rush down his forehead, into his eyes, and across his cheeks. They hold him by both arms, guns pointed at his head. He doesn't resist. He just hangs his head. He probably knows what will happen next. They grip his arms tight, walk him outside to their SUV, throw him inside, and are gone.

"Thomas, I can't believe this happened again. Intelligence thinks they've been watching us for almost a month. I don't understand how he got inside this house. You've got to put us somewhere safer.

9

My family could have died tonight." Dad's voice surges. He closes his eyes and shakes his head. "No, I'll be there in the morning. I want to talk to him myself. We're all coming, so don't send protection. See you in a few hours."

"What do you mean we're all coming?" I ask as he hangs up the phone.

"We've got to go to DC tonight," he answers, his fingers quickly punching in the code. The steel beams unlock and the door opens. "Grab your go-bag. We're not coming back here."

I stand frozen in the panic room. We're not coming back? No. Not again. I watch him, dazed, as he walks away from me. I force my body to chase after him into the weapons room. "What? Why?"

"They know where we are," he answers sternly without turning around.

"But I just started the school year and I actually like the girls in my class and I have a precalculus test on Monday and . . ." I babble. Words are just tumbling out of my mouth. I'm not even sure what I'm saying.

"Reagan, this is not negotiable." He turns around and shouts in my face. I stop in my tracks and close my open mouth, surprised by his anger. He raises his arm, pointing toward the panic room. "Were we even in the same room? Did you not just see what happened? If he hadn't tripped the alarms on the property, we'd be dead right now. We're not safe in Philadelphia anymore. He's just one assassin. If they know where we are, they'll send twenty more before morning. I'm not going to stay here and watch my family die. We have to leave. Tonight!"

I hold on to the air in my chest until my lungs burn. Philadelphia

10

was just starting to feel like home. And there they go again, ripping me away from my friends and my school and the life I was building here. The worst part is, I'll never get to say good-bye. No farewell party. No note. No explanation. I'll just disappear. Like all the times before.

I'm so sick of this. We've moved so many times, I'm losing count. Seven times? Eight times? I was just starting to feel a sense of normalcy here but saying those words out loud will just piss Dad off. I'll be reminded that I'm not normal. That I have a gift. That I was born to do this. It's a phrase I've heard so many times, I've memorized my parents' inflection and the way they always emphasize the word *born*. I was *born* to be one of them. A Black Angel.

I dig my nails into the palms of my hands and watch helplessly as Dad climbs the back staircase. His pounding footsteps tell me this conversation is over. We're leaving. And there is nothing more I can say.

ONE

"REAGAN, EVERYONE IS GOING ON SATURDAY," Harper says, in between bites of overcooked meat loaf and runny lunchroom mashed potatoes. "You'll be, like, the only senior not there."

"I'd rather eat glass," I say, taking a long swig of Vitaminwater. I ran six miles before school and my body is in dire need of electrolytes. I can feel it. I hate getting up early to train, but it's a million times better than waiting until the afternoon. I'd much rather be hanging out with Harper or studying with Luke, but skipping is not an option. I made that stupid mistake only once and that was enough for me. My parents were the kind of pissed that bypasses the yelling and screaming phase and goes straight to the silent treatment and punishment. They gave me a training session the next day that made my legs shake for an hour. A twelve-mile run followed by five hundred push-ups, a thousand sit-ups, and two hours of Krav Maga. Pure hell. In most households, I'm pretty sure that'd be considered child abuse. But what was I supposed to do? Call Child

Protective Services? Tell them my parents forced me to work out for six hours because they're operatives for a part of the CIA the world, even most of the US government, doesn't know about and I'm training to be an operative too? I don't think so. So every morning, I pull my butt out of bed at five on the dot to train before school.

"I don't understand why on earth you would want to miss one of Mark's parties," Harper counters, tucking a loose strand of her long, wavy blond hair behind her ear.

"You know my two party rules," I reply, counting them down on my fingers. "Number one: Drinking Mad Dog 20/20 will make you sicker than eating at a strip club buffet. Number two: No good ever comes from attending a Mark Ricardi party."

Mark's gatherings at his parents' estate outside the New Albany Country Club community were sort of famous. I've only been to one of his parties and left before things got totally out of control, but the stories that come out of that house . . . my God. People always end up going skinny-dipping in the pond or losing articles of clothing (or just their dignity) during tequila-induced twerk-offs. Someone always gets into a huge fight or breaks something or cheats on their girlfriend. People always leave Mark Ricardi parties with the taste of expensive liquor and regret in their mouths.

"We'll take a vote when Mal gets here," Harper says and takes a swig of her pop.

"I'll take a vote right now. All those in favor of not holding your best friend's hair back while she throws up in the master bathtub, please raise your hand," I say, throwing my hand straight up into the air. Harper narrows her hazel eyes at me then smiles, exposing the tiny gap in her two front teeth that I love and Harper hates. She says she wishes she would have gotten braces back in middle school when everyone else's teeth were jacked up. She's thought about getting one of those clear plastic retainer things to fix it, but I continue to talk her out of it. I think the gap makes her look like a supermodel.

"Hey, that was the easiest party-fail cleanup ever," Harper says, reaching across the gray laminate table to slap down my hand.

"It was disgusting," I reply, my arm still high in the air. "I almost threw up next to you and I was stone-cold sober."

"You're so the good little mom of the group," Harper says, batting at my hand again. "I totally H your G's right now."

"You totally what my what?" I ask.

"H your G's," Harper replies and rolls her eyes. "Hate your guts."

"No way, you totally L my G's," I say and laugh. Love how we both do that. Abbreviate things to the point people don't know what in the world we're talking about. We have some regulars, like RTG, which means "ready to go." PITA means "pain in the ass." SMITH means "shoot me in the head." Those are probably the favorites, but we both come up with ridiculous new ones every day that make our friends roll their eyes. But whatever, it's our thing and we like it so WGAS? Translation: Who gives a shit?

"Hey, MacMillan," a voice calls at me from the lunch line. I turn around to see Malika carrying a blue lunch tray. "Share my nachos?"

"Always," I answer and spin back around.

MacMillan. Out of all my Black Angel cover-up last names, Mac-Millan may be my favorite. I've always been Reagan. But I've been lots of Reagans. Reagan Moore. Reagan Bailey. Reagan Klein. Reagan Schultz. No one has ever known my real name. Reagan Elizabeth Hillis. It's been so long since I've said my real name out loud that sometimes I have to think about it. It sounds ridiculous that I'd actually have to use any brainpower to know my name, but while it's only for a fleeting moment, sometimes I do. I've heard my mother say the older she gets, the more she really has to think about how old she is. When you're seven or seventeen, you never have to think about your age. She says as you get older, there's that split second where she has to ask herself, *Wait, am I forty-eight or forty-nine?* That's how I feel about my real name. And the more new last names I get, the longer that beat is in remembering who I really am.

It always happens the same way. As soon as I'm comfortable with a last name, I'm forced to forget it. My parents' cover will be in jeopardy or we're being watched and we'll have to get out of town. And every time we load up the car in the middle of the night and pull down our street for the last time, I feel like a piece of me is stripped away. I've never told my parents that. I don't want to make them feel bad. But it's like a version of myself—Reagan Moore or Bailey or Schultz or whoever I was there—dies and becomes a splintered shadow for anyone who ever knew that Reagan. When I get my new name and new cover story, it's like that Reagan—that fractured piece of myself—never really existed. I don't talk about it. I don't tell anyone the truth about where we were or what my life was like. I have to make up a whole new set of lies and repeat them over and over again until they become truth. I make the girl I was just a few months ago disappear.

"Hey, girls," Malika says, setting her tray down next to me. She lifts up her left leg to climb over the bench, forgetting about her very short red skirt.

"Holy inappropriateness," Harper says, covering her eyes with both hands.

"What'd I do?" Malika asks, settling into her seat.

"You kind of just gave the entire school a look at the goods," I say and pat her bare knee.

"Well, it's not like I'm not wearing underwear," Malika says and throws her slick black hair over her shoulder.

"Yes. I like the pink flamingos, Mal," Harper answers and gives her a wink.

With a Japanese mother and Pakistani father, Malika is hard not to notice in WASP-y New Albany, Ohio. Plus, she's what I like to call stupid pretty. So beautiful, she strikes you dumb and stumbling.

"Malika, what do you think this is, a strip club?" a voice says from behind me. I know who it is before I even turn around. Everyone knows the low, raspy voice of Madison Scarborough. "But then again, it's nothing half the guys in this room haven't seen before."

"Hey, I'm only a make-out slut," Malika says, pointing a finger to her chest. "I don't take off my clothes."

"Whatever. A slut is a slut," Madison says, rolling her startling blue eyes. I open my mouth to zing her but she's already turned on her heel to head to the field hockey girls' table.

"Don't worry," I say, linking my arm with Malika's. "I'll get her back later."

I learned how to hack into computers during one of my summer training camps in China. In about ninety seconds, I can hack into the school's computer system and change grades, attendance records, anything. It's child's play compared to the other systems

I've mastered. By tonight, Madison will have a D in physics and the field hockey captain will be promptly benched for Saturday's rivalry game against Upper Arlington. I'll change it back Monday. Madison totally deserves the D for all the mean-girl crap she pulls on a daily basis. But I only use my spy skills for short spurts of vengeance evil.

The rumor-spreading, shit-stirring Madison Scarborough is what bonded us last year. I noticed Harper and Malika on my first day of school. Malika because she's gorgeous and Harper because she has the type of effortless coolness money can't buy. But they didn't hang with the field hockey and lacrosse crowd, the self-anointed "popular" girls. They were what Madison and her friends liked to call "fringers." Invited to the big parties but never the exclusive sleepovers or birthday dinners. They were known around school but never the center of attention. They quickly became my target group of friends. I needed to get into a small, uncomplicated group and blend as quickly as possible, so when I caught wind of terrible rumors Madison was spreading about them, I knew it was my chance.

Madison has had the same boyfriend for over a year. A preppy lacrosse senior who wears salmon shorts and mirrored sunglasses at parties and uses the word *summer* as a verb. Even with a d-bag boyfriend, girls think twice about getting involved with anyone Madison's ever dated. When Madison's ex-boyfriend asked Harper to homecoming, she spread a rumor that she was a lesbian and that none of the field hockey girls felt comfortable sharing a locker room with her. Then when Madison heard that Malika kissed a guy who dumped her two years ago, she started a rumor that sweet Malika made a sex tape even though Mal had never even had sex. Still hasn't.

During study hall, I hacked into Madison's Twitter account (@PrincessMaddie. Cue the eye roll) and had Mal and Harper help me compose a stream of hilarious apology tweets to every person she'd ever terrorized. They were deleted twenty minutes later but that act cemented my place in our little group.

I almost hate to admit that my motive to get into the fringers was part of my training because I sort of love everything about them. I love that Harper eats all the orange and purple Skittles because she knows how much I hate them and how her shoelaces are always coming untied because she refuses to double-knot. I love how Malika is deathly afraid of spiders but has seen every slasher film ever made and how she's still a virgin but has a hilarious goal of making out with a guy from every continent. They've become real friends now and not just part of my never-stand-out strategy.

"Got to love a guy in uniform," Harper calls over my shoulder and whistles a loud catcall. I turn around in time to see Luke Weixel's creamy cheeks turn a dusty rose. He shakes his head at Harper, his lips crinkling into a crooked smile before turning his pale blue eyes to me.

It's uniform day for the Junior ROTC and Luke looks extra sharp in his dark pants and tan button-down shirt, decorated with colorful medals, arc pins, and accolades. Six foot three with hair the color of summer hay and defined cheekbones, Luke always has girls swiveling in their seats or craning their necks to stare, but he looks especially stunning in uniform. It's not just the way the uniform makes him look but how it makes him feel. He stands a little taller, walks a beat faster, and smiles a little wider in that uniform.

I raise my right hand to my forehead and give Luke a tiny

salute. His crooked smile cracks wide, unmasking a pair of dimples so charming, even if you were mad at him, one smile would make you forget why. We hold each other's stare for a moment before he steps out of the lunch line and heads for our table.

"Hi, girls," Luke says, sliding into the seat next to me. He purposefully bumps his shoulder into mine, the right corner of his lip rising into a sideways smile. "Hey, Mac."

Luke is the only one I let call me Mac.

"Hey, soldier," I reply, my voice shyer than I expected it to be. Luke rests his strong arms on the table next to mine. Our skin is separated by my thin cardigan, but even the slightest touch from him manages to make my body buzz. Harper eyes the two of us and from the slow rising smile on her face, I know my olive skin is turning crimson.

"Luke, help us," Harper says, pulling her wavy hair into a messy bun. "Reagan is refusing to go to Mark Ricardi's party."

"What?!" Malika practically screams then pouts. She loves a good and rowdy Mark Ricardi party.

"Oh, come on, Mac," Luke says, his smile still lopsided but wider, exposing his white, perfectly straight teeth. Orthodontists make a good living in this town. "Mark's parties are always epic."

"Yes. Epic disasters," I rebuff but can't help but match his grin. It's annoyingly contagious.

"How about this?" Luke negotiates. "We go, sit in the corner, and watch the disasters unfold together."

Luke and I have done that before. Sat shoulder to shoulder at parties, laughing as we make up the dialogue between fighting couples and drunk lacrosse girls. My stomach, even my face hurts from three-hour giggle sessions with him.

"Pleaaassseeeee," Malika begs, her eyes closed and hands collapsed together in painful prayer.

"Okay, okay," I say, throwing my hands into the air in defeat. The three of them cheer in unison and exchange a round of high fives.

"I better eat if I want to make it to lab on time," Luke says, standing up from his seat and resting his hand on my shoulder. "See you in a bit."

Luke's fingertips graze against my shoulder blades as he turns on the heel of his freshly polished JROTC boot and walks toward the lunch line.

The rush that takes over my body every time I'm near Luke drains from my blood and as he disappears from my sight, my sharp senses return. Every muscle in my body tightens as I turn to my left and lock eyes with a man whose stare is so penetrating, I can feel it from hundreds of feet away. He's tall and strong, his eyes intense and dark, dressed in a janitor's navy-blue uniform. But I've never seen him before. He holds my stare for a moment, then looks away. He fumbles with the garbage bag in his hands, struggling to open it up. I watch as he tears at the black plastic, gets frustrated, and throws it to the ground. As he looks back up at me, a hundred pins prick my spine. My eyes follow him as he spins around and plows his way toward the dining hall door, knocking into a student with so much force, her face winces in pain. I wait for him to stop or look back or apologize. But he doesn't. He puts his head down and keeps going.

TWO

"REAGAN, WHAT'S WRONG?" MAL SAYS AND GENTLY touches the top of my hand, making my body flinch. I finally take my eyes off the door and look down at her. I hadn't even realized I'd stood up.

"Nothing," I say and shake my head. "I just . . . I forgot my lab homework in my locker. Harper, I'll see you in AP bio."

Before they can say another word, I grab my messenger bag off the ground and walk quickly toward the exit sign that hangs beneath two sets of double doors. I have to stop myself from running. I don't want to freak everybody out.

I push open the door and get sucked into a sea of underclassmen heading to their next class. *Where did he go?* My neck cranes as I search both ends of the hallway, catching the top of his dark hair as he takes a sharp left down one of the main halls.

My training kicks in and I break out into a slow jog. I bump shoulders with a younger girl. "Sorry," I yell out without stopping. I don't want to lose him. I rub my hand on the outside pocket of my messenger bag and feel the outline of my "calculator." The Black Angels weaponry team designed and built it just for me. A push of a button activates a secret compartment and out slides a serrated knife. I almost forgot it today. I walked out to my car without it, debated just leaving it at home, but turned around and went back inside. My parents' constant badgering to always be armed no longer seems like one of their annoying ticks. It's for moments just like this; when every bone in my body feels like it's splintering and my mind is screaming.

I push past underclassmen and eventually they start to get out of my way. I reach the hallway where he turned. His dark, long hair and large frame give him away in this crowd of freshmen and soph-omores. Our eyes lock and his face twists into a scowl. Before I can take another step, he pulls open the door to the gymnasium and slips inside. I jog down the hallway, my heart pounding, adrenaline buzzing through my body. I slip my hand into the pocket of my bag just enough to feel the top of my calculator with my fingertips. I reach the door, pull on the metal handle, and step inside, the door slamming shut behind me with a loud, metallic clang.

The gym is dark and empty. I take a few cautious steps toward the basketball court, my boots echoing against the vaulted ceiling. After a few steps, I stop and listen. My lungs tighten in my chest as I hold my breath. I hear the slight rustle of clothing followed by slow and quiet taps. He's on his tiptoes somewhere in the black. Most would never be able to pick up on that, but after years of intense training, I recognize the sound of someone trying desperately not to be heard. I slowly let out my breath and take three steps back, pushing my body up against the cinder-block walls. *Don't let him attack you from behind,* I hear my mother's voice in my head. I reach inside the pocket of my bag and push the button at the top of my calculator. Out slides the handle of my knife. I listen again to the quiet tap, tap, tap on the hardwood floors. A door at half-court swings open with a shrieking creak and light pours from the equipment room. A dark image walks into the light and just as quickly dips back into the shadows. The outline of a silhouette has been swallowed by the black, but I can hear heavy footsteps walk closer and closer to my side of the gym. I grab the handle of my knife, pulling it out of its hidden compartment and up to the edge of my bag.

"Who's there?" I push out from my tight throat, my voice bouncing off the two-story ceiling.

No one answers me. The footsteps get louder and louder. My stomach twists, and fear tingles up and down my arms.

"Who's there?" I repeat, my voice booming.

I hear a crack and then a soft buzz above me.

"Reagan? What are you doing?"

The dim glow from the overhead light reveals Coach Hutta, dressed in shorts and a polo shirt two sizes too small, standing twenty yards away from me near the massive overhead light switch. My knees lock. I stand there frozen, my hand still wrapped around the handle of my knife, as my eyes scan the gym. I expect to see the stranger cowering in a corner or running out the back door. But he's gone.

"Sorry, Coach. I just . . ." My mind races for a quick lie. I let go of my knife and feel the weight of it drop down into my bag. With my free hand, I reach into the pocket of my jeans, pulling out the five-dollar bill I was going to use to buy a brownie at lunch. "I saw one of

24

the janitors drop some money in the hallway. I was just running after him to give it back. I saw him slip in here. Have you seen him?"

"Oh, you mean Mateo?" Coach Hutta asks, his brow furrowing over his beady eyes. "The new janitor? Dark-haired guy?"

"Yes," I reply, my tense shoulders falling half an inch.

"Yeah, he just came into the equipment room," Coach Hutta says, his hitchhiker thumb pointed over his shoulder at the open door. He steps toward me, his stride wobbly and wide. When he reaches me, he snatches the five-dollar bill out of my hand with a smirk and puts it in his pocket. "Don't worry. I'll give it to him."

Great. Out of my mind *and* five dollars.

The double doors to the gym fly open behind me and a group of freshmen come running inside, their chatter and giggles drowning out the buzz of the industrial overhead lights.

"Better get to your next class, Reagan," Coach Hutta calls out over his shoulder as he makes his way toward half-court where his students are sprawled out on the floor.

I nod even though he's no longer paying attention. Coach Hutta blows on the whistle that's permanently draped around his thick neck, and the chatter dissipates. I turn around and head for the door.

"Aren't you a lucky group of students? Today we will do your favorite thing in the world. A timed mile run," Coach Hutta announces. The class groans in unison before erupting into a series of complaints and excuses.

It was nothing, my mind whispers. *You're worked up over nothing*.

I pull the strap of my messenger bag tighter against my shoulder. I breathe in deep, trying to release my rigid muscles and untie the remaining knots in my stomach. But they won't budge.

As I reach the double doors and put my hands on the cool steel bar, those hundred pins prick my back once again. I can feel eyes on me. I whip back around, my long ponytail smacking me in the face, in time to see the edge of a man's silhouette slipping out the back door and disappearing from my sight.

THREE

DROP IT, I TELL MYSELF AS I WALK DOWN THE NEARLY empty hallway. *It was nothing.*

I take another deep breath, trying to calm the anxiety I feel tingling up my fingertips and toes. But the daymare comes anyway. His dirty hand over my mouth. A serrated knife pressed to my throat. His humid breath whispering threats in my ear. I can almost feel the cold steel of his blade on my flesh; tiny, warm drops of his spit in the curve of my ear. I close my eyes and try to make it go away, but the horrific scene continues to play out in vivid detail. He pushes the knife harder against my neck, nicking my skin and drawing blood. I try to run, but my hands and feet are tied. I try to scream, but only a muffled cry echoes against steel walls.

Stop, stop, stop, my mind begs for it to be over. I put my right hand over my face and violently shake my head, trying to erase the scene, as if my brain is an Etch A Sketch that can be cleared with a few shakes. The daymare finally begins to break apart.

"Are you okay?" I hear a voice say, pulling me back into reality.

Luke is standing in front of me, his eyes wide, his right arm reaching out to steady my shoulder. I lower my hand from my face and silently hope he hasn't been watching me long.

"Yeah," I answer quickly and return my fingers to my temples. "Just a migraine, I think."

He squints and cocks his head slightly, examining my face. I force a smile that would satisfy most, but Luke knows me well. Probably too well. My Black Angel psychological training doesn't always work on him.

"You sure you're okay?" Luke asks again, moving his hand from my shoulder to my back, his fingertips slowly running along the curve of my spine.

"No, I'm totally fine," I say and shake my head, my brain searching for a lie. "When I get stressed, I get a migraine."

"What are you stressed about?" Luke asks.

"I guess I'm . . . uh, just . . . nervous about my interview at Templeton this weekend," I stumble through my lie. With Luke, the lies don't fall as easily off my tongue. It's unnerving. He has a way of almost pulling the truth out of me. Almost.

"Ahhh . . . the dream school," Luke repeats another lie I've told him. He returns his hand to my shoulder and gives it a friendly squeeze. "You'll do great, Mac."

"Thanks. The premed program there is unbelievable," I answer more confidently, sticking to the carefully crafted script of my cover. We begin slowly walking down the quiet hallway toward the biology lab. "I guess I'm just a little nervous about blowing the interview."

"Come over Friday night and we'll hang out and do some interview prep," Luke replies, nodding.

"Okay," I say, his invitation parting my lips. "Thanks so much."

"No problem. Prepping helps. I was so nervous for all my interviews at West Point. The last interview for the nomination with the congressman was intense. I hope I didn't sound like an idiot."

"I'm sure you did amazing," I say and place my hand on his strong, exposed forearm. And that's all it takes. One little touch and that spark runs through my body. I keep hoping that this rush will disappear. But it doesn't. That ache is always there, lingering below the surface of my skin, waiting to rise.

"Given any more thought about the kind of doctor you want to be?" Luke asks. We've talked about it a few times but I can never narrow it down. Probably because the dream for me isn't real. My future is all but written.

"Maybe an ER doctor," I answer, which is only half a lie. If I did choose to go to college instead of the Black Angel Training Academy, that's the type of doctor I'd love to be.

Technically, I have a choice. When I turn eighteen, I must choose between college and a normal life or the training academy and the Black Angels. But for me, there's really only one choice. My parents don't just hope I'll go to the training academy. They expect me to go. Everyone does. My name has been at the very top of the academy's list since I was ten years old. *Born to be a Black Angel.* The words have been burned into my brain since before my first bra. Even if I wasn't the academy's golden child, the pressure to go would be high. The children of Black Angels become Black Angels. It's a tradition that's almost never broken. My parents are both first generation but they are the exception rather than the rule. Most Black Angels are third, even fourth generation. Children of Black Angels are trained by their parents from the moment they learn what Mommy and Daddy really do for a living and by the time they turn eighteen, they are more than ready for the academy. There's no need for CIA training on The Farm when you've been practicing martial arts since you were four and shooting high-powered assault rifles since age ten.

There's honor in what they do. I know there is. They save people's lives, they rescue hostages, stop terror plots, take down the bad guys. They're as close to superheroes as you can get. But there's a list of cons that come with the admirable pros. And after Philadelphia, my secret con list is getting longer.

"Thank God," Harper yells across the biology lab as we walk through the door. I raise my finger to my pursed lips in an effort to get Harper to zip it. Mr. Bajec is several lab tables away, his back turned to us. He hasn't noticed we're late. She gets my signal and presses her lips into an oh-crap smirk.

Luke and I take a few quick steps across the lab, throw our bags on the ground, and hop on our lab stools just in time.

"Don't forget, test tomorrow afternoon, everybody," Mr. Bajec says, turning around to face the class. I turn on my best I've-been-here-the-whole-time smile and nod. He turns his attention back to the lab.

"That was a close one," Harper says, letting out a breath.

"What are you doing?" Luke asks with a laugh.

"Yeah, are you trying to get us detention?" I ask, pulling my blue biology notebook out of my messenger bag.

"Sorry, but it's dissection day and if you think I'm touching that slimy frog, then we might as well take the F on this lab," Harper exclaims, pointing down at our dead frog, his four legs pinned down, waiting to be cut open.

"It's fine, I'll do it," I say, snapping on a pair of latex gloves and grabbing the lab scissors out of her hands. Harper hops up on the metal stool next to Luke and neatly prints our names on the top of our lab sheet.

"Sorry I'm a pretty shitty lab partner," Harper says, leaning her arms onto her notebook.

"Don't sell yourself short," Luke says, watching as I begin to cut into the belly of the frog. "I think you add a certain something to these dissections."

"Spunk," she says and smiles.

"And vomit sound effects," I say and point my gloved finger at her. "I couldn't get through the lab without those."

"Thank God you're going to be a doctor or we'd be super screwed," Harper says, and I have to stop my muscles from flinching. I've been lying my entire life. It's scary how second nature it is to me but when my friends repeat my lies back to me, sometimes the guilt rises hot and prickly on my skin.

I open up the frog's stomach to reveal thousands of tiny black eggs. "I guess this one is a female."

Harper glances up from her notes and doubles over when she

sees the glistening cluster of eggs. "Oh my God, that is so disgusting," she shrieks, then chokes on something in her throat.

"Mac, would you rather have to eat all those frog eggs or..." Luke begins.

"Stop it, Luke. That's so gross," Harper says, smacking him hard on the arm with her notebook. "Do your stupid 'Would You Rather' game with Reagan later when I'm not wanting to die."

Harper throws her hands over her eyes as I grab one of the scalpels and scrape out all the eggs.

"When I go to med school, I'll have to dissect a person," I say, staying on script. I cut a few inches more and open up the frog to reveal its heart, liver, and stomach.

"Seriously? Oh my God, no lie, I feel runny mashed potatoes coming up my throat. This isn't fake throw-up. This is real. Please change the stomach."

"The stomach?"

"The subject. Please change the subject," Harper says, squeezing her eyes shut and grabbing on to her midsection.

"You are so dramatic, I love you," I reply and giggle.

"Mr. Weixel, can I see you for a moment, please?" Mr. Bajec says, adjusting his dark-rim glasses and motioning with two quick flicks of his fingers for Luke to meet him at his desk.

An uh-oh look flashes into Luke's eyes for a moment, but with a quick shrug of his shoulders, it's gone. "Last name *plus* the worst words a teacher can possibly utter, all in one sentence," he says with a smile. Luke hops off his stool, his hands smoothing the front of his uniform. "Lucky me."

I watch Luke for a beat too long as he walks away. I know it's too long because I can feel Harper's eyes on me, a small smile creeping up her face.

I break my stare, remove my frog-slime-covered gloves and take the lab sheet out of Harper's hand to start working on our notes.

"Why is Mal so into going to Mark Ricardi's party?" I ask quickly before Harper can start in on me. "She practically burst into tears when she found out I didn't want to go. There's got to be more in it for her than spiked cider."

Harper sighs, probably disappointed that she missed her window of opportunity to bust me on my Luke-induced staring problem. "The real deal on Mal is that she heard Peter Paras is bringing some hot Australian guys from his soccer travel league to the party."

"I should have known," I say and smile. Mal's continent goal. She's got Africa and Europe crossed off the list after making out with a South African swimmer in town for a competition and a French boy while on vacation. She's been saying that Australia and South America are her next big gets.

"Well, Luke certainly got you to change your mind. No surprise there," Harper says, her voice teasing, her eyes on my face, careful not to look down at the frog.

"What's that supposed to mean?" I ask, my eyes back on our lab notes. I scribble down the location of the heart and lungs.

"Oh, stop trying to BS me," Harper says, cocking her head to the side. "It's me you're talking to. Seriously, what's going on with you guys?"

"Nothing. We're RGFs," I reply, staring hard at my notes and instinctively pushing my lips into a disinterested pout. I refuse to give Harper a reaction. But I can feel my heart beating in my ears. Not fluttering either. Pounding.

"RGF? What?" Harper's nose, eyes, and brow squish together as she tries to decode my abbreviation.

"RGFs. Really. Good. Friends," I say and look up at her. Her eyebrows arch sharply over her hazel eyes as she shakes her head slightly, not believing a word I'm saying.

That's not a lie. Luke and I *are* really good friends. He's probably the first real close friend I've ever had. Granted, I haven't been in one place long enough to make too many close friends. We've been in New Albany just over a year and that's our longest run in a new city since I started high school. But it's not just the length of our post. From day one, we just sort of fit together.

I love Malika and Harper. They make me happy. They really do. But there's something about being with them that makes me feel lonely too. I can never really be myself with them. I can't really be myself with anybody. It's ingrained in me to lie, to stick to the cover story and blend in no matter what. And I feel guilty about that. Because they *think* they know me so well. They *think* because they can finish my sentences they know everything about me. But they only know Reagan MacMillan; the quick-talking, tough girl I created. Sometimes I wonder which parts of my personality are really me and which ones belong to the pretender.

But with Luke, it's different. There's nothing forced or strategic about our friendship. He's gotten to see glimpses of the real Reagan. And that scares the shit out of me. Because I know how quickly it could all be torn away from me. How quickly I could be torn away from him. There's no such thing as a happy ending for a girl like me.

"Come on, Reagan," Harper says quietly, glancing over her shoulder to make sure Luke is still out of earshot. "You guys are so cute together. He broke up with Hannah months ago. I don't know what you're waiting for. I can just tell by the way he looks at you he—"

"Harper," I interrupt as her words compress my lungs, making each breath labored and painful. I don't want to hear this. "He doesn't look at me like anything. I don't want to ruin our friendship."

"You know some things are worth ruining," Harper replies, reaching out to touch my arm with her fingertips, her nails painted a shade darker than my gray cardigan. "You can't tell me you haven't at least thought about starting a relationship with him or maybe—"

"There is no relationship," I cut her off again, pulling my arm away a little faster than I meant to. I snap new gloves onto my hands, pick up the scalpel, and slice into the frog's heart. "Next stomach."

"Next stomach?" Harper repeats, scrunching her forehead.

"Next subject."

FOUR

I PUSH OPEN THE SCIENCE BUILDING'S HEAVY DOOR
and walk out onto one of the school's smaller quads. New Albany
High School looks more like a college campus with its deep redbrick
buildings, towering white columns, domed roofs, and manicured
lawns. I glance at the giant clock on the gym and it reads 2:10. Love
end-of-the-day free periods. I have just enough time to finish my
calculus homework in the library before the final bell.

I pull on the strap of my messenger bag and step out from under
the overhang and into the sunshine. The leaves have turned muted
shades of yellow, red, and orange. They're about a week away from
their peak. Out of all the places I've lived, Ohio falls are by far my
favorite. Apple picking, pumpkin patches, corn mazes, and haunted
houses, the kind of unspoiled normalcy you'd find in a Norman
Rockwell painting.

As I cross the quad, something catches my eye: a wispy mess of
blond hair, a small body cowering in a corner near the entrance to
the gym. It's Claire Weixel, Luke's little sister. Her tiny hands grip

her books. She holds them to her chest like a shield. I squint and hold my hand up to my forehead, blocking my eyes from the glare of the afternoon sun. And then I see them. From behind a white column, three girls emerge and surround Claire. My body stiffens but I watch from a distance, just to make sure I'm not being super overprotective. The leader of the group digs her meaty hands into Claire's thin shoulder, shoving her into a dark corner most teachers can't see. Claire's back hits the coarse bricks and a look of pain crosses her pale face.

"Oh, hell no," I say under my breath.

"Come on, give it up," I can hear the tall, thick leader say as I run up behind the group. "Give it to me now or I'll make you wish you were never born."

"Seriously? That's the best line you've got?" I say, putting a hand on the girl's hunched shoulder, pushing her aside. I step in front of a trembling Claire, my hands on my hips, and get a better look at the group. The leader is tall and strong with long dark hair and almond-shaped eyes. She's got about fifteen pounds on me but could honestly pass as my sister. Same coloring, same build. But that's where our similarities end. The leader and the rest of her little crew look like they stepped right out of Central Casting with their torn jeans, dirty hair, and I'm-so-tough-you-should-be-scared scowl on their faces. I can't help it and start to giggle. "Wow, really? What's it like to be a walking stereotype?"

"What'd you say to me?" the leader asks, looking me up and down.

"I mean, seriously, did you steal all your lines *and* your wardrobe from a Lifetime original movie or something?" I ask and roll my eyes. "If you're going to be a bully, can't you come up with something a little more original?"

"Get out of here," the leader says, trying to get around my athletic frame.

"Leave her alone," I say defiantly, my tongue slowly wrapping around each word.

"No, she owes us Spanish homework," the leader says, adjusting her thick flannel shirt that's too heavy for the unseasonably hot day.

"Reagan, it's okay," Claire's soft voice says from behind me. "I told them they could copy my homework."

"That's right, now give it up," the leader thunders, reaching around me and punching a book out of Claire's hand. The heavy textbook lands with a thud on the concrete and papers scatter at my feet. It's taking a considerable amount of strength not to knock this girl out.

"Don't you touch her," I snap, my finger pointed inches away from the girl's nose.

"Get your finger out of my face," the leader says, batting away my hand.

"Touch me again, and we're going to have real problems," I assert, doing my best to keep my voice cool and calm.

"I'm warning you, Reagan," she says. "Back off. This has nothing to do with you."

"She has everything to do with me. She's my friend. Now you back the hell off and leave her alone," I say, inching closer to her.

"Fine. I was going to beat her wimpy ass, but instead I'll beat your skinny ass." The leader clenches her fists, cracking her knuckles one by one against her open palm.

"Are those little knuckle cracks supposed to be intimidating or something?" I ask, raising one eyebrow.

"Most people take it as a warning before I pound them into the ground."

"I'd really like to see you try," I say and laugh.

"Are you seriously laughing at me right now?" the girl asks, taking a step back. "Don't you even know who I am?"

"Nope," I say and shake my head. "I don't even know your name, so you'll have to excuse me if I refer to you as 'that bitch whose ass I kicked' from now on."

That did it. The girl's dark eyes fill with even more fury as she lunges for me, her right fist clenched and heading straight for my face. I can feel Claire's body tighten beside me. But before the girl's fist can reach my jaw, I grab her thick wrist with both hands, spin her around, and twist her arm behind her back. The girl whimpers with agony, her arm struggling to break free as I push her up against the wall, smashing her face into the coarse brick.

"Holy . . . ! Stop! Please, let me go," the girl begs as I push my knee into her back.

"If you ever, and I mean *ever*, touch Claire again, I won't just twist your arm," I whisper harshly in her ear. "I'll break it. You got me?"

"Yes, yes, I promise. Please let go," the girl cries out. I loosen my tight grip and let her free. One more twist and her bone would have snapped in two. What I really want to do is use one of my Krav Maga take-downs on her; rapid-fire punches to the stomach, then the kidneys, then her temple. I want to wrap both hands around her forehead and slam her to the ground. But that'd probably be frowned upon.

"So much for being the tough girl, huh?" I say as the leader runs for the cover of her friends. The girl shoots me a death glare, color rising to her pimpled cheeks, as her two friends begin to laugh.

"Shut the hell up," the beaten bully yells, pulling on their arms. "Come on, let's go."

"Oh my God, Tess, that girl really kicked your ass," one of the girls says as they walk away.

"I could have taken her," Tess snaps. Name mystery solved. The group argues about the likelihood of Tess beating me up as she drags them out of earshot.

Claire's small hand touches my shoulder. I turn around to see her still shaking, causing my heart to involuntarily clench. She used to tell me about girls picking on her and never inviting her to sleepovers or birthday parties, but I had no idea girls were putting their hands on her.

"Are you okay?" I ask, pulling her into a hug. Claire puts her tiny arms around my back. As she rests her head on my shoulder, a few teardrops escape her eyes and soak through my cardigan and onto my skin.

"They do that to me all the time," Claire says, her voice soft.

"Why didn't you tell me? I would have stopped them," I ask, pulling out of our hug and looking into her dark brown eyes. Whatever Claire is feeling, it's written in her big doe eyes. She cannot fake it and she never tries. And today, her eyes say she's lonely.

"I didn't know when to tell you," Claire says, looking down at the ground.

"You can always just knock on my door. I live literally twenty steps away from you." We had counted once last spring. Luke, Claire, and I figured out how many steps it took to cross from my house to their house. Twenty steps walking. Fifteen steps running.

"I just didn't want to bother you with it," Claire answers with a one-shoulder shrug. "We haven't hung out in a while. Guess you've been busy."

My stomach twists into a guilty knot. It's true. It's been months since I spent quality time with her, introducing her to bands, listening to her talk about the boys she liked. I've been spending more and more time with Luke and less and less time with her. I should have noticed the impact that was having on her. Claire's incredibly sweet and smart but that's where the similarities between her and Luke end. She doesn't share any of her brother's popular-boy traits. Just a last name everyone knows and a reputation she can't live up to. I should have been looking out for her, protecting her. I've completely failed.

"Did you tell your brother?" I ask, taking her cold hand into my own.

"Oh, I don't want to tell him," Claire replies, shaking her head. "You know how overprotective he is. Who knows what he'd do. I don't want to get him into trouble with West Point."

The first time I ever saw Luke, he was sitting on the back porch with his sister. She was wiping tears from her eyes as he consoled her on the back steps. They sat together, looking out into the backyard, his big arm around her tiny shoulders. It was such a sweet moment between a brother and his little sister that when he looked up and noticed me at the window, I almost fell I backed away so fast, embarrassed by my intrusion.

"I'm so sorry," I say and bite down on my lip.

"It's okay," Claire says, even though it's not.

"You can always talk to me, okay?" I say, giving her hand a squeeze.

"Okay," Claire says. She drops my hand and leans down to pick up the books and papers that have scattered on the ground between us. I get down on one knee to help her.

"I'd better go. Thanks for rescuing me."

"Of course," I say, handing over her notes and homework. I wipe the knee of my jeans as Claire walks away. After a few steps, she turns around.

"Don't feel bad about not hanging out with me," she says, looking back at me. "Luke's just being a hog. I'm probably betraying a little brother-sister confidence here, but I think he really likes you."

I feel my jaw unhinge. Harper's been teasing and prying for months now but Claire's much closer to the source. Claire and Luke are as close as a brother and sister can get. They had to be with a career-long, high-ranking military officer for a father. The number of cities they've lived in are only surpassed by the number of framed photographs of Colonel Weixel shaking hands with the congressmen, senators, and generals that wined and dined him during his military days. He's retired now. Well, as retired as he'll ever allow himself to be. He's a special operations consultant and still spends months at a time overseas advising military leaders.

Because of Colonel Weixel's training, I watch what I say in front of him. He's warmer than you'd expect a man of his military status to be, but I know beneath that thinning white hairline is a brain trained to analyze every word and action, just like mine.

Claire's confession ping-pongs around my skull. I refuse to let her words settle into place. I'm ill prepared to deal with this. Luke is not something I can quickly evaluate and categorize like I do with everything else in my life. I feel my pulse quicken, my vein pounding inside my neck. I bite my lip and study my feet, not wanting to see what's written in Claire's big eyes and not wanting her to see what may be written in my own.

"I'll see you later, okay?" I say, hoping to end the conversation, not wanting to hear what Claire might say next. I glance back up and try to give her a smile, but it feels crooked on my face. Her lips part to speak; she searches my face and thinks better of it. She closes her mouth, waves, and hurries away. I press the long breath I'd been holding through my lips and dig my fingers into my hips, pushing down any hint of the emotions threatening to break free from the box I lock them in and keep in the darkest corner of my body. I dig my fingers even harder into my hip bones and the flood retreats. I settle back into the comfort of numbness and breathe again.

I look up at the sky. White puffy clouds are moving quickly across the blue. I feel for the double hearts on my bracelet, hold the cool metal between my finger and thumb, step back into the sunshine, and head to the library.

FIVE

"I WANNA REWRITE MY HEART AND LET THE FUTURE in. I wanna open it up and let somebody in." Harper is behind the wheel of her Range Rover, driving down the tree-lined streets of the New Albany Country Club community and singing along to an old Miike Snow song from my Spotify playlist. Actually, it's a playlist Luke made me. He's always making me little playlists with songs he knows I'll like.

"I love indie artists who stay indie artists," Harper says, turning down the music. I crack a half smile. Harper hates it when the indie musicians she loves show up on Top 40 radio. Harper likes to pretend she's above celebrity gossip and pop culture, but I've found *Us Weeklys* under her bed. It's ingrained in me to know every inch of my environment and the people I surround myself with. But I'm also kind of a snoop. So I know all about her secret tabloid subscription and the fact that she's downloaded an embarrassing number of baby-faced, floppy-haired boy band songs and hidden them on a secret playlist. I've never called her out because she'd be mortified. So I let her keep up her too-cool-for-school act. I guess it's not totally an act. She really doesn't care what people think and never tries to impress anybody. But still, I wonder how much of it she's faking. How much we're all faking.

The song finishes and Frank Sinatra's "Fly Me to the Moon" comes on. A slow smile creeps up my face as I look over at Harper, knowing what will come next. She shakes her head, her wavy hair swinging from side to side, and laughs.

"You officially have the world's weirdest music collection," Harper says, pulling past the lavish New Albany Country Club. We're not members but Harper's and Luke's families are. My parents occasionally let me escape my Saturday training sessions for a dip in the Olympic-size pool or a match on the clay tennis court.

"I think the word you're looking for, my love, is eclectic," I say and sing her a few lines of Frank. "In other words, hold my hand. In other words, baby, kiss me." I push together my lips and make a kissy face for Harper. She laughs and blows me a kiss back.

"The Wombats are coming to the Newport next Friday night," Harper says, winding her way around the ninth hole of the golf course. The warm October day has brought out plenty of polo-shirt-wearing golfers hoping to squeeze in one more round before gray, cold November skies roll in and the course closes for the season. "Carlee Abernathy's brother is bartending that night and said he could hook us up with tickets and a little drinky drinky. Want to go?"

"Depends. If my parents are out of town, totally. If they're home, definitely not."

"So when will you know if you can go?"

"Next Friday."

"What? We can't get the tickets day of. How do you never know their schedule?"

"They're journalists. They go where the story is and they go when it's happening." The journalist thing was their new cover. My dad was supposed to be a photographer, my mother a writer, for the Associated Press. Saying they worked for the AP made it plausible for them to have to leave at a moment's notice, be gone for long periods of time, and never have a byline in the *Columbus Dispatch*. It was a great cover. CIA operations officers usually pose as diplomats while out on assignment, but anyone in the Special Activities Division, especially Black Angels, gets the best and most detailed cover stories. Because unlike CIA officers, who really only collect information from foreign agents, Black Angels are the ones who are in true danger on a daily basis, even on American soil. They're the group the government pretends doesn't exist and the president doesn't even know about. Well, he probably knows *something*. He's the president, after all. But there's sort of a don't-ask, don't-tell policy with the Black Angels. He knows there is an underground group the CIA calls on to handle the messy stuff the government doesn't want to lay claim to, but he doesn't want to know any details. It's the knowing that could get him in trouble and get Black Angels killed.

"How's your NYU application going?" I ask. Harper wants to go to one school and one school only so she's applying early decision.

"Almost done. God, I hope I get in. I'm so freaking excited to get out of this cow town," Harper answers, coming to a stop to let a golf cart full of forty-something men cross in front of her to reach the next hole. The driver gives us a polite wave with his golf-gloved hand.

"Come on, it's not that bad," I reply, suddenly defensive of New Albany. I must admit: I thought of Columbus as a cow town before I moved here, but it's really grown on me. I've lived in so many different places. Big cities like Los Angeles, Philadelphia, and Chicago and small border towns like Derby Line, Vermont, and Laredo, Texas. Columbus has been a perfect happy medium for me.

"There's no culture here. No art, no diversity," Harper says, sticking her left arm out her open window and letting her hand ride the wave of the wind.

"What about the Short North? You can't walk down a block of High Street without running into three art galleries."

"Well, there's no outlet here for someone like me who's interested in filmmaking. Maybe after I finish film school and make a few hit indie films, I'll come back and shoot one here or something. Culture this place up a bit," Harper replies. The song changes and Louis Armstrong serenades us.

Harper has her whole life figured out. NYU film school, then move to LA and become the next Sofia Coppola. She knows exactly what she wants to do and she's so excited about it. She beams every time she talks about the future. Luke too. He's wanted to follow in his dad's military-boot-size footsteps and go to West Point since he was a kid. I think if they both had it their way, they'd fast-forward through senior year and get on with the next chapter of their lives. I envy that. Their hopefulness. The fact that their futures are theirs to create. I'm so jealous of it sometimes my body aches. My life has never felt like my own. And my future certainly doesn't belong to me.

Harper pulls off the main artery of the country club community and onto Landon Lane. Enormous oak trees create a canopy of crisscrossed branches and bright red leaves. Each Georgian brick house is more stunning than the next. Everything in New Albany is brick. No exceptions. It's very *Pleasantville*. All my friends complain about it but I secretly like the order and perfection—the manicured lawns, beautifully kept flower beds, and miles of white picket fences.

Our New Albany house is by far my favorite of all the homes I've ever lived in. The brick is a rustic red-and-white wash; it makes the house look like it's been standing since the 1700s even though it's less than a decade old. Two white columns hold up the roof over the small front porch and black shutters frame every window.

"Still on for eight at Luke's to study AP bio?" Harper asks as she pulls into my driveway. I pop open the door handle.

"Yup. I've got to ace this one if I want to get an A in the class, so no fooling around this time, Harper," I say, grabbing my messenger bag and waving my finger at her. If procrastination was an Olympic sport, Harper would win the gold medal. Last time we all studied together, we spent the first ninety minutes watching YouTube videos and flipping through Instagram.

"Oh, whatever," Harper replies, rolling her eyes and fluttering her long lashes. "You're, like, the smartest person I've ever met. You get an A on every test you take yet freak out constantly that you're going to fail. It's annoying to us B students."

"I got a B on that calculus test," I say, a smile inching up my face.

Harper fake strangles me from across the front seat console and the smile sticks.

"Oh my God! Let's call TMZ! Reagan MacMillan got a B once on a test," Harper replies and gives me a wink. "And by the way, I know for a fact . . . it was a B plus."

"Truth," I say and hop out of the car.

"Later, smarty-pants."

I close the door and walk up the brick path that leads to my porch, turning my head toward the sky. The days are getting shorter and the sun is starting its daily dip toward the horizon. The white puffy clouds are turning a caramel cream and the blue sky is streaked with orange and gold.

Harper gives the horn a quick honk before driving out of the cul-de-sac and down my street. Fallen red leaves blow backward and dance together as she speeds away. I watch her taillights blink red at the stop sign. She turns the corner and heads to her street on the other side of the country club.

I put my hand on the doorknob, but a noisy motor stops me cold. I turn back around in time to see an unmarked gray van pulling slowly down the main street. It pauses and someone in the driver's seat looks down our cul-de-sac. I strain my eyes to try to make out the person behind the wheel but the trees are casting shadows and I cannot see their face. I feel an uneasy knot tighten in my stomach. I step back out onto the porch and bounce down my front steps but just as I reach the sidewalk, the tires squeal and the van speeds away.

I shake out my arms, hoping to quell the nerves pulsing between my muscles. I open the heavy wooden front door and walk into the two-story foyer, immediately locking the door behind me. I lean my back up against the smooth wood, suddenly out of breath, my mind racing. Do I tell Mom and Dad about the van? Do I tell them about the janitor? What will they think? What will they say? My paranoia has been so much better. Mom and Dad are finally letting me stay at home by myself without Aunt Sam when they go on missions. They finally trust me to control myself.

When we moved from Philadelphia, every car I didn't recognize on our street, every person who walked onto our property who I didn't know, even someone who just looked at me too long would send my heart racing or close up my throat. I was convinced the hitman was still going to find us and that we'd never be safe. But every car, person, or look could be explained away. My brain—I couldn't trust it. It played tricks on me. I've done my best to hide the paranoia and anxiety. My parents think it was just a fluke. A rough patch after the hitman. They don't know I'm still struggling. That it's escalated.

This spring, I noticed someone following me. Or at least, I thought he was following me. This was after two false alarms, so I kept it to myself. I put the fear and anxiety in my little box, pushing it into the numbest part of my body. But when Mom and Dad were on a mission, I was mid-makeup routine and suddenly couldn't breathe. I started sweating and my chest was pounding so hard, I could have sworn you could see it beating through my shirt. I grabbed the cold granite countertop with my clammy hands, my arms and legs trembling. I thought I was having a heart attack or dying or something. I lowered myself down to the icy tiled floor, my back up against my wood cabinets, and sat there, begging my throat to open back up so I could suck in a full breath. Aunt Samantha found me, curled up on the ground, a few minutes later. She laid me down on the floor and put a cold washcloth on my burning forehead, asking me to describe my symptoms.

"What's wrong with me?" I asked, staring up into her warm blue eyes.

"You're having a panic attack," she answered very quietly. She sat on the floor next to me, stroking back my dark hair, telling me it would pass and I was going to be okay. Once my legs stopped trembling, she helped me off the floor and insisted I lie in bed.

After two hours of lying side by side, watching over-caffeinated anchors on morning talk shows, I was finally feeling better. I could breathe again.

"What was that all about?" I asked, turning my head to face Sam. She twisted her strong, lean body to face mine, settling her head back down on my extra-fluffy pillows.

"I don't know," Sam said, shaking her head slowly. "I've never had one but I know they can be really scary."

"It was," I replied, my voice quiet. We stared at each other for a few seconds, waiting for the other to speak.

"I know what happened in Philadelphia is weighing on you," she said, grabbing my arm, rubbing the fabric of my blue shirt between her thumb and index finger. "But you're safe here."

"I know," I replied, even though I didn't believe her. Not for a single second.

"I don't want to put pressure on you, my love," Sam said, picking

51

at the errant fuzzies on my bedspread. "But if you suffer from panic attacks, we'll need to tell your parents and they may want to stop your training. Or at least think about not having you train for rescues and take-downs."

Sam explained that panic attacks and anxiety would cloud my brain and alter my judgment, making it unsafe for my teammates and me in the field. She never said it out loud, but I could read between the lines. Have another panic attack and I'd be out of the Black Angels.

"Please," I said, grabbing Sam's hand. "Don't tell them. Not yet."

She didn't. And I learned to bury the fear.

That panic attack was my first and only. But what's taken its place are the daymares. They creep into my brain, sometimes without warning or even a trigger. I've coined them daymares because they're like the vivid nightmares that startle you straight up in bed, panting and sweating, except I'm awake. I haven't said a word about the daymares to anyone. Perhaps it's normal. Perhaps everyone has these worst-case scenarios play out in their minds. Just not as vivid and violent as mine. I could ask, but I don't think I want to know the answer. Because then it's just one more thing on a very long list that makes me abnormal.

We've been perfectly safe in New Albany for over a year now. So what would I even tell them? A janitor looked at me funny today? A van pulled down the main street slowly? People do that all the time, gawking at the million-dollar homes. No. I won't say a word. It's all in my head. Again.

"Mom, Dad?" I call out. Nothing. I walk down the hardwood

hallway. The heavy strike of my heel is the only sound. My natural walk (or as natural as a walk can be when you've been trained to walk a certain way since practically your first step) is silent. I'm a sidler. I scare the shit out of people when I show up at their side in stealthy silence. So to alert Mom and Dad to where I am in the house, I walk hard. Like hear-you-two-stories-and-five-rooms-away hard. When I walk hard, Dad likes to call me Elefante, the Spanish word for elephant. When he hears me coming down the hallway, the bone of my heel slamming into the floors, he sings out "Elefan-teeee." It always makes me laugh.

I stick my head inside the kitchen, then inside the family room. The only two rooms they're ever really in. I swear I can count on one hand the number of times we've stepped foot in the living and dining rooms. I stop and listen again for the hum of a TV or the shuffling of feet somewhere in the house. It's silent.

The garage door opens with a whiny creak. I walk down three concrete steps and stand in front of locked steel cabinet doors. I flip open the keypad and enter in our six-digit code. I hear the steel beams unlock. I pull hard on both of the metal handles, separating the heavy cabinet doors and revealing wooden steps. We've had a secret door in every house we've ever lived in. CORE always finds us a house with an unfinished basement so they can transform it into our gun range, weapons room, martial arts studio, and, of course, panic room.

"Hello?" I yell down the stairs, and the sound of gunfire answers me. I close the secret door behind me and bounce down the steps. I stand on the last step and smile as I watch my parents in their

Ralph Lauren knit sweaters and jeans. They look like just your average mom and dad except for the pistols they hold in both hands. My mom's blond hair is bobbed. Not a soccer mom haircut or anything, but an I'm-totally-in-my-forties-and-too-busy-for-anything-high-maintenance haircut. She's thin and tall like me, but that's really the only thing that we physically have in common. I don't really look like my dad either. He has chestnut hair and big, light brown eyes while mine are deep brown and more almond-shaped. Our family pictures are always funny because I look like I don't really belong. I'd swear I was adopted if it wasn't for the family photos of me actually coming out of my mother. Gross.

Bang. Their shots rip through the paper target. Right to the heart and head.

"Nice shot," I say loudly as they go to reload. They both turn around and smile when they see me.

"Hi, Reagan," my mom says and takes off her protective headphones. "When did you get home?"

"Just walked in," I say, crossing the room to get to work. There's no such thing as idle time in the basement. When I'm down here, I should always be training. I grab my M4 carbine off the counter that holds my weapons and kiss Mom's waiting cheek. "Harper and I went to Starbs after school and she just dropped me off."

"What's Starbs?" my father asks, wrinkling his brow. "I don't speak teenager."

"Starbucks," I say and smile.

"Hey, no coffee for us?" he asks.

"Sorry, Dad," I reply, sitting down at the weapons assembly table behind them. I look the assault rifle over and begin the process of stripping it to clean it, a weekly must-do to avoid jams and misfires. "I didn't think vanilla lattes would pair well with gunpowder."

"Good point," Dad says, looking down at his phone. He's always on that thing. I've even seen him checking it while brushing his teeth. He's constantly connected to CORE.

"So, how was school today?" Mom asks.

"Took a calculus test, got an A on my AP modern European paper," I say, popping out the assault rifle's magazine with a loud crack. "Threatened to break the arm of a girl who was bullying Claire. You know, the usual."

"You da woman, Rea Rea," Dad says, giving me a thumbs-up with one hand and picking up his Glock 27 pistol with the other. I swear I could tell my dad that I discovered the cure for cancer and he'd give me the same response. *You da woman.* It's his little annoying but sort of adorable way of showing pride.

"You weren't using Krav Maga in school, now, were you?" Mom asks and crosses her arms, not exactly excited that I almost snapped a girl's bone in two.

"I mean, nothing ridiculous," I say, visually inspecting the M4's upper receiver and chamber for any ammunition.

"Reagan..." she starts.

"Just one move, Mom. She was going to punch me in the face. And besides, I'm not going to let people mess with Claire."

"Well, good for you," Mom says with a small smile, brushing a loose strand of hair out of her eyes. "You're a natural rescuer. I've been telling you that for years. Black Angel is in your blood." Of course. I resist the urge to roll my eyes. They always have to slip that in.

"I got an email from the Templeton admissions guy about my interview Saturday. What time are we leaving?" I ask, pushing the upper portion of the M4's bolt catch, sliding the bolt forward. "My interview's at two but I'd like to make sure we're there by one so we can walk around the campus."

"Sorry, hon, but you'll have to go without us," Dad announces casually, crossing the room and grabbing another clip for his pistol off the shelf. "Mom and I have to leave for DC tonight."

"What? But I've had this interview planned for months," I say, looking up from my weapon.

"You know how missions are," Mom says with a small shrug. "We can get called to headquarters at any moment."

"What's the big deal?" Dad asks, reloading his magazine with a sharp click. "It's not like you're going to college anyways."

My breath catches, sharp and jagged, in my chest. Of course he'd say that. They've never even bothered to ask if this is the life I want. I was told casually over dinner at thirteen that when I turned eighteen, it would be my choice. But it's never been brought up again. The path they've chosen for me is rammed down my throat at every opportunity. I'm not asking for much. I'd take even a flicker of concern over what I want for my future.

"I know. I just wanted you guys to see the campus with me," I say, lowering my weapon and my voice, trying not to get upset. I know it won't do any good so what's the point? The anger I want to feel is already replaced by defeat. I pick up my M4 and cross the room to the weapons shelf. God, I freaking hate this. It's more than Dad's dismissal. It's the fact they can't show up for anything. Why even make plans? We almost always have to cancel them. Family vacations, Christmas, Thanksgiving, it doesn't matter. The Black Angels come first and always will.

"Sorry to disappoint you, Reagan," Mom says, her voice uncharacteristically quiet. I turn to look at her; the corners of her mouth are pointed down and her eyes are heavy. I shake my head, press my lips together, and look away. I've been hearing "sorry" my whole life. Sorry for missing your birthday, sorry for leaving you on Christmas Eve, sorry for missing your play. But there are some pains they've never even acknowledged. Sorry you've basically been raised by Aunt Sam, sorry you're always in danger, sorry for forcing you to lie every single day of your life, sorry for making you choose between this life and a normal one, sorry you don't even know what normal is. I'm sick of their sorrys. The ones they say and the ones they never will.

Bang. My father is shooting at a fresh dummy target. Clearly, he cannot feel my disappointment like my mother can. She is still looking at me, her gaze heavy, willing me to look at her. I place the M4 on my shelf and walk toward the martial arts room.

"Reagan," my mother says in between gunfire as I walk away, but I pretend I don't hear her. I don't want to turn around and have her see the broken look I can feel on my face.

I pull on my training gloves and stare at the quote that's been painted, thick and black, on the wall of every martial arts room we've ever had:

"To whom much is given, much is expected."

It's become the Black Angels' unofficial mantra. We are given so much. The best of the best training. Beautiful homes. Envious paychecks. But more than that, genetically inherited abilities and the power to do so much good. For the last decade, the quote empowered me. It was something I told myself proudly. But lately, it's felt more like a loose, guilt-inducing knot around my wrists.

I turn to face the dummy, but Mom is standing in the center of the mats, her green eyes wide and fixed on my face. She opens her mouth to speak, the words rolling around her head but not off her tongue. She presses her lips together. Her face changes, her eyes narrow, and her body hardens. She tries again.

"Take-downs from a choke hold," Mom says as she moves toward me. She puts her fingers tight around my neck and pushes me hard against the wall, the quote centered above our heads. "Let's go."

I look into her eyes for a beat. But she tightens her grip on me. I guess there's nothing more to say. I push down hard on her arms to my right then slam her head to the left. I lift my knees to hit her in the groin and stomach over and over again until her hold on me slips and I can push her away.

"Good. Again," Mom commands, wrapping her strong hands around my throat from the side. I've done this so many times, the synapses in my brain don't even fire. My body knows what to do. With one hand, I pull at the fingers around my neck while with my other I simulate slamming into her groin then elbowing her in the chin to get away. Three seconds and I'm out.

"Good. Again." Mom runs at me from the side, pulling me into a choke hold. I don't resist. I let her body and gravity pull us closer together. I punch one hand against her groin and reach around with the other to pull her head back, slamming her onto the mat. The echo of her back crashing against the plastic pad bounces off the cinder-block walls and polished concrete floors. Mom struggles to pull in the last wisps of air that I forced from her body.

"I'm so sorry," I say and extend my hand down to her as she catches her breath.

"Don't be sorry. That was perfect." Mom's rosebud lips break into a smile. She reaches up and takes my hand. "Again."

SIX

BUZZ. MY PHONE VIBRATES ON THE CREAM-AND-BLACK
granite sink top next to me. I touch the screen to read a text from
Harper.

> Leaving my house in a few. Just flipping through
> Instagram. Zedd posted a couple amazing videos.
> Must watch before studying. PS GET ON INSTAGRAM!

I'm not on a single social media channel. Can't be. It's one of
the Black Angels' strictest policies. I'd be way too traceable if I was.
The last thing I need is for someone in my new life to find a picture
of me from an old life with a different last name. It's hard to keep
track of all the lies as it is. So I just pretend that I'm completely too
cool for social media and that I hate having my picture taken. People
buy it.

I pick up my phone and text her back.

Harper! No Instagram. No Vines. No Snapchat. No Pinterest. No Twitter. Biology!

I stare at my phone and wait for her reply.

I love messing with you. xo

I smile and delete the message like always. I'm paranoid my parents check my texts. In fact, I know they do. We are three trained killers, but three natural-born snoopers.

I look back at my reflection in the bathroom mirror. I've struggled to give my long dark hair a little bit of body and pinned a few pieces back with bobby pins. But it just won't sit right. I'd normally put it up in a bun or a ponytail and call it a day but Luke loves my hair down. He also likes it when I . . .

Stop it. I look at myself in the mirror and shake my head, slapping my forehead with the palm of my hand. I have to stop thinking about him like that. I have to stop hoping for something. For his sake and mine.

"Stop sabotaging yourself," I say in a singsong voice to my reflection as I turn out the light. I shake out my arm, trying to crush the butterflies in my stomach. I never understood that phrase until I met Luke. I always thought it was an eye-rollingly annoying way of saying you like someone. But the first time he touched me, I felt them. All he did was pull me in for a half hug after we beat some neighbors in a game of soccer. He ran the tips of his fingers up and down my arm. Up and down. Slowly. My stomach tied into a million little knots. My heart pounded hard and fast in my ears. I had to remind myself to breathe. And a year later, that's still the feeling I get every time we touch.

Clunk, clunk, my boots hit the hardwood floors.

"Reagan," Mom calls out and I immediately regret not doing my Black Angel walk.

"Crap," I say under my breath. I can tell by the way she says my name that she's going to want to talk about missing the trip to Templeton and I just don't feel like it. I don't have the energy to "talk it through." She always wants to "talk it through" so she can feel like she's doing her job as a mother, but really I think she just wants me to tell her it's all right and that I'll be just fine without them. And so I do it. Every time I follow the script and tell her what she wants to hear so she can bury the guilt and sleep at night.

"Reagan, can you come here, please?" she calls out again. I sigh, dig my heel into the floor, and turn around. I walk toward the opposite end of the hallway, following the light that pours out of her open bedroom door and onto the dark wood floors.

She looks up when I enter the room. She is so pretty, my mother, with her ivory skin and wide-set eyes. Her makeup is off and a plush cream robe is pulled tight around her thin frame. A small black suitcase is open on their dark gray linen bedspread. My mother is neatly folding articles of clothing and placing them inside. It's a mixture of normal clothes—jeans, sweaters, T-shirts—and black clothes, or what I like to call their "kick-ass gear."

"I take it by the size of the suitcase you won't be gone long this time," I say and walk across the cream carpeting to the dark leather chair in the corner. I sit down, throwing my legs up on the matching ottoman, crossing them in front of me.

"Those boots better be clean, my love," Mom says, eyeing my boots on the leather ottoman.

"Don't worry," I answer, looking at the soles of my feet. "I went tramping through mud and cow manure a week ago. Should have worked its way off the boots and onto all the cream carpeting in the house by now."

"No need to get smart," Mom says, doing a double take with my outfit. She's used to seeing me in PJs or sweats by this time of night. Not a red scoop-neck long-sleeve T-shirt and dark skinny jeans. "Where are you going?"

"Just to Luke's to study for our AP bio test tomorrow," I answer, gesturing toward the window that overlooks the Weixels' home.

"Don't you think you should stay in tonight?" she asks with a sigh. She likes Luke. But I don't think she loves how much time we spend together.

"He's got the notes for a couple of the classes I missed when I was in DC with you guys," I answer. Pulling out the Black-Angels-make-me-miss-school card usually shuts her down.

"Okay," Mom responds, semisatisfied.

"So, how long will you be gone this time?" I ask and nod toward the suitcase.

"Not very long," she answers and returns to her folding. "Couple days is all."

"Why can't people need saving when we don't have plans?" I ask, trying to keep my tone light and this conversation short. Mom looks up from her packing. Her intense eyes are uncharacteristically sad and I know guilt is twisting her stomach into knots. *Good*, I think, then immediately feel guilty for being glad that she feels guilty. It's a vicious cycle.

"Sorry we can't be there Saturday," she says, leaning her hip on the side of the bed. She looks down at my father's socks, unfolds them, and then refolds them.

"It's fine. I understand," I say and shrug, following the script.

"It's all part of your cover anyways," Mom says, waving her hand through the air, brushing it off and with it, any feelings I might have on the subject. "Just go with a friend or something."

"Yeah. Sure," I reply with a weak smile. It's not even a question for them where I'll be next year. And every time they talk about my future with steadfast certainty, the knot that's been anchored to my stomach since Philadelphia pulls tighter and tighter.

"I'm also upset we're going to miss the country club's fall gala with Harper's parents," Mom says without looking up from her packing.

That's what she's upset about? I dig my nails into the palms of my hands and take a breath. I close my eyes and try to concentrate on the rise and fall of my chest. Sometimes I want to scream at them. I want to wave my hands around the weapons room and shout "You chose this life." The moving, the cover stories, the lying, the danger. They weighed out all the pros and cons and chose this. I don't have that luxury.

My mother lived my dream. She's absolutely brilliant. Graduated from college at twenty and went to medical school at Johns Hopkins. She was a practicing trauma surgeon for less than a year before she got recruited by the CIA. She was one of the CIA's top operatives when she was promoted to the Special Activities Division, the most secretive operations force in the United States. That's where she met my dad. They became partners and eventually fell in love and got married. They both became so well trained and so well respected in the SAD that before I was born, they were asked by the government to go completely underground and become Black Angels, a promotion that is almost unheard of if you aren't grandfathered in. They've been living a double life for almost two decades.

"So, what's the mission anyways?" I ask after calming my nerves.

"You know I can't really tell you very much, Reagan," Mom answers and crosses the room. She opens the top drawer of her dresser and pulls out two simple cotton bras.

"So, tell me what you can," I say, uncrossing my arms and running the tip of my finger along a deep crease in the armchair's soft, worn leather. I follow one crease down the length of the arm and then back up again. I look up at my mom. She is pressing her lips together, thinking about how much she should give away.

"Mom, if you guys want me to do this, don't you think I should know the truth about some of the missions?" I say, my eyes returning to the crease. "It's only fair I know what I'm getting myself into."

"I know it is." My mother's voice is low. She sounds tired and overwhelmed by what lies ahead of her.

Mom takes a breath and sits down on the bed. "A Colombian drug lord, Santino 'El Martillo' Torres, kidnapped five American tourists on Tuesday and is demanding that some of his men that are in federal custody in the US be returned to Colombia. One of the men is his brother. Until they're freed, he's refusing to let the hostages go."

"I'm assuming the US won't release them."

"Of course not. They're convicted drug smugglers. Plus, you know the government won't negotiate with terrorists, and they certainly aren't going to negotiate with a thug like Torres. We have to get in there, and soon, because Torres has said if his men aren't released by Monday morning..." She pauses and swallows the emotion I'm surprised to hear bubbling up her throat. "If the US doesn't let them go, he plans on executing all the hostages during a live webcast."

"Holy shit," I whisper. My mom doesn't like me to swear, but she lets it go. "You think he'll actually do it?"

"They don't call him 'the hammer' for nothing. He's killed plenty of people before."

"So why are they calling on the Black Angels? Seems like something the Special Activities Division could take care of, right?"

"Probably, but it's a little tricky," Mom says, sweeping her blond hair out of her eye. She runs her finger down her jawline and stares past me. "For one, your dad and I were on the team that took down Torres's drug ring in the US."

"You put his brother in jail?" I ask.

Mom slowly nods and I immediately think about the janitor. Their enemies have tried to find us before and I'm sure they'd do it again. But before I open my mouth, she continues. "Torres has three brothers. They are his most trusted advisers in the cartel and just as crazy and dangerous as he is, so I'll sleep a little better with one of them in jail. The other reason we have to go is one of the Americans being held hostage is Senator Taylor's eighteen-year-old daughter Anna."

66

"What?" I exclaim and my stomach drops. "How'd he get his hands on her?"

"She was backpacking through South America with friends. Intelligence is still trying to figure out how Torres tracked her down. They have a few theories. Since Senator Taylor is one of the few officials who actually knows about us, he wanted only the best team out there to save her."

"Where's he keeping her?"

"I can't tell you that information, love." Mom stands up and goes back to folding clothes. "It's classified. I've probably told you too much already. If everything goes according to plan, we should be in and out of Colombia in a couple days."

Mom places the last bit of clothing into the suitcase and gets started on the weapons. I crane my neck to see what is on the bed. Knives, pistols, ammunition, zip ties, and earpieces are all perfectly lined up. Seeing them, knowing what they'll be used for, makes my stomach hurt. I look up at my mother's face. Her body is here but I know her mind is very far away. When it comes to missions, she's usually unemotional and detached—she has to be or she'd crumble. But I can tell this one has gotten to her. It's seeped underneath her skin.

"Why do you do it, Mom?" I ask, my voice barely audible. I watch the muscles in Mom's neck tighten. She looks up from packing and our eyes truly connect for the first time in a while. Sometimes when she looks at me, I feel like she's looking through me. I'm guilty of that too. I don't always see her. We see each other now.

"Why do I do what?" she asks even though she knows exactly what I'm asking.

"Why do you do all this?" I say and motion toward the

weapons on the bed. "You're risking your . . . I mean you've never even . . . you don't know her. You don't know anyone you rescue. So why do you do it?"

We hold each other's stare and I wait for her to say something. The silence between us is heavy with the question I've always wanted to ask and the answer she wasn't sure she'd ever have to give.

She clears her throat and finally speaks. "She's somebody's daughter. The other people I've rescued . . ." Mom pauses and raises her hand to her chest. "They're someone's mother or brother or aunt. They mean something to somebody. And I don't want them to die like that. I don't want them to die alone and afraid and begging for their lives. Not if I can do something to save them."

"Aren't you scared?" I ask. My voice is thin, like the words aren't even coming from my body.

"I'd be lying if I said no. But I know more than anything else in my life, this is what I was meant to do. This was my life's purpose."

A short and shallow breath fills my lungs. Of course she'd say that. She'll always pick them. I look away, breaking our connection.

When I finally look back, her face has fallen and I wonder if it's because she can read the hurt on my own. I know she loves me. I hear it in the way she says good morning and good night; I feel it in her hugs and the way she strokes my hair when I'm upset. It's love, but it's a different kind of love; one that has competition. A second-place kind of love.

I clear my throat. "You're very brave, Mom," I say, going back to the script.

"So are you," Mom replies. "To whom much is given, much is expected."

"Yes. I know," I say with a nod.

"It's a calling, Reagan. One few hear and one even fewer have the talent for. You're one of the lucky ones, aren't you?" Mom says, picking up her weapons case. She holds my gaze as the words wash over me again and again, knocking me back like a tidal wave. *It's a calling. It's a calling.* My stomach compresses its painful knot.

It's the closest she's ever been to asking me if this is what I want. But her tone is rhetorical. She expects a one-word answer. Yes. I open my mouth to reply then close it. She stands there frozen, her arms hugging a black weapons case to her chest, waiting for me to respond.

My phone buzzes loudly and I have never been so thankful for a text in my entire life. I pull my iPhone from my bag. Luke.

On your way?

"Who's that? Luke?" Mom asks, lowering her eyes as she lays her weapons case back on the bed, tucking her knives and pistols inside.

"Yeah," I answer and slide the phone back into my bag. "Just wanting to know if I'm coming over."

"You know I like Luke," Mom says, quickly glancing up at me and then back down at her weapons. "I just want you to be careful. You guys are from two different worlds and ... I just don't want to see you get hurt. Either of you."

Me too, my mind whispers but I force a smile.

"We're just friends," I say for what feels like the tenth time today. I jump out of my seat and cross the room to where Mom is still packing weapon after deadly weapon. I put my hand on her shoulder.

Her robe feels like a cloud on my skin as I lean in and kiss her cool cheek. She puts her hand up to my face and pats the side of my head. I pull away and wait for her eyes to meet mine. They don't.

"Aunt Sam will be checking in on you," Mom says, methodically packing rounds of ammunition in her case.

"Okay," I say and turn around, walking toward the doorway.

"Be careful while we're gone, okay?" she calls after me.

"You be safe too," I answer.

As I reach the hallway, I raise my hand to the door frame and look over my shoulder as Mom slips her last remaining round of ammo in its holder. There's something about her that seems so small tonight, like she could be folded up and fit inside the tiny silver box that holds her wedding rings.

"I love you, Mom," I say softly, just as I've done before every mission. Mom finally lifts her head, her eyes meeting mine, and there's something about them that makes my bones ache.

"I love you too," she says, then looks back down at her case. I watch her for one more moment. I take in her faint smile lines and the way her blond hair brushes along her jawline when she moves. I hold on to that image and file it away. I turn back around and walk down the dark hallway, skip down the steps, open the door, and run the fifteen steps to Luke's house.

SEVEN

THE COLD AIR PIERCES MY LUNGS AS I CLOSE MY FRONT door and bounce down the steps into the mellow October morning. A delicate mist hangs in the air and a cloth of silver dew clings to the blades of grass. The sweet, heavy summer air is long gone, replaced by the smell of earth, clinging desperately to its last precious weeks of life.

Luke stands at the edge of my driveway dressed in athletic shorts and a maroon New Albany High School lacrosse sweatshirt. His full lips separate into a wide smile when he sees me and I can't stop my own from turning up at him. I never invited him to go running with me. He just kept showing up at the end of my driveway at 5:45. But now I can't imagine him not striding along next to me, pushing me to go faster.

"I was about to send a search-and-rescue team," Luke says, tapping on his Fitbit.

"What am I, a whole minute late?" I tease, bumping my hip into his.

"Two minutes late," he says, extending his arm to show me the time. "Bed feel too good this morning, Mac?"

"Just too comfy," I lie with a yawn. Little does he know, I've already done thirty minutes of Krav Maga and fifteen minutes of target practice.

We take off down Landon Lane, our feet crunching the red leaves that cover the sidewalk like a crimson carpet.

"You ready for the AP bio test?" Luke asks as we run to the end of our street and hit the bike paths that crisscross throughout the neighborhoods and along the golf course.

"As ready as I can be," I say with a laugh. Harper didn't stick to her promise and we found ourselves looking through Snapchat and Instagram in between trying to memorize the difference between structural isomers and geometric isomers. "I'm really not in the mood for a test today. Mr. Bajec's tests are so painful."

"Would you rather have to take an AP bio test every single day for a year," Luke says with a sideways smile as he begins our favorite, silly game. "Or scrub the gym locker room toilets with a toothbrush once a week?"

"Oh gosh," I answer, my voice and breath beginning to strain as we run up a hill. "The test, I think. I don't know what you boys are doing in that disgusting locker room."

"Okay, how about this one?" Luke asks as we reach the crest of the hill. "Would you rather have a bear claw as a hand or a mermaid tail as a foot?"

"Bear claw all the way," I answer and tuck a dark strand of hair that fell out of my ponytail behind my ear. "I'd be so super strong."

"But you'd be hairy."

72

"True enough," I reply. "I think I'd still take the claw. Hairy hand and all. Okay, how about this one? Would you rather be stuck on a desert island by yourself or with someone you hated?"

"Oh man, I don't know," Luke says and shakes his head. His blue eyes smile at me before his lips do. "Can I have your bear claw hand? Just in case I need to kill the person I hate when they get on my nerves."

"Sure," I answer with a laugh. Luke and I have probably asked each other about one thousand stupid "would you rather" questions and I never get tired of them.

"Are your parents excited to tour Templeton with you tomorrow?" Luke asks as we run past New Albany Country Club. There are a lot more cars in the parking lot than I expected at this hour but then I remember what day it is. Hot Yoga Instructor Friday. Harper may have even pulled her butt out of bed for the gorgeous Australian's six a.m. class.

I press my lips together and shake my head. "They're not coming."

"What do you mean they're not coming?" Luke asks, his eyes growing wide.

"They got called out on assignment," I answer and shrug my shoulders two inches too high. "A protest in South America or something."

"You bummed?"

"Nah, it's okay. No big deal. Work is work." I'm lying. To Luke and to myself. I know exactly what I'm doing; trying to pretend like I don't care so that I can trick myself into actually believing it when really my body is sore from the sting of their dismissal.

"So who's going up with you tomorrow?" he asks.

"No one. Just me," I answer, attempting my best chipper, it's-all-good voice.

"No way," Luke says, furrowing his brow and shaking his head. "I'm going with you."

"You don't have to do that. It's an hour-and-a-half drive. I'll be fine," I reply and push up the sleeves of my sweatshirt. "Besides, you've got JROTC stuff on Saturdays."

"It's okay. I'll skip it."

"Won't you get in trouble?"

"Maybe a little bit. A few extra chores at the office will fix it."

"I don't want you to get in trouble for me."

"I'd love to get in trouble for you," Luke says, his voice a little less playful than I was expecting. But when I glance at him, the scarlet apples of his cheeks rise and he smiles.

"Okay," I say with a nod and look away. I sink my top teeth into the side of my lower lip to keep from smiling. My heart is pounding. I can't tell if it's this hill or the rush of endorphins or Luke.

"Come on, race you to the top," Luke says, grabbing my wrist, his chin nodding toward the top of the hill. "On the count of three: one, two, three."

Our legs sprint up the hill, our stride in sync. Luke has over six inches on me and his long legs begin to gain ground. I reach out and tug very gently at the bottom of his sweatshirt and he swats me away.

"Mac, you cheater." He laughs, playfully putting his hand to the top of my chest, slowing my pace.

"Now you're the cheater," I holler and pull even harder at his sweatshirt, finally breaking his rhythm. One more tug and I zoom past him, my muscles burning, my pounding feet begging for rest, Luke's long legs nipping at my heels.

My body leans forward, breaking through imaginary finish-line tape, and I pump both fists in the air like I just won the Olympics, the imaginary crowd going wild.

"I win, I win!" I yell, jumping up and down on the pavement while Luke bends over, hands on his knees, smile on his face, his chest rising and falling in rapid succession.

"You did win," Luke replies between gasps of air while I dance in celebration. "Look at you. Even if you hadn't cheated, I think you still would have won."

"Hey, you cheated first," I say, my hand on my hip, my finger playfully wagging in his face.

"No way, you started it," he says, finally standing up straight, the dimples in his cheeks crinkling as he grins.

"That was minuscule compared to your arm bar," I reply, giving his shoulder a slight shove.

"Yeah, yeah. Whatever. You win, Mac," Luke concedes, throwing his arm around my neck and pulling me closer. Even after a run, he smells good. A mixture of leaves and body wash and cinnamon gum. I instinctively wrap my arm around his waist and play with the strings on my sweatshirt.

We walk in comfortable silence, amber leaves crunching at our feet. I look up at the tree-lined path, its branches set ablaze for nature's most beautiful performance art. Fall is the world's way of begging for one last colorful celebration before the bleakness of winter.

A gust of wind breaks through the stillness of the morning, whipping my hair and sending the tree branches swaying. Luke pulls me closer to him and rubs my shoulders and even though I'm warm, I begin to shiver.

"You too cold? Do you want my sweatshirt?" Luke says, tightening his grip on me with one hand and pulling at his sweatshirt with the other, accidentally pulling up his T-shirt, exposing his defined, athletic stomach.

"No, no, I'm fine." I wave off his offer, trying to stop my body from shaking but it won't obey. My blood is pumping and I can feel heat streak across my cheeks.

The rumble of a loud motor spins my body around. A gray van. But is it the same gray van? People in New Albany are always renovating or calling in carpenters or plumbers, so I can't be sure. As it drives closer, I identify and file away its distinguishing features. Charcoal gray paint job. Ohio plates. No windows on the sides. Early 2000s model. GMC. My eyes strain to get a look at the driver but the sun has yet to climb over the horizon. The van quickly passes beneath a streetlight. It's only for a fraction of a second, but long enough for me to see a face I don't recognize staring back at me. Long black hair, a sharp jaw, and dark, probing eyes that make my warm blood run cold. The van picks up speed as it drives past us, turning down Route 62 before I can get a clear shot of the license plate.

"Mac, are you okay?" Luke asks, staring down at me, and I realize I've stopped moving. Stopped breathing too. "What's the matter?"

"Nothing," I say, looking up at him with a forced smile that hurts my cheeks.

"You're still shaking," he says, his fingers wrapping tighter around my shoulders.

"I guess I'm cold after all," I answer and pull out of his grasp. I give the bottom of his sweatshirt a tug. "Come on. Race you home."

EIGHT

"YOU DON'T KNOW ME, BUT I'M YOUR BROTHER," I sing along to the record in the bonus room over the Weixels' four-car garage. I grab one of the remotes off the rustic wood coffee table and pretend it's a microphone. I hop on an ottoman in the corner and sing the lyrics at the top of my lungs. At the chorus, I leap off my perch like a rock star and point at Luke, stretched out on the rich chocolate-brown leather couch, laughing at me.

"Takin' it to the streets," Luke sings along to the record with me.

"Takin' it to the streets," I sing the Michael McDonald part, shaking my shoulders to the beat while I jump from side to side.

"Takin' it to the streets," he sings, banging on the fake piano on his lap.

"No more need for runnin'," I sing dramatically into the remote and drop to my knees.

"Takin' it to the streets," Luke half sings, half laughs.

"Oh, oh-oh, nah, nah," I sing from the ground, my eyes closed.

When I look back up, Luke is lying down on the deep leather sofa, laughing and clutching his stomach. I love it when he laughs like that. So hard no sound comes out of his mouth and he fights to breathe.

I giggle and take a running jump for the other end of the couch, landing with an ungraceful thud. It's after midnight on Friday night and we're on Mountain Dew number four and record number six. Claire is sleeping at her grandma's house and Colonel and Mrs. Weixel are out of town. So we can be as loud as we want.

"Oh my God," Luke says, still laughing but trying to catch his breath. He sits up and leans against the arm of the couch. "I love it when you're silly, Mac."

I shrug and throw my dark hair over my shoulder. "I guess you bring out my silly side." Luke smiles and I can tell he likes that.

"Are we the only two seniors in the world sitting around on a Friday night listening to the Doobie Brothers?" he asks.

"Probably. But proud of it."

Luke and I have the same eclectic music taste. Singers and standards. Top 40 Pop. Jazz. We like it all. But we have a special place in our hearts for the bands of the seventies. Chicago. Doobie Brothers. Steely Dan. We've totally confiscated all of Luke's parents' old records. Playing air guitar to the Doobie Brothers' "China Grove" or acting out the scenes from Chicago's "Saturday in the Park" like two total goofballs (Luke does a fabulous man selling ice cream) has become our weekend favorite. I live for these silly moments. When I'm not the chosen Black Angel child. When I'm just Reagan. Or as close to whoever Reagan really is.

Luke shakes his empty pop can on the coffee table and stands up. "Want another one?"

"No thanks," I answer and nuzzle my warm face up to the cool leather of the couch. "I think I better quit it on the Mountain Dews if I want to fall asleep tonight."

Luke comes back from the wet bar in the corner of the room and hands me a bottle of water.

"Here you go," he says and flops back down. I love this couch. It's so deep, two people could sleep side by side without a problem. I remember when the Weixels bought it last year; the delivery guys spent a good hour trying to figure out some way to get it through the back door, up the back staircase, and into the bonus room. Once it was finally in place, Luke and I volunteered to break it in and spent the entire night listening to music and watching movies. The leather was pristine then; now it's soft and worn. I run my fingers along the dark creases and wonder which lines were made by us during our many Friday and Saturday nights.

"So when do you find out about West Point?" I ask and open up the bottle of water.

"I find out if I get the Congressional nomination soon. I'm getting kind of nervous," Luke says and reaches for one of the remotes. He points it at the receiver and turns down Michael McDonald's voice so we don't have to yell.

"How will you find out?"

"A letter in the mail will let me know if I got the nomination," Luke replies and scrunches his face.

"What?" I ask.

He shrugs. "Just funny to think that a single piece of paper will decide my entire future."

"You'll get the nomination," I reassure him, reaching out to touch the top of his smooth hand. I hold my fingers there an extra beat and feel that familiar rush. I lean forward and put my bottle of water on the coffee table, breaking our connection.

"I hope you're right," Luke says, pressing his full lips together. His lips are such a pretty shade of watermelon pink, they almost don't look real. They're the lips you'd expect to see in the pages of GQ or on a movie star, not on an eighteen-year-old army brat.

"They'd be fools not to take you. You were accepted into the Summer Leaders Experience this summer, which makes you a shoo-in," I say, counting his accomplishments on my fingertips. "You're the leader of your JROTC class, you're on your way to being valedictorian—"

"Alongside you," Luke interrupts me and I wave him off to continue counting.

"You've been training with your dad since you were a kid, you know everything there is to know about weapons, and you're a terrific shot," I finish. A few months ago, Luke took me to the gun range he and his dad practice in at least twice a week. I of course pretended I had never shot a gun before and had Luke give me a lesson. My first shot was an accidental dead-center bull's-eye. Another Luke-induced mask slippage. Luke just about lost his mind. Beginner's luck, I called it. The rest of the clip was all over the place. Pretender mask locked firmly back in place. Luke ripped a massive hole in the bull's-eye of his paper dummy. I know great training when I see it and Luke's got the goods.

"Thanks, Mac," Luke says, placing his hand on my exposed ankle. "I appreciate the vote of confidence. It's a competitive nomination. I get nervous every time the mail comes. I just want it so . . . I just hope I get good news soon."

His sweet face, hopeful and anxious all at once, hits me square in the gut. All those accolades are going to get him into West Point, I know it. But it's his heart that will make him a high-ranking officer someday. I've been envious of his passion for the future; the fact that serving our country, as hard a life as it is, is what he wants to do more than anything. But now I realize he may have exactly what I've been missing. And I wish I could ask him for a piece of it.

"How about practicing your interview questions?" Luke says, removing his hand from my ankle. Even with it gone, I can still feel the warmth and weight of his fingers on my skin.

"Yes!" I exclaim, tucking my legs toward me and pulling my spine straighter on the couch. I brush my hair over my shoulders, widen my eyes and my smile, trying to look the part of an interviewee.

"Perfect," Luke says, sitting up from his lounging position, trying to match my sudden change in posture. "Okay. First question. If you were an animal, what kind of animal would you be?"

I laugh and lean forward. "Really?"

Luke nods. "They ask weird questions during an interview."

"Gosh . . . ummm . . ." I say, pulling my legs closer to my body. "I don't know. Perhaps a lion. Or a cheetah. Some type of big cat that can run really fast and take down anything in its path. How about you?"

"A zoo animal," Luke says without missing a beat. A laugh bubbles up my throat. I watch his thick lips curl up into a smile.

"Out of all the animals in the world you're going to go with a zoo animal."

"Don't you think zoo animals have the best lives ever?" Luke says, his pale blue eyes dancing. "If you're a lion out in the wild, yeah, you're at the top of the food chain and all, but you have to chase after your own food. You're constantly worried about some other lion killing you or stealing your lady lions. That's stressful. A zoo lion, you just hang out all day. People bring you big slabs of meat. It sounds great."

In between giggles, I weigh in. "I don't know. I think the life of a house cat is the best animal life ever. Your entire day consists of people petting you, followed by a long nap and then maybe looking out the window or lying in the sunshine."

"Yeah, but you could get stuck in one of those weird cat families that dress you up in American Girl doll clothes and sing 'I love you a bushel and a peck' while they dance around the house with you."

"That sounds oddly specific," I say, raising one eyebrow at him. "And like someone speaking from experience."

Luke casts his face down, his blond hair falling into his eyes, and slowly shakes his head in pity. "Poor, poor Patches."

"You dressed your cat up in doll clothes," I exclaim, reaching out to grab his wrist. "What's the matter with you?"

"And hats," he adds, which makes me explode in laughter. "Straw hats. Bonnets. Tiny baseball caps. It was mostly Claire, but sometimes I helped. It was not a good life for that poor little thing."

I'm laughing so hard now, my entire face actually hurts. It's not just Luke's delivery and timing that always makes me laugh. It's his face too. It's just so cute. Sometimes he'll say something, not even meaning to be funny, and I'll start giggling.

"Okay, next question," Luke announces as we finally get our giggle fit under control. He reaches for an open bag of Lays potato chips sitting on the coffee table. He shoves a handful of chips in his mouth and between bites asks, "If you were a chip, what kind of chip would you be?"

"These questions are ridiculous," I say and smack my palm to the center of my forehead.

"Hey, I'm just trying to prepare you," he answers with a shrug and a smile and passes me the bag of chips.

"Okay, what kind of chip would I be?" I say and crunch down on the salty chip, letting the oil coat my tongue while I think. "I'd be Ruffles."

"Why Ruffles?"

"The ridges mean I'm a little complicated but I'm versatile. You can dip me into different situations, just like a Ruffles chip, and I'm adaptable. Also, I'm just delicious."

"That's a very good answer to a very stupid question," Luke says with a grin and steals back the bag of chips. "Okay, rapid-fire questions. Don't think. Just answer. Ready?"

"Ready," I answer, stretching my legs back out and slapping my knees.

"French fries or Tater Tots?"

"Tater Tots."

"Name three things in your personal hell."

"'Who Let the Dogs Out' on repeat, the constant stench of B.O., and being force-fed meals of tuna balls."

"You mean meatballs?"

"No, tuna balls," I say and swallow the gag threatening to rise up my throat. "My Sicilian grandmother makes meatballs out of tuna fish whenever we come and visit because they're Dad's favorite, and the thought of them alone makes me want to die."

"That sounds awful," Luke says and shakes his head. "Okay, you get one superpower. What is it?"

"Teleportation."

"Who's your biggest role model?"

"My mom."

"What's your biggest strength?"

"My loyalty."

"What's your biggest weakness?"

"My anxiety," I say without thinking. Luke's blue eyes flash surprise. *My anxiety.* I can almost see the words floating away from me, white and fluffy, like they were written by the tiniest skywriting airplane. I immediately wish I could lasso them with my tongue and pull them back.

Luke's eyes blink and regain their shape. The room is quiet for two long breaths. "I didn't know you felt that way," Luke replies, choosing his words carefully. I swallow the nerves climbing up my throat.

"Well . . . it's not like a diagnosed problem or anything," I say, my eyes darting away from Luke's sweet, concerned face. I stare over his shoulder at the dark window that overlooks my even darker house. "I'm just a worst-case-scenario thinker sometimes. I wish I wasn't."

"I get it," Luke replies. He takes a breath and places his warm hand on my ankle. "I think you try to come off as Miss Carefree. But I can see that mind of yours working overtime."

"You can?" I ask, my eyebrows rising even though I'm not surprised.

"Yeah," he answers, his fingers doing figure eights on my skin. "I don't like it when you pretend you're someone you're not. I just want you to be you. Good. Bad. Anxious. I'll still be here."

We stare at each other, enveloped by stillness. I hadn't even noticed that the record was over. I open my mouth to speak, then close it. I look across the room at the record as it spins and spins in silence.

"Promise?" I ask, my voice soft.

"Promise." Luke's fingertips run up and down my smooth skin and my eyes return to his. My entire body buzzes.

I don't know if it's Luke's touch or the fact that he may be the only one who actually knows me but suddenly, every trace of air is drawn from my lungs. He takes his hand off my ankle and my skin begins to throb. I want to tell him to put it back. To keep touching me and never stop touching me. I've been keeping him at arm's length for so long. For his own good, I know. But tonight, my long list of reasons to push him away shrinks and blurs and crumples.

My body begins to shake, just like this morning, and I don't know why. I pull my arms to my chest and wrap them around my shivering body.

"You cold?" Luke asks.

"I must be," I say, trying to stop my teeth from chattering.

"Come here." Luke scoots his body over, patting the empty spot on the couch next to him. I crawl down to his side of the couch and place my head on the fluffy pillow, my face pointed at the blank television and still-spinning record player. Luke wraps his strong arms around me, warming my cold, goose-bump-prickled skin. "Better?"

"Yes, thanks," I say, resting the back of my head against his chest. I feel his body rise and fall with every breath, and my stomach flips onto itself over and over again, like kneaded dough. We need a distraction and fast. "How about a movie?"

Luke reaches for the controller next to him and flips on the TV. "*American Beauty* is in the DVD player, I think. I know you like it."

"Sounds perfect," I say as he pushes the play button. As the opening credits roll, Luke pulls me tighter, resting his chin on the top of my head.

"One more question," he says. "Favorite moment?"

"In life?" I ask, turning toward him and he nods. I scan my brain. Before New Albany, my life was an endless *Groundhog Day* of training and school where I was pretty much ignored. We've moved so many times, spur of the moment, it was hard to break into a group of friends in the middle of the school year. My parents would always say I was destined for bigger things than being invited to a sleepover or birthday party. But that wasn't exactly comforting when I'd sit in class listening to everyone else make weekend plans, and silently hope someone would ask me to come along.

But all that changed here. Something clicked. This place, the people. My life before New Albany felt like a dress rehearsal until I got to the academy. That's when my life was supposed to start. But here, I sometimes forget that I'm a Black Angel. I forget about the path that was plotted for me before I was even born. I no longer feel like I'm floating outside of my body, watching it happen: a spectator in someone else's life. Here, I feel alive.

Luke nudges me then smiles, waiting for my answer. "I don't know," I say and shake my head. "I don't know if it's happened yet. What about you?"

"Mine hasn't either," Luke answers and brushes my dark hair out of my face. "But this one is pretty up there."

Every word vibrates against my ear and pulses through my brain. I slowly nod and look down, getting lost in the deep blue of Luke's sweater, as his fingertips slip beneath my hair, running up and down the back of my neck. Up and down. Up and down. Goose bumps rise over every inch of my body and I wonder if he can feel them; wonder if he can feel this. A jolt buzzes through my body as his fingertips trace the length of my spine. There is silence but no still-ness. The room feels like one big electrical circuit. I can almost feel the atoms ping-ponging off my skin and onto Luke. I look up at him, my brown eyes finding his blue. My heart races, my lips throb. His honey-blond hair hangs over his eyes and I have to fight the urge to reach out and touch it, smooth it back into place.

"Mac, I . . ." Luke begins.

"My name is Lester Burnham," the opening monologue of *American Beauty* blasts through the speakers, cutting him off. I turn my body back around and release the breath I've been holding in my chest. His hand slides down my arm as every muscle, every cell,

every atom (we're talking molecular-level yearning here) is screaming at me to kiss him, but I can't.

I've been praying for this feeling, this rush, to fade. But it won't.
It taunts me, strengthening with every touch. I shouldn't let his
fingers dance on my skin. I shouldn't let him hold me like this. I
shouldn't even be here. But I can't not be here. I can't not touch
him. I can't not want to kiss him. And I don't think he can either.
Because no matter how much my mind begs for this feeling to
weaken, it always feels the same. And right now, it feels impossibly
good.

Luke runs his fingers up the length of my arm as we watch the
movie in silence, my skin continuing to pulse. I beg my body to fall
asleep. Eventually, it obeys and I fade into black.

NINE

WARM LIGHT POURS THROUGH THE WEIXELS' BONUS room windows, stirring me awake. The TV screen on the entertainment center is black but a low hum cutting through the stillness of the room quietly confesses it's still on.

Luke's body fusses next to me and I realize the pillow I thought my head was resting on is really his arm. *Oh my God, oh my God, oh my God.* I'm waking up. Next to him. No, not even next to him. Practically on top of him.

I squeeze my half-open eye shut. I can hear him rub his palm on his face, followed by a yawn and another long eye rub. My mind debates opening my eyes and wishing him a good morning, but the practical part of my brain wins out and I stay "asleep." His hand carefully moves my head from his arm and onto the oversize pillow. The leather on the couch whines as Luke slowly pulls his body up. His movements pause and the room is quiet. I can feel the weight of his eyes on me and I wonder what he's thinking. I feel his body lean in closer. I breathe in his sweet skin as he brushes a piece of hair out of my eyes and away from my face. I've never had the privilege of smelling Luke first thing in the morning, but his scent is strangely intoxicating. Maybe even better than a freshly showered Luke. He lingers near me for another moment and I take in another breath, trying to decode its mixture. Muted notes from his body wash, a deodorant that's most likely advertised as smelling like an "Ocean Breeze," and the tiniest hint of sweat, stirred up from one of his dreams. I kind of want to grab him and tell him to stay so I can smell him a little longer, but I'm pretty sure that crosses the fine line from quirky girl next door (literally) to just plain weirdo.

The weight of the couch shifts as he carefully climbs over me. I hear Luke rummage through a cabinet and return, placing a thickly knitted blanket over my body. He opens the bonus room door and quietly closes it behind him. I listen as his feet shuffle against the hardwood floors of the hallway until they disappear. The low buzz of the TV fills the quiet room once again.

I open my eyes and search for a clock in the room. A big, rustic silver clock hangs near the wet bar: 9:21. We still have a couple hours until we should head up to Templeton.

I rub my face with the heel of my palms and wonder how bad I look right now. I pull myself off the couch and the wood floors creak beneath my feet. I wander to the mirror over the console table and look at the face reflected back at me in the glass. My dark hair is a little ratted and mascara has smeared underneath my bottom lashes, but not as terrible as I feared. I run my fingers through my hair and pull it into a low ponytail. I carefully wipe the mascara under each eye with my index finger and grab my purse for reinforcements. Thank God for Listerine strips and Rosebud's lip balm.

I open the door and walk down the long wooded hallway toward the back staircase that leads to the kitchen. As I climb down the carpeted stairs, I can hear the clink of Luke's metal spoon against the side of his ceramic cup. A few steps farther down, I pause. He's whistling. I squish my toes into the thick carpet and listen. It sounds familiar: a Christmas carol I just cannot place even though the lyrics are on the tip of my tongue. I hear him whistle the last bar of the song. There's about a two-second pause and he starts the carol again. I smile and bounce down the last few steps. When I enter the kitchen, he winks at me, keeps whistling, and hands me a cup of freshly brewed coffee. I love that he doesn't stop whistling or even say good morning. It's like we're in the middle of a playful morning routine that's been going on for years.

"A little early for Christmas carols, don't you think?" I ask, taking a seat at the enormous white-and-gray marble island.

"I whistle that song all the time," Luke answers, sliding the creamer and the four packets of sweetener (yes, four) he knows I have to have in my coffee toward me. "June, December, October. Doesn't matter. It's my go-to whistle."

"I've never heard you whistle it before."

"That's because I usually only whistle in the privacy of my car or home. No need to subject others to my random whistling."

"What's that carol called again? I know it and it's driving me up the wall that I can't remember the name," I say, glancing down at my coffee. Steam rises, licking my face, as I stir cream into the elegant white mug, transforming the almost black liquid into a warm caramel.

"'Good King Wenceslas,'" Luke answers and begins singing the lyrics. "Good King Wenceslas looked out on the feast of Stephen."

"That's it!" I say and pick up where he left off. "When the snow lay round about deep and crisp and even."

"Super random, I know," Luke says, shaking his head and taking a sip of his coffee.

"So random but I love it," I reply and blow at the rising steam before taking my first sip. I let the warm liquid coat my tongue and run down the back of my throat.

"You sleep okay?" Luke asks, reaching across the island and grabbing the creamer, adding a drop or two more to his cup.

"Yup," I say with a nod. "How about you? I don't snore or anything, do I?"

"No, no snoring," Luke answers, his mouth curling into a half smile, his dimples threatening to crease. "You did sleep on me most of the night, though."

"Sorry," I say, my cheeks growing hot. "You make a good pillow."

"Don't worry," Luke answers. "I'm happy to be your pillow anytime, Mac."

I cover up my smile by taking another gulp of my coffee. I glance at the digital clock on the oven. "I better go get ready," I say, hopping off the bar stool and grabbing my purse off the kitchen table. "Leave in like an hour or so?"

"You got it."

"Taking this with me," I say, raising the coffee cup in my hand.

"Okay, see you in a bit," Luke says as I slip out the Weixels' kitchen door and walk the eighteen steps to my back kitchen door (we counted that one too). With every step, my legs feel heavier and heavier. I hate being in my house alone. I put my key in the door and turn it. I push open the door and the alarm immediately wails. The high-pitched shrill pulses, bouncing off every wall and crawling underneath my skin. I have thirty seconds to turn it off before it bypasses police and sends a message straight to CORE. I slam the door, put my coffee cup and purse on the granite island, and run into the mudroom where the state-of-the-art security keypad is installed. I type in the ten-digit code and the alarm finally ceases its piercing cry.

I run my fingers along the slick countertops and look around the dark kitchen as I take another gulp of coffee. The refrigerator hums for a few seconds then clicks off. The house is quiet again. A shiver shakes my body. It feels a good ten degrees colder in here than it does at Luke's but when I check the hallway thermostat, it reads seventy. I pull my sweater tighter across my body and climb the curved staircase toward my bedroom. The clack of my boots on the hardwood hallway fills the house and I picture Dad yelling out, "Elefanteeee."

As I pass the open guest room door, something out the front window catches my eye. A gray van sits idle, exhaust spewing from its tailpipe. I walk into the room and creep closer, dropping to my knees to peer out from the right bottom corner of the windowpane. The van is parked three doors down in front of the Saldoffs' house and in the driver's side mirror, I can see someone sitting in the front seat.

A buzz shakes my body and I jump to my feet. I place my hand over my rapidly beating heart and feel my chest rise and fall as I catch my breath. It's just my phone vibrating in my pocket but I'm jumpy as hell all alone in this place. I pull out my phone. Aunt Sam.

"Good morning," I say into the phone and walk away from the window.

"Well, good morning to you too," Sam replies. "Glad to see you make an appearance in your own home."

I glance up at the ornate picture frame on a high bookshelf in the corner of the guest room. But it's not a picture frame. It's a camera. We have cameras in every room of the house. Except bathrooms, because . . . eww.

"Hi, Sam," I say, giving the camera an exaggerated wave. "Have you been watching for me all night?"

"I checked the cameras a few times," Sam answers. "But just got an alert that the alarm went off so figured you were home now."

"I'm home."

"So. Where were you?"

"Harper's," I answer a little too quickly.

"Reagan?" Sam questions, her voice adding about ten extra *a*'s to my name. Who am I kidding? She always knows where I am.

"Luke's," I say and sigh. "I was at Luke's."

"The truth comes out. Hymen still intact?" Sam asks with a laugh.

"Sam!" I shout into the phone, which only makes her laugh harder. She was Aunt Sam to me growing up. She took care of me and protected me like I was her own child. But the last few years, we've dropped the aunt and she's become more like a big sister. An annoying, pestering, always-questioning big sister.

"I'm still waiting for a response," Sam says and I can feel her smiling on the other end.

"Of course my hymen is still intact! Luke and I are just..." I stammer into the phone. I want to say friends but I don't even believe my own lie. "Well, I don't know what we are but nothing happened. Mountain Dews were drunk, records were played, and clothes stayed on."

I flop down on the expensive white-and-silver bedspread that I'm not really supposed to sit on, much less lie on.

"At least take off your shoes," Sam says, clearly still watching me through the camera. "You know your mother will kill you if you get anything on that bedspread."

I roll my eyes but comply. "Are you going to tell her?"

"About the bedspread or showing up at home with bedhead from Luke's?"

"Both?"

"No. Promise," Sam says and pauses. "But Reagan, I do think you need to think about what you're doing."

"What do you mean?" I ask even though I know exactly what she's talking about. I lean to my left to glance back out the window. The van is gone. Maybe the Saldoffs are having work done on their house again. For a moment, fear begins to creep into my brain but I force it back out.

"Just everything with Luke," Sam says and takes a big breath on the other end of the phone. "I haven't said anything because I just wanted to see where your friendship with Luke went ... but I think you need to be careful. Because if you want to go to the academy and become a Black Angel, it's going to get really complicated with Luke. I know you don't want to hurt him."

"Of course I don't," I reply, my heart painfully constricting at the thought. I press my lips together and scan the room. My eyes land on an old picture of Mom and Dad on the nightstand. I reach out and touch the edge of the silver frame. It's a candid shot from their wedding day. They got married on the beach in Florida. Dad's sitting in an oversize Adirondack chair and Mom's perched comfortably on his lap, her arms draped around his neck, her forehead pressed against his as she laughs. Dad's steadying her arms and smiling so wide. They look like they're in the middle of having the best conversation of their lives. It's my favorite picture of them and I've never really known why. Maybe because it just feels so real or perfectly unperfect. Like that's what love really is; that back and forth, give and take. She says one thing. He says another. She laughs. He touches her arm. If you're lucky, it's in those simple moments you find complete happiness. And that's how you want to spend the rest of your life. Forever in the middle of a conversation with the person you never, ever get tired of talking to.

"Listen, Reagan. We all want you to be a Black Angel," Sam continues. "You were *born* for this. But I also want what's best for you. So listen to your heart. What does it say?"

I take a deep breath and slowly shake my head. Of course Sam is the only one who even bothers to ask.

"That I should do this," I answer quietly. A lump begins to grow thick in the back of my throat but I will it down and it obeys. "That I owe it to my parents and my country to be a Black Angel."

"But what do you want, Reagan?" she presses further. "Don't think about what your mom and dad want. What do *you* want?"

To stay in the light. To leave this dark and dangerous life. Or at least have the power to choose.

"I don't know," I lie. I'm thankful I'm lying down because I can feel my legs weakening, trembling under the weight of my thoughts, my words, my lies. I push my head further into the plush decorative pillows, no longer perfectly arranged on the bed. Sam is quiet on the other end of the phone. I can hear her breathing, hear her thinking.

"What are you so afraid of?"

My eyes close as I listen to the sound of my breath going in and out of my lungs. I'm scared of everything. I'm scared of angering my parents and wasting my talent if I choose college. I'm scared of a life full of constant fear and alienation if I choose the Black Angels. I'm scared of never falling in love and never being happy.

"I don't know," I lie again, my voice soft and distant.

I hear Sam sigh on the other end of the phone followed by the click, click, click of her biting her thumbnail. One of her emotional ticks. I wonder if she even notices she does it but I certainly do. She stays silent, waiting for me to get uncomfortable and fill the quiet with the truth. It's a psychological secret we both know. Cops and reporters know it too. Watch any interrogation or interview. They stay quiet because people hate silence. It makes them squirm. They'll almost always fill it with the words on the tip of their tongue, even the words they don't want to say.

"You only get one life," Sam finally says. "No one's going to be able to give you a road map and you can't live it for somebody else. You've got to live it for you."

"But my parents, my training—" I begin.

"Reagan, I'm not going to lie to you," Sam cuts me off. "Your talent is unprecedented. It would be a huge blow to the agency if you didn't choose this life. But if your heart isn't in it, you'll be no good to us either."

The early warning sign of tears sting the corners of my eyes. I quickly close them before those salty drops have a chance to fully develop. I keep my eyes closed and breathe deep, digging my fingers into my hip bones and forcing them back down.

"The moment will come when you'll know what to do," Sam finally says. "When it does come, pay attention. Don't close your eyes. Don't let it slip away."

"Okay" is all I can muster.

"Good luck at Templeton," Sam says. "I'll be here if you need anything. Love you, Reagan."

"Love you, Sam," I say and touch my screen to end our call. I toss the phone to my side, fold my hands across my rib cage, and feel shallow breaths forcing my body up and down. I've never really bothered to think about what I want for my life. It's never felt like an option. Becoming a Black Angel is the only future I've ever known. But the thought of your future shouldn't make you physically ill, should it? I've blown it off as nerves. As lingering paranoia left over from Philadelphia. But maybe it's more than that.

My fingertips run along my left hand until they reach the bracelet on my wrist. I press the hearts between my fingers and try to steady my breath. I have to make a decision, I know I do. Sam just handed me a ticking bomb and time's about to run out.

TEN

"OLD TEMPLETON IS THE OLDEST BUILDING ON CAMPUS," Katie, our Templeton sophomore tour guide, says, standing in the shadow of the massive stone building. With its proud spires, heavy wood doors, and arched windows, Old Templeton is the crown jewel of the gothic-style architecture on campus. "Old Templeton provides housing for upperclassmen and is said to be one of the most haunted buildings here. So hopefully you won't mind if your roommate is a friendly ghost or two."

The small group of parents and prospective students politely chuckle at what can only be a canned joke Katie repeats on every tour. I look up at Luke with a smirk. His blue eyes return my silly smugness with a wink.

"Well, that concludes our tour of Templeton College," Katie says, clapping her hands together. "Hope you enjoyed it and hope you have a wonderful day exploring our beautiful campus."

If Katie was hoping her handclap would signify the end of our hour with her, she was mistaken. A foursome of uptight, East Coast, old-money parents in expensive trench coats and heavy knit sweaters swarm Katie and immediately begin firing off questions before she even has a moment to breathe.

"The acceptance rate is twenty-three percent, so how good do your ACT scores have to be? What were your ACT scores?"

"Tell me about the sororities on campus. Does Templeton have Delta Gamma? I'm a legacy."

"What's the food like here? Is it all organic? Do you have sushi?"

"I'm not pleased with the size of the rooms here. Could we purchase two rooms? And make one room a closet and dressing area for our daughter? Maybe knock down a wall?"

Their children, a blond Chanel-bag and pearls-wearing girl and disinterested-with-the-world boy with black eyeliner and a lip ring hang back and watch as their parents elbow each other for Katie's attention.

Luke raises his chin in their direction and says, "Helicopter parents."

"Seriously. They look like the kind of parents that call and yell at HR when their kids don't get chosen for an internship," I reply with a laugh.

"Internship! I wouldn't stop there," Luke says as we watch Katie frantically try to answer their incessant questions. "They probably call the hiring manager at whatever hedge fund they want them to work at when they don't get hired in their late twenties."

"Poor, poor preppy princess and emo kid," I say with a sympathetic smile. "Maybe if they both go here, they'll bond over that and date."

"That guy looks like preppy princess's parents' worst nightmare,"

Luke replies as we turn and walk toward the other side of campus where Luke's truck is parked.

"You're probably right," I answer. Our conversation falls into a comfortable quiet as we walk down Middle Path, its pebbles crunching under our feet. Middle Path is Templeton's main artery and runs the length of the entire campus. On either side of the path, trees, thick with the passage of time, hold tight to leaves that are so orange and yellow and red, they look like they're on fire.

"If heaven has seasons," I say, my face tilted up, soaking in the vibrant colors, "this must be what fall looks like."

"I was thinking the same thing," Luke replies, his gaze matching mine. "It's beautiful here."

My head nods in agreement. Templeton is like nowhere I've ever been, with its monstrous gargoyles, pointed arches, and peaked roofs. This part of Ohio is all rolling hills and forests and cornfields. Its "downtown" consists of a family-run grocery store where students pick up chips and energy drinks, a post office, a coffee shop, and a school bookstore. It's the type of place where people don't lock their doors and nothing bad happens. Very different from the life I have in front of me.

"So what's the verdict?" Luke asks as Templeton's one-hundred-year-old church bell rings, its heavy, alluring clang announcing a new hour. I look up and down Middle Path and think about all the students who have loved that bell and suddenly my body aches for memories I haven't even had.

"I love it," I reply, which is not a lie. Templeton feels like home or something. Or at least the feeling I think people mean when they say it feels like home. I've moved around so much, I don't think I know what that feels like. But I think it's when your heart knows before your head that this is where you belong.

"Good," Luke says with a relieved smile. "West Point is only a few hours' drive. I'd miss you if you were on the other side of the country."

His words, always uncalculated and sincere, twist my stomach into a million little knots and I can feel my heart constricting under the weight of agony and hope.

"Me too," I reply, my voice quiet.

"Hey," Luke says, grabbing my arm. "I dare you to belly flop into that pile of leaves."

Luke points toward an enormous mountain of leaves on the edge of Middle Path, waiting to be bagged up.

"Luke, you know better than to dare me to do anything," I reply, a slow smile creeping up my face. In the last year I've done a series of pirouettes in the middle of AP bio, meowed at complete strangers in the mall, and stood up and licked my plate clean in the middle of the Cheesecake Factory, all on dares. This one is child's play. I rock back on my heels, then take off running and leap headfirst into the colorful pile. Crimson, burnt orange, and gold leaves explode around me, then float back down, covering my face and body. I laugh and blow at a yellow leaf that landed on my lips.

"I give you a nine-point-five." Luke cups his hands around his mouth and calls out to me from down the path.

"A nine-point-five?" I reply and sit up as best I can in the shifting pile. "What the hell? That was a ten."

"Your technique was good but you lost some style points," Luke yells, shaking his head with a smile. "You didn't point your toes during entry into the pile."

"Well, what are you waiting for?" I ask and slap the massive pile next to me. "Show me a ten."

Luke's smile cracks even wider. The pebbles on Middle Path scrape loudly against his shoes as he runs toward the pile of leaves. He leaps, arms outstretched like Superman, legs spread, toes pointed, next to me, and the colors explode like harvest fireworks.

"A definite ten," I say and laugh, picking a red leaf out of his blond hair. "Only you could make belly flopping into leaves look so good."

I lay my body back down, settling in next to Luke, my torso parallel with his. Our legs brush. I wait for him to pull away but he doesn't move. So we lie there, wrapped thick in our soothing silence, as a gust of wind stirs the leaves that hang defiantly to their branches. A few break free and pinwheel to the ground to join their fallen brothers and sisters.

"I love fall," Luke begins, spinning a freshly fallen leaf back and forth in his hand, changing its shade from bold red to light red. "But it's sort of the Sunday night of seasons."

"What do you mean?" I reply, furrowing my brow.

"You know that feeling you get in the pit of your stomach on Sunday night? When the weekend is over and you know you have to go to school the next day? That's what fall is. As great as it is, it's sort of tainted because you know that suckiness is right around the bend."

"I love the way you think." I laugh and put my hand to his chest.

"Would you rather," Luke begins, "have a billion dollars or know all the secrets to the universe?"

"Secrets to the universe," I answer confidently even though pretender Reagan would say money. Luke gets the truth. "What about you?"

"Same," he says with a nod, turning his face back toward the sky. "There's so much I want to know."

"Like what?"

"All kinds of stuff. Like, do you think there are parallel universes?"

"I don't know. Maybe."

"Do you think in a parallel universe somewhere we're having this exact conversation?"

"I don't know. Maybe in another universe we haven't even met."

"Or maybe in another universe we're not having this conversation because we already know that there are other parallel universes. Maybe in some other dimension, we're watching this very conversation right now." Luke turns his face to me, his dimples deep, his hair thick with leaves. He raises his eyebrows twice and asks, "Did I just blow your mind?"

"You know, Luke, for someone who has never smoked pot, you sure do ask a lot of puff, puff, give questions," I reply with a laugh.

"I know," he says with a shrug, the swaying trees casting shadows on his beaming face. "Don't you like my ridiculous questions?"

"I love your ridiculous questions," I say and throw a pile of leaves at his face. Luke closes his eyes as the reds and yellows and oranges make impact. I laugh as he shakes his face free of my leaf missile attack.

"Mac, don't even start that game." He smirks and throws a pile of leaves in mine, the colors flying all around me. "You know you'll lose."

"Oh yeah," I reply and I push my body up. I grab an enormous pile next to me with both arms and bury his entire face. "What are you going to do about it?"

"Oh, you're dead, Mac!" Luke's muffled voice and laugh comes from below my pile but before he can make his next move I jump on top of him and playfully punch his side before dumping even more leaves on top of his face.

"Not so tough now, huh?" I say, tickling his sides.

"Mac, stop!" He laughs, squirming and shaking the leaves off his face. "Mac, you know I'm ticklish."

"Of course I know you're ticklish," I reply, reaching for another fistful of leaves, but Luke grabs me by my wrist, pulling me off of him and rolling me onto my back.

"No, Luke," I squeal, my eyes closed, my head shaking from side to side. He laughs and playfully pins down my other arm, the leaves crunching beneath the weight of our bodies. He throws a pile of leaves on my face. I spit and laugh and promise, "I'm gonna get you, Luke."

"You started it," he whispers in my ear, his warm, sweet breath lapping at my cool skin, a chill pricking every last goose bump on my body.

My eyes open and find his and suddenly, I'm no longer laughing. I'm no longer breathing. I get lost in the paleness of his eyes, the curve of his lips, the weight of his body on my own. And even before he moves his hand up my wrist to lace his fingers with mine,

I know exactly how it will feel, as if it's happened a thousand times before.

Before I can speak or think or breathe, Luke is wrapping his hand around my neck. As he pulls us closer, I feel a rush of happiness and helplessness. A surging tide of heat washes through my blood, causing whatever limbs that remained strong to go limp. And as his lips gently brush and linger on mine, the contact sparks, hot and bright. I press my lips to his teasing mouth and the world goes dark. He kisses me, softly at first, with an aching sweetness. Then his warm lips crescendo with such intensity, my hands are forced to cling to his sweater, trying to find something solid in the dizzying darkness. My heart hammers in my chest and blood rushes through my body, drowning out any sound except the beat that swishes in my ears. I dissolve into his body, wrap my arms around his neck, and press him closer. His lips taste like cinnamon and are soft and fierce all at once. His feather-light fingertips trace the back of my neck and every part of me is electric.

Our lips part and Luke rests his forehead on mine. I open my eyes to see him looking back at me. And through our blurry closeness, I see his lips rising into a smile, matching mine.

"You know how we talked about favorite moments?" Luke says, his voice soft and out of breath.

"Yeah?" I whisper.

"This might be mine." He smiles and leans in, and I fall once again, hard, into his kiss.

ELEVEN

"SO MARK'S PARTY TONIGHT, RIGHT?" LUKE ASKS AS we pull his black truck into his driveway. "You want me to drive you?"

"I'll just meet you there. I promised Harper I'd go with her," I say and squeeze the hand I haven't let go of since Templeton. The ninety-minute drive home, I've studied him, my mind taking snapshots of the way his full lips part and his defined jaw moves as words spill out, one by one. The way his cheeks flush and his dimples crease when I make him laugh; the feel of his warm lips on my hand as he kisses my skin. I collect each moment and file them away.

"I'm glad I came up with you today," Luke says, turning the car off next to the old basketball hoop, rising tall out of the cracked asphalt.

"Me too," I answer, rearranging our fingers for a firmer grip. Luke reaches out, tucking a long strand of my dark hair behind my ear, allowing his fingertips to linger and trace the skin beneath my chin, sending shivers up and down my body.

Luke looks down at our entwined fingers and touches the sterling silver bracelet on my wrist. He runs his fingers along the delicate linked chain until he reaches the double heart charm. He holds the dangling hearts in between his thumb and index finger, leaving his warmth and fingerprints on the cool metal.

"Your mom's bracelet," Luke says and my eyes widen with surprise. "For good luck, right?"

"How did you know that?" I ask.

"You told me once," he answers with a smile. "Last year when we were sitting in chemistry. You were nervous about our test and kept playing with your bracelet. I asked you where you got it and you said it was your mom's. That it brought her good luck growing up and so she gave it to you. And now you always wear it for good luck."

"You remember that?" I reply, truly astonished he remembered that passing comment so early in our friendship.

"I remember everything," he says, running his smooth hand across my cheek and through the tangle of my hair before pulling hungrily and sweetly at the back of my neck. I inch closer, savoring the smell of milk and honey on his skin, the way his nose grazes against mine, the hot, syrupy air between us just before our lips touch. The space between us pulses and my heart skips every other beat. As our lips meet, my hands glide along his strong chest and pull at both sides of his sweater. He's right next to me but it's not close enough. I taste him and every part of my body buzzes. His fingertips graze against my cheek, float down my neck, and slip into the delicate hollow of my shoulder. I lose all sense of time.

As we kiss, the tight knot anchored to the pit of my stomach begins to melt. My worries and longings and fears dissolve, the pain swimming to the edges of my body until they disappear. In its wake floods a secret hope that's been lying dormant, untapped and buried, at the center of my chest. I guess that's what happens when you kiss the only one who really matters. Nothing else does.

Our lips part and our foreheads lean together. Luke is mirroring my smile and I struggle to catch my breath. He leans in and kisses me sweetly one last time, stroking the side of my face before letting me go.

"I'll see you later?" he says, more a question than a statement. I pop open the door handle and hop onto the asphalt.

"Yup," I say, exhaling shakily, still recovering from his kiss. "I'll see you later."

I close the door and slowly walk across the Weixels' manicured lawn. My heart fluttering in my chest, I draw in the deepest of breaths, trying to quell the heavy buzz that numbs my arms and legs, for fear I might faint.

My head is deliciously fuzzy, unable to form complete, coherent thoughts. A few words cycle on repeat, round and round in my skull. *It happened. It finally happened.* Incredible Luke. Impossible me. As I climb the steps of my front porch, I wish I could freeze this moment, when the possibility of us drifts in the air like a hopeful pink balloon.

I put my key in the front door and push it hard, expecting to hear the wail of the alarm, but I don't. My perked ears hear the clang of coffee cups on the stone island and hushed tones in the kitchen. Crap. They're home.

I carefully close the door, trying not to alert them of my

presence but they're Black Angels for crying out loud. They hear everything.

"Reagan?" my mother's voice calls out to me.

"Hi. Coming," I cry out cheerfully and take three giant, silent steps toward the hallway mirror. My cheeks are flushed and my mouth is bright red. My dark, normally sleek hair is wild and my mascara is smudged beneath my bottom lashes. I totally look like a girl who has been kissing the boy next door, and they'll know it in two seconds if I don't fix this. I run my fingers quickly through my hair and wipe the mascara from beneath my eyes. I slather on a thick coat of lip balm and hope they'll think I'm just wearing colored lip gloss. My cheeks . . . what can I do about pink cheeks . . .

"Hello? Daughter?" my dad calls out now.

"Coming," I say and pull out my phone. I look down, faking a text, as I enter the kitchen. "Sorry. I was just texting with Harper."

I slip my phone back into my pocket before they can see I'm lying. Mom raises her eyebrows at me anyway from her seat at the island. Dad stands opposite her in dark jeans and a black sweater. He smiles, grabs me, and hugs me tighter than normal.

"Favorite daughter," he says and kisses me on top of the head.

"Only daughter," I answer and return his tight squeeze. "That was a quick trip."

I drop my purse on the floor, give Mom a hug, and take a seat on the stool next to her at the island.

"We missed you. Did you miss us?" Mom asks, running her hand through my hair.

"Yes. I wept uncontrollably," I say and smile.

"What'd we miss around New Albany?" Dad asks, leaning against the counter with his strong, callused hands.

"Not much. Same shh . . . stuff. Different day." I glance over at my mom with a sheepish grin on my face. She gives me "the look."

"Nice girls like you don't swear, Reagan," she says, shaking her head.

"Yeah, yeah. You love me and my potty mouth," I reply and wrap my arms around her shoulders.

"I certainly do not. I did not raise you to sound like a truck driver," she says. I give her arm a squeeze and feel her wince. I pull my arms away and stare at her, waiting for an explanation. She doesn't give me one. She stares straight ahead and takes a sip of her coffee, her thin blue sweater falling down her arm and exposing a sliver of a white bandage.

"Mom, what happened?" I ask, touching her arm. I run my fingers along the little grooves of the wrap. She shoos my hand away and pulls her sweater down, hiding it from view. "What happened?" I ask again, this time with a little more force.

"Nothing," she says, refusing to meet my eyes. "Just some bumps and bruises. All part of the job, sweetie."

I look at my father. He stares down at the counter, drumming his fingers on the side of his coffee cup.

"What's going on with you guys?" I wait a few beats. Silence. "Did something happen on the mission?" I ask, trying to keep my voice calm.

"Why would you think that?" Mom asks after a few silent

seconds, her eyes fixed straight ahead, staring blankly into the backyard.

The lightness we shared when I first walked in was a facade. With each moment that ticks by, it begins to crack and the darkness they're hiding slowly slips out, encircling the room like a thick smoke, licking the corners, the cabinets, and the granite until it reaches my chest, tightening my lungs with every breath.

"Because you're acting super weird. I know when something is wrong," I answer. "So what's going on?" They share a look. One that says, *Should we tell her?*

"Nothing that concerns you, baby," Mom finally says, her voice soft and still. I roll my eyes and stand up from the stool.

"You know, I'm really sick of this," I say and point at my chest. "Childhood ended for me a long time ago. You want me to put assault rifles in my hand and kick down doors and rescue people like you do, fine. But start by telling me the truth."

My fist knocks against the stone counter. My mother jumps and my father's eyes widen, surprised by my anger. They're used to me rolling my eyes, saying "Whatever," and walking out of the room.

"Who do you think you're talking to?" my father snaps at me, his sharpness forcing my body back into the chair. "We will tell you what you need to know and that is it, do you understand me?"

We sit in impenetrable silence. My eyes dart between Mom and Dad, studying their weighty eyes, their tight lips, their strained breaths. Whatever they're hiding, it's heavy.

"That's not fair," I finally say, my voice quiet.

"Well, guess what? Life is not fair. Out of everything we've encountered in the last twenty-four hours, you have the fairest of lives," my father replies, his voice raised, his tone bitter. The joy I felt five minutes ago seeps from my blood and is replaced by a flash of panic. It burns sharp and hot and thick against the walls of my veins, tensing every muscle.

Dad stares at me, his eyes angry, before he shakes his head and walks out of the room. His feet shuffle down the hall and the door to his office slams shut. I listen as his body collapses into his old desk chair. It squeaks under the weight of his 225-pound frame and the house is silent again. Mom stares at the doorway, like she's hoping Dad will come back to help her explain.

"Mom," I say, placing my fingers gingerly on her arm. She turns around, but her glassy green eyes still won't meet mine.

Mom starts then stops. She takes a deep breath and wrinkles her brow. I watch her put the words together in her head before she speaks.

"We are going to have a Black Angel watcher with you for the next few days," Mom says, reaching out and touching the shoulder of my thin red jacket. She straightens it and pulls it closer to my chest, dressing me like she did when I was little.

"Why do I need a watcher?" I ask, staring at her, waiting for her to stop fidgeting and look at me.

"Don't worry. They'll be completely undercover with you at school," she says, still playing with my coat. "You won't even realize they're there. And I need you to carry your weapon with you wherever you go from now on."

My weapon. Holy shit. We have a no-gun rule outside of the house. Sure, I have my little knife contraptions the Black Angels made me and weapons stashed near the school. But never, ever have I been told to carry my gun.

"My gun? Bodyguards? I don't understand. Why do I need them?" I press her again.

"I also need you to memorize all the codes that identify you as a Black Angel," Mom continues, staring straight ahead and ignoring my questions. "Our code right now is BA 178229. If anyone is questioning you or you need to get yourself out of trouble, just repeat BA 178229."

BA 178229. BA 178229, my mind repeats over and over again until it's locked in.

"My code name is Red Sunrise. Dad's code name is Black River. Sam's code name is Beacon. Your code name is Shadow."

They've never told me my code name before. I didn't even realize I had one.

"Mom, what is happening? Why are you telling me all of this?" I demand, grabbing her carefully by the shoulder and forcing her to look at me. Her eyes finally lock with mine. They are no longer glassy. The sadness has been replaced with something else, an emotion I cannot put my finger on.

"Just in case," she says, her voice firm and cool.

"In case of what?" I ask, each word tightening my throat.

Mom takes a deep breath and gets up from the stool. "Just in case is all, Reagan."

Before I can say another word, she slips out the garage door and closes it behind her. I hear the secret door slide open and she is gone.

I sit frozen in the kitchen, the refrigerator humming behind me.

The searing heat I felt in my stomach with Luke has been replaced by a series of tiny knots, tied so tightly, it's impossible to move. I slide Mom's coffee across the sleek granite and take a sip. I stare into the cup and it's then I get a flash of what I saw in Mom's eyes. What had replaced the sadness and guilt: It was fear.

TWELVE

WHAT THE HELL HAPPENED OUT THERE? WHAT IS GOING on? Who is after us? How long until we leave?

The nerve endings in my brain are violently thrashing, my mind spinning with questions my parents refuse to answer. I sat alone in the kitchen for ten minutes, drinking Mom's coffee, watching the garage door, listening to the squeak of Dad's chair, waiting for one of them to reappear and explain why I need my gun and body guards 24/7.

They never came back. Fine. I'll find the answers myself.

As I sit down at my computer, the terror I've been trying to push away slashes deeper, making each breath a labored effort. I should have known as soon as I walked in the door, their soft voices in the kitchen, their tight smiles, the tension pulsing off their bodies, ping-ponging against the cabinets and countertops. They're unequivocally shaken and won't tell me why. They've been on a gazillion missions. Sometimes stuff goes wrong. But this time feels different. I've never felt this undertow of fear before.

I force my brain to focus on what Mom told me about the mission and the details come flooding back. Anna Taylor. Santino Torres. Drug lord. Colombia.

I type Anna Taylor's name into Google and one hundred headlines pop up. The top one reads:

Senator Taylor's Daughter Killed During Rescue Mission

The words knock me back in my chair. *Shit.*

I click on the CNN article. A picture of Anna smiling, her arm wrapped around her father, stares back at me. She's absolutely stunning with long blond hair, sky-blue eyes, and a bright, wide smile. A white play button at the center of the photo beckons me to hit play. So I do.

A brunette anchor appears on screen, filling in all the missing details. "Anna Taylor, the daughter of millionaire businessman turned US senator Josiah Taylor, has been killed during an attempted rescue from Colombian cartel boss Santino 'The Hammer' Torres. Taylor, along with four other Americans, had been abducted earlier this week and held hostage in exchange for the release of three Colombian drug dealers in federal custody here in the United States. Sources are reporting that an unknown group raided the compound in the early morning hours and successfully rescued Taylor's two traveling companions, Stephanie Litton and Jen Meredith, all former students at the Sidwell Friends School in DC, as well as Massachusetts couple Richie and Mila Barcelona. The rescue team was unable to reach Taylor before she was shot and killed. Anna Taylor planned to attend Georgetown next fall. She was just eighteen years old."

They lost someone. They lost a senator's daughter no less. My parents rarely lose someone they are trying to save. I can count on one hand the number of people that have died on their watch.

"Oh my God," I whisper as I feel the gravity of what this could mean for the Black Angels and my parents, the shit storm from the media, the repercussions at CORE. But there has to be more. This can't be the only thing that happened. There has to be something else that has my parents so petrified.

Tears threaten to climb up the back of my throat but I swallow hard and let my training take over. I take a deep, full-bodied breath and fall back into numbness. Holding this tragedy far away is the only way I can function. I refuse to let it break through my skin, soak into my body, and affect me. *Turn off emotions, push away the poison*, I hear my mom's voice in my head. And so I do.

My fingers bang at my keyboard, typing in *"Rehenes Estadounidenses"* and "Santino Torres." Several Colombian newspapers pop up. I scan the headlines. The newspaper in Santa Marta, Colombia, called *El Informador* has a headline that reads *"El hijo de Santino Torres se murió en rescate de rehenes."* Translation: Santino Torres's son killed in hostage rescue.

That's it.

"Holy shit," I whisper, raising my fingertips to my temples. I click on the headline and begin to scan the article.

Take-down in Santa Marta.

Unidentified American Group.

Alejandro. Four years old. Shot in head by rescue team.

Died in father's arms.

Anna Taylor. Forced to her knees.

Cried and begged for her life. Shot execution style.

Her body abandoned. Her flesh set on fire that night. A promise from Torres.

"*Venganza, venganza, venganza. Muerte a los Americanos.*" Revenge, revenge, revenge. Death to the Americans.

Bile rises up my throat as I realize that Torres must have leaked this entire story in hopes the Americans would find it and heed his warning.

At the bottom of the article, Alejandro's dark eyes haunt me; his sweet smile crushes me. He was so small. Why did he have to die? Collateral damage. That's what the Black Angels would call him. He was just collateral damage. But he wasn't. He was a little boy. They'd justify it and say he'd grow up to take over his father's drug empire. But how do they know? Maybe he'd grow up and become a doctor or maybe a lawyer or a teacher and do good to offset the evil of his father. He was only four years old. He still had a chance.

My stomach has been tied into so many knots, I feel physically ill. The wall I've built around me begins to chip and crumble; my body begins to tingle. My arms, my legs, my feet, my hands feel disconnected from me somehow.

We're leaving. We're leaving, my mind taunts. I can feel it in my bones. We're twenty-four hours away from going into hiding. Forty-eight if I'm lucky. The room spins, dread tightening my lungs, and I can't breathe. I want to slow the clock that's counting down the minutes I have left in this house, in this life, but it ticks by at double speed.

My wobbly legs stand up from my desk chair. The walls around me begin to melt, coming closer and closer and a sudden rush of heat blisters my skin. I have to get out of here, go for a run, something.

I tear open the bottom drawer of my dresser, pulling out yoga pants, a sports bra, and a T-shirt. I glance over my shoulder and out the window. The sun is just starting to set, its warmth retreating as our part of the world spins into darkness. I grab my red jacket in case I get cold.

I slip on my shoes and walk into the dark hallway. Mom and Dad's door is closed, a sliver of pale light lining the crack at the bottom. I can hear the hum of their voices but cannot make out what they're saying. Or more important, what they're plotting. A shiver pricks at my spine, sending my body shaking, at the thought of what's next. A two a.m. wake-up call. A frantic search for my go-bag. A silent drive down our street, my face pressed to the window, as I watch my house, my life, disappear.

I pound down the stairs, pull open the front door, and practically throw myself into the darkening night. The cool air hits my flushed face and finally I can breathe.

The leaves crunch under my running shoes as I head out of my neighborhood and down one of the bike paths. I pick up the pace and turn on the running mix Luke made me last weekend. A hollow, harsh violin floods my ears, followed by an explosion of drums and a rap beat.

My feet strike the pavement and with each line I push myself to run a little faster, my stride a little longer. I run past the small downtown and toward the bright lights of the high school track.

Once I reach school, I'm surprised to see dozens of cars in the parking lot. I thought the track would be empty. I take out my earbuds and hear female voices. The cross-country team is in the middle of the field, laughing, talking about their weekends while they stretch their tight quads and massage sore calf muscles. I reach the iron gates and grab the cold metal with both hands. I know I should turn around, head back to the path or pick a different route. But I stay there and watch them. I lean my warm cheek against the cool black bar, wishing I was in the middle of the field with them instead of looking in. A wave of loneliness rushes over my body and even though I'm sweating, I feel cold.

Every fall I ask my parents if I can run cross-country. I don't know why I even bother asking anymore. The answer is always no. My training is too important, they say. I'm in far better shape than any of those girls will ever be, my dad always tells me. But it's never been about the running or the competition or being in shape. I just wanted to be part of something normal, something that was mine.

The crisp evening air punctures my lungs. At first, I think something is wrong. I put my hand on my chest and breathe in again. The air cuts through me, knife-sharp, as I inhale. I realize then that the crushing pain I feel isn't just in my lungs, it's in my veins. Anger tingles down my arms and up my legs.

I do my best to bury the anger. Mask it as sarcasm or annoyance. But watching the girls in the middle of the field, I can't find a way to make fun of it or brush it off. Because I'm not annoyed or irritated. I'm freaking pissed off.

It crushes me, wave after wave after wave, one right after the other. It doesn't trickle in, it floods. I'm angry that my childhood ended at ten. I'm angry that my parents pulled me out of ballet and soccer and that training took over my life. That summers were spent learning languages and martial arts, and weekends were spent shooting and running and strength training. I'm angry that playing outside with my friends was a luxury and that leaving them in the middle of the night was something I was told to just "get through." I'm angry that my mind is riddled with daymares and that the fear of another panic attack lingers with every anxious breath. I'm angry I might be taken away from the only person who's ever really seen me, maybe even loved me. That I have to bury every emotion and pretend everything is okay. God forbid I cry or get mad or show that I'm human. I feel like a zombie, a robot. My entire life, I've followed their every order, forced on a million different masks, and I'm just so tired. I'm tired of feeling half dead.

My mind takes over my body. I don't even realize what I'm doing until I shake the fence with so much force the gate slams shut. The bone-chilling sound of metal crushing metal echoes against the empty bleachers, silencing the entire cross-country team. I stand there frozen as their ponytails whip around. They stare at me, their mouths open, like I'm a monster. And maybe I am.

I take three steps backward and turn around, running at almost full speed toward the sidewalk. My feet pound back down the hill and my heart beats just as fast. Fury tightens my lungs and numbs my lips. I take deep breaths in and push bad air out as my legs sprint the mile back to my house. My body fights me, wanting to give up, but I just keep running.

I flip open the keypad and punch in the six-digit code, unlocking the secret door to our basement. My feet pound down the stairs, relieved to find the basement empty and cold. I head straight for the punching dummy, rage bubbling and burning my skin. My hands are shaking. I can't even be bothered to put on training gloves. All I want to do is smash the dummy's face.

I tear off my jacket and throw it to the floor. A piece of paper flies from a pocket and pinwheels to the ground.

It's folded, its edges torn. I pick it up, unfold it, and recognize the half-cursive, half-printed handwriting immediately. Luke's. Inside the note are four words. *I'm falling for you.* I hold the note in my hand and read the words over and over again. The tears I've been struggling to contain rise, burning the corners of my eyes.

"No," I whisper and close my eyes. "Please, no."

I breathe in once, twice, then attack the dummy. Punch after punch after punch the dummy bounces back to me, mocking my strength, unmoved by my rage.

You're leaving him, you're leaving him, my mind hisses with every violent punch.

The tears crawling up my throat finally break free, rolling hot and thick down my face. I don't swallow them or fight them or even brush them off my face. For the first time in years, I let them fall.

Through glassy eyes, I hit the dummy again and again until I cannot take it coming back to me one more time. "Goddammit!" I scream and shove the dummy with so much strength, it falls with a deafening crash to the floor.

Pain shoots sharp and searing through my muscles, sending me to my knees.

"Please don't," I whisper as the tears fall faster and turn into full-body sobs.

Please don't take me away from him. I pull my legs up to my chest and bury my face in my knees. The pain I've been dreading the most finally breaks free from its box, poisoning my blood. The body-guards and passcodes and guns are just the beginning. If Torres isn't found immediately, there will be a significant increase in our threat level and there's just no fighting it. We'll be forced to disappear.

I hug my knees and rock my body back and forth on the icy concrete floor. I cry for Anna Taylor and Alejandro and Luke and my parents and me. My ribs begin their slow ache and my dark hair becomes matted to my cheeks. I pull at the wet strands and open my eyes, catching my distorted reflection in the glass gun case. My eyes are swollen and mascara runs down both cheeks.

"I cannot do this," I whisper as I force my tears to slow. My cheeks are hot from sobbing, but the tears that cling to the skin around my eyes are growing cold.

I will myself to get up. My hands push down on the smooth concrete, forcing my body to rise. I cannot stay here. I have to take care of this. Before it's too late.

THIRTEEN

AS HARPER AND I WALK ARM IN ARM TOWARD MARK
Ricardi's house, my senses are heightened. The sound of pebbles
scraping against the sidewalk seems louder, the smell of Harper's
sugar-and-citrus perfume is stronger, and the October air feels
cooler. My training has taken over, forcing me to focus on my next
move.

Just do it, Reagan. Do it for him.

"My giirrrllllsss," someone yells from an open window. I look
up. Malika is waving wildly at us from a second-story window. "Get
your butts in here immediately."

"We're coming," Harper yells back.

"She's drunk already," I say, snapping pretender Reagan to attention. *Act normal. Act normal,* I repeat until I'm able to force a
smile. "I call not babysitting her tonight." I rush to touch my nose
before Harper does, a little game of "not it" we both play. Harper
touches her index finger to her own nose, but it's too late.

"Ugh! You suck, you know that?" she says and bumps her hip into mine. "You're so watching her at the next party."

"Fine, fine," I say as we climb the brick steps that lead up to Mark's ginormous house. We're still several feet away, but I can feel the beat of the hip-hop flavor of the month coming from inside. The music intensifies as I push open the heavy front door.

"Well, this doesn't look like one of Mark's intimate affairs," Harper says as she surveys the scene. "I think the entire senior and junior class is here."

"And half the sophomore class too," I reply as we weave our way through the packed foyer. I scan the crowd, surprised by the number of young faces, and lock eyes with someone I didn't expect to see. Tess. Claire's bully. Her hair is straightened and she's wearing a little makeup. She looks pretty. I raise my eyebrows at her and she immediately bolts down the stairs that lead to the basement. As she should.

Our boots clack against the white marble floors. There are elements of old money in this house. Antique furniture, sterling silver frames, and expensive-looking art. But there are signs of new money too. Enormous plasma-screen TVs, embarrassingly large portraits of Mark and his family, and the biggest chandelier I've ever seen in my entire life. Very look-at-us.

I pull Harper across the great room and head straight for the kitchen. If I'm going to do this, I need more than my training. I need liquid courage.

The white-and-gray marble island is littered with half-empty beer cups, lip-gloss-stained wineglasses, and empty liquor bottles.

I take two red cups off the counter, inspecting their questionable cleanliness, ready to down a beer.

"Shot, ladies?" a guy I recognize from the soccer team asks, carrying a tray of shot glasses with pale pink liquid.

"What is it?" I ask.

"Vodka with a splash of cranberry," he says and pushes the tray toward me. Shots are better than foamy beer. I grab two shots off the tray. Harper holds out her hand to take one from me but I down them one right after the other. The vodka burns my throat and waters my eyes. Once my vision clears, I see Harper's mouth come unhinged. I rarely drink, let alone double fist shots.

"Holy shit," Harper yells over the music and smiles. "You're in rare form tonight. What happened to Mama Reagan?"

"I left her at home," I yell into Harper's ear. "Your turn to play mom."

"Okay by me," Harper says with a smile, putting her shot back on the tray. "I'll take it easy. So how was your day with Luke?"

Just hearing his name pulls me out of my numbed state. My muscles tighten and my stomach twists until it's pretzeled and heavy beneath my skin.

"Fine," I say quickly and turn away. I don't know what's written in my eyes but I don't want Harper to see. I look out the large window over the farmhouse sink. The light in the room and the darkness outside has turned the window into an imperfect mirror. My reflection stares back at me, but my silhouette is hazy, my features hollow.

"Everything okay?" Harper asks, pulling at my arm.

"Everything's great," I lie and give her a sweet smile that turns my stomach even more than the vodka sloshing around inside.

"Harper!" Malika yells as she takes four giant steps across the kitchen, grabbing Harper by both of her hands. "Come on. Peter Paras brought a bunch of his super-hot Australian teammates and I've been telling one of them all about you."

Before Harper can even agree to play wingwoman, Malika is grabbing her by the arm while running down the list of his hot-guy stats: Tall. Dark eyes. Dark hair. Six-pack. Harper grabs me by the hand and pulls me past the flip cup tournament and into the crowded great room. The field hockey girls are bouncing around, dancing and lip-synching to a Taylor Swift song while frat boys in training sit on the deep leather sectional and cheer them on. I can think of about a thousand other places I'd rather be than here. But I have to stay. I have to do this tonight.

My eyes scan the room, looking for a target. Sitting with the group of Australian soccer boys is a dark-haired guy I don't recognize. But he's looking straight at me. His lips crack into a lazy smile as soon as our eyes lock. Perfect.

As I walk toward him, a wave of claustrophobia hits me hard. I take deep breaths through my nose to try to center myself, use my training to stay sane. But it's hot and loud in here and I feel the party encircling me like a snake, waiting to strike. A few more steps, a few more breaths, and I'm at his side. I swallow the panic crawling up my throat and flood my blood with one more breath of oxygen. The numbness returns. It's go time.

"Hi, I'm Reagan," I say, taking a seat and extending my hand.

"Nice to meet you, Reagan," he says with an Australian accent. "I'm Oliver."

"Love that accent," I say, touching his arm and turning on the charm.

"Not as much as I love a gorgeous American girl," Oliver replies, the right side of his lips turned up. Tall with sculpted features, a smooth-as-a-statue complexion, and athletic body, a compliment like that from a guy like Oliver would make every girl in this room lose their minds or consciousness or both. But his words prick at my skin, threatening to shatter my numbed state. My muscles begin to twitch; my brain pleads with me to run. To stop this. But I can't.

"What are you drinking?" I ask, nodding toward a glass tumbler filled with dark liquid.

"Spiced rum. Want a sip?" Oliver says, offering me his glass. I take it and gulp. It's smokier and smoother than the vodka but still burns my throat.

"Not bad," I say and take another gulp. I need more alcohol before I lose my nerve.

"A gorgeous American girl who can drink," Oliver says, leaning in, his breath in the hollow of my ear. "Double bonus."

Oliver puts his hand on the top of my knee and I let his fingers linger. His touch is strong. Respectful, but not soft and gentle like Luke's. After today, I can't imagine anyone else's hands on me. I look down at the dark hardwood floors as the heavy weight of guilt settles at the bottom of my already-sore stomach. When I look up, Harper is staring at me from four soccer players away. She cocks her head to the side, *What are you doing?* written in her narrowed eyes.

I turn away from Harper's questioning gaze and lean into Oliver. "So what do you think about Ohio so far?" I yell in his ear over the music.

"Very different from back home," Oliver replies, steadying his hand on my arm as he leans into me. "But I like it. It's really pretty here. And I keep finding better and better things to look at."

Oliver pulls back, revealing a smile so unfairly handsome, it'd probably help him get away with murder. I can't tell if it's the sight of his stunning white teeth or the precarious concoction of liquor in my stomach or the thought of what I have to do next, but suddenly, I feel nauseous.

Someone in the corner turns up the music several notches and the party is in full swing. Harper and Malika pass around a bottle of Mad Dog 20/20 with the rest of the soccer players. Madison and her crew have turned the enormous blue stone coffee table into their own personal dance platform and about thirty other juniors and seniors are holding red plastic cups in the air, dancing around them.

Just then, I spy Luke standing in the kitchen, checking his phone and looking out into the crowd—looking for me. He hasn't seen me yet. But he's about to.

"Want to dance?" I ask Oliver, willing my lips into a pretender smile.

"Absolutely." Oliver stands and holds out his open palm to help me up. I place my hand in his and as we walk, he laces his fingers with mine. His hands are soft but our grip is clumsy and forced. Still, I don't pull away.

Oliver leads me out to the middle of the dance floor. I throw my arms around his neck and dance to the beat. Oliver wraps his hands around my waist, slowly pulling me closer and closer as the bass crescendos.

After a song and a half, I spy over Oliver's shoulder to see Luke's eyes locked on us. I quickly look away. Time to make my move.

I tug at Oliver's neck and swing my hips from side to side, our bodies colliding with every note. As we dip in unison, he pulls at my hips and I let my body fall into him. I feel Oliver's hot lips on my cheek, his hands gripping the back of my waist. I run my hands along his shoulders and across his strong chest, tears scratching and bullying the back of my throat. I take a breath and pull at Oliver's shirt until our lips are centimeters away.

Do it, my mind demands.

And so I do. I let the Australian kiss me while I swallow the scream in my throat.

With one kiss, I destroy Luke. But even as I betray him, my heart, beating and bleeding within me, calls his name.

I pull out of the kiss and immediately regret looking at Luke's fallen face. His pale blue eyes turn glassy before his gaze leaves mine. And as I watch him shove his hands in his pockets and walk out of the room, a tightening knot of sorrow grows under my breastbone.

The broken look on his face shatters any remaining trace of numbness and my skin feels like it's wrapped in scalding barbed wire. Every cell within me wants to run after him. My brain is on fire, shrieking at me. Begging for me to explain that falling in love with him ... letting him fall in love with me ... soon the pain will be ten times worse.

I crane my head toward the foyer and watch Luke quietly slip out the front door. My job is done. This mission, a success. I want him to hate me. But he'll never hate me as much as I hate myself. Tears sting my eyes as Oliver comes in for another kiss. I push him away and break free of his grasp. I walk quickly across the great room, grab the Mad Dog straight out of Harper's hands, put it to my lips, and chug.

FOURTEEN

"NO! I DON'T WANT TO GO. I WANT MORE MAD DOG,"
I announce, several octaves too high for the dark and silent streets of
New Albany's most expensive neighborhood. Harper loops her
arm in mine and I try to pull away.

"No more Mad Dog," Harper says, tightening her grip on me.
"Let's get you some coffee at the diner."

"No, I want Mad Dog," I whine, throwing my head back in the
air and looking up at a blur of stars, glittering pinholes in a black,
cloudless sky.

"Reagan, nothing good happens when you drink Mad Dog, remember?" Harper says, guiding me to her parked Range Rover. "It's
your party rule for a reason."

Harper eases me into the front passenger seat. She closes the
door and climbs in the driver's side. The motor turns on and a warm
blast of air hits my face. I lean my head against the cold window as
we pull down the street, lined with impressive estates.

"I want to go home," I say, as the alcohol begins to weigh heavy on my eyelids.

"No way! Your parents will kill you," Harper exclaims, turning left onto Route 62 and away from the country club neighborhoods. "Let's get you some food or something."

I close my eyes as Harper drives the seven miles out of New Albany and into neighboring Gahanna where the Dead End Diner sits at the end of, you guessed it, a dead end street. Open twenty-four hours, the Dead End has been owned by the same family for over sixty years and has become a Columbus institution. You can get a cheeseburger at nine in the morning and coffee and eggs at midnight if you want. The owner says he doesn't even have a key to the place anymore since they never close. Even on Christmas Day.

As Harper pulls into the gravel parking lot, I open my eyes. There are a few cars parked in front of the classic fifties diner that looks more like a train car than a building. I look for Luke's truck. The Dead End is his favorite. He's not here.

"Caffeine awaits you," Harper says, turning off the SUV and hopping down on the gravel. We walk in silence up to the front door, her hand placed gently on my shoulder blade. The crunch of the gravel and the buzz of the Dead End's neon sign fill the space between us, drowning out the silent questions that have to be running through Harper's brain. *How could you? What's wrong with you?* I asked myself the same questions while downing a half a bottle of Mad Dog that looked like Windex and didn't taste much better. Mad Dog tastes like somebody liquefied blue Jolly Ranchers in cough syrup and then mixed it with rubbing alcohol. The taste still lingers on my tongue.

A couple tables are occupied. One booth holds a group of teenage boys I don't recognize, scarfing down big plates of fried eggs and hash browns. In the back, a twenty-something couple share loving gazes and a plate of fries. Vom. A Gahanna cop sits on a red stool at the cream Formica counter, sipping a cup of coffee and reading yesterday's newspaper.

Harper and I slide into our favorite booth next to the cigarette machine that even with Ohio's strict smoking laws, the Dead End still keeps.

We don't even bother to look at the menus. Rachel, the forty-something night shift waitress, brings freshly refilled pops to the boys three booths behind us. She sees us and walks over to our table.

"Hey, girls," Rachel says, pulling a pencil out of her messy bun. "French fries with a side of ranch and coffee?"

"Please," I answer, fighting the urge to lay my head on the table while Rachel grabs two ceramic cups and one of the pots behind the counter. The cups clang, clang, clang with every step back to our table. She places them in front of each of us and pours.

"Reagan, you look like you've had a long night," Rachel says, studying my face. She fills my cup, slides it closer to me, and places the pot on the table. "I'll leave this for you ladies. French fries will be up in a few."

The Dead End's fries are the best. Hand cut and generously seasoned. I know I should get something in my stomach to soak up the alcohol but I'm not very hungry. In my Mad Dog state, I almost forget why. But Luke's shattered face comes back to me. Pain crawls up my body, tightening my muscles and squeezing my lungs. I deserve it. I deserve every gut-wrenching breath. There's no such thing as a happy ending for a girl like me. How selfish am I to forget that?

I pour cream into my coffee and stare at the swirling patterns until the milk takes over, infusing itself into the hot liquid, turning its black hole a caramel cream. I can feel Harper's eyes on me, the air between us dense with questions she's too good a friend to ask and answers I'm too broken to give.

"So . . ." she says, breaking the silence. "What are the chances Mal gets some rare form of mouth herpes after making out with that Australian guy?"

I spit out a laugh. Harper always knows exactly what I need.

"From what I saw, he was pretty cute," I answer and bring the coffee to my lips. I blow at the steam before taking a sip.

"Yeah, too cute for me," Harper declares, stirring cream and sugar into her cup. "You can just tell he's banged a ton of chicks, right? He's got that look to him."

"Well, I think Malika won't let things get too far with that guy," I answer and fold my hands in front of me. "Maybe just a kiss so she can scratch another continent off her list."

"She's freaking hilarious," Harper says and shakes her head.

"So what else did I miss tonight?"

"You mean while you were downing a Mad Dog basically by yourself?"

"Exactly," I answer with a nod.

"Let's see," Harper says, tapping a finger to her forehead. "My Australian soccer player seemed like a nice guy until he spotted

Madison wearing a dress about an inch from her vag. He took one look at her, turned to his friend, and yelled 'dibs' right in front of me. So that was awesome."

"What an asshole," I reply and take a gulp of coffee. "Would you like me to beat him up?"

"Not necessary but thank you for the kind offer, darling," Harper answers with a wink. "Let's see, what else . . . Owen cheated on Annie with some skanky freshman, the Goldach twins broke some really fancy, expensive crystal vase in the foyer, and I heard Renee puked all over the wine cellar after she and Jenna chugged a two-thousand-dollar bottle of wine."

"See. I told you nothing good happens at Mark Ricardi parties."

Without a word, Rachel slides a hot plate of fries in front of us and steals a full bottle of ketchup from the table behind us before disappearing to tend to the couple in the corner who have taken their cuteness to new obnoxious levels by sharing the same side of the booth.

"What are you glaring at?" Harper asks with a mouth full of fries. She follows my gaze and nods in their direction. "Are you sending your eye daggers to that couple over there?"

"I just don't understand people who sit on the same side of the booth," I say, still glaring. She's leaning her head on his shoulder; her long blond hair (perhaps a little too long. Like 1980s-music-video-star long) cascades down both their backs. He's looking down at her, smiling sweetly. I freaking hate them.

"Yes, same side of the booth is super annoying," Harper replies, turning to face me. "Can you really not spend a single second not touching each other that you have to sit side by side and make the rest of us uncomfortable-slash-hate-your-guts?"

"Same with couples who only refer to each other as 'babe' or worse, 'bae,'" I add and roll my eyes. "'Just chilling with my bae.' Please do the world a favor and stop talking."

"What about the oversharers?" Harper says, shoving another fry in her mouth. "Like, I do not need to hear about how hot you are for each other all the time. Keep that inappropriateness in your bedroom or basement or Toyota Corolla where it belongs."

I nearly spit my coffee back into my cup. Harper smiles back at me, a fry hanging out of her mouth as I continue our rant. "What about the couples that feed each other? Every day at school, I watch Alex literally spoon-feeding Sophie soft serve. And not just a taste. No, no. Like, a bowl of swirl ice cream. What is she, a baby?"

"Or how about the ones that constantly try to finish each other's sentences? Jesus Christ. Let them speak!"

"Or the couples who wear coordinating Halloween costumes. Or substitute every 'I' statement for 'we.'"

"The worst," Harper says and shakes her head. "Seriously, kill me if I ever become like that."

"Don't worry. I will," I reply, bringing a fry to my mouth. They're crunchy and salty and soak up Mad Dog's washer fluid taste.

"Do I get to strangle you if you become one of those couples too?" Harper asks, dipping a rare soggy fry in her overflowing cup of ranch.

"You won't have to," I answer and force a sharp laugh. My eyes cast down into my coffee cup. "I'll never be happy like that."

"Of course you will," Harper replies. "Someday."

"No," I answer quietly and shake my head. "I won't."

My eyes drift back to the couple just as he brushes a long strand of her hair off of her cheek, gently tucking it behind her ear. His fingers trace along her jaw and my entire body goes cold. My words are true. I've destroyed the only person in the world who could make me that happy.

My vision blurs, tears welling in my eyes without warning. I try to push them down but it's too late. Harper's face changes. She's seen them. Harper reaches her hand across the table and takes my cold fingers into her warm palm. She's never seen me cry.

"Reagan, why did you do it?" Harper asks, confirming she'd watched it all.

"You wouldn't understand," I reply, shaking my head and staring hard into my cup of coffee.

"Try me," Harper says softly. "I've always known there's something special between the two of you. It's electric when you guys are in the same room. You . . . I mean, you're always happy, I guess. But you become more awake or alive or something next to him."

"What does it matter?" I ask, swallowing the sobs that are clawing up my throat, leaving the delicate flesh jagged and sore. "This time next year, he'll be at West Point and I'll be God knows where. It's too complicated."

"Look, Reagan, I'm no expert on relationships," Harper says, squeezing my hand tight in her palm. "But I do know one thing. There's no such thing as perfect. But there's always the chance of wonderful."

The tears fall faster now. Luke wasn't just my best friend. He saved me. He opened my eyes to a world I didn't know could exist for a girl like me. Being with him made me realize that I'd been confined to a dark, lonely room. A prison the Black Angels had built for me. When I met Luke, he unlocked a door I didn't even know was there. He took my hand and guided me to the other side and I saw what my life could be. But now I'm locked back inside that windowless room. And I don't know if I'll ever find a way out again.

FIFTEEN

"ARE YOU SURE YOU DON'T JUST WANT TO SPEND THE night?" Harper asks as she pulls into my driveway. Her headlights hit the garage door, creep up the sides of the house, and spill into my parents' bedroom. I look up at their window. The curtains are closed. Thank God. "It's almost four a.m."

"Positive," I answer and climb out of her car. It's dark and silent out, but navy blue is beginning to frame the star-dotted black sky, the sleeping world on the cusp of a new day. In an hour, the sun will shed its golden ribbons and I'll be forced to face everything I've done in the last twelve hours. But not now. Now, I just need sleep.

"Call me tomorrow," Harper says, the right side of her face rising into a small smile. "You'll be okay."

I nod once in agreement even though I don't believe her. I close the door without saying another word and stand frozen, my feet glued to the asphalt, as Harper backs out of my driveway and rolls down Landon Lane. I watch her taillights blink red twice as she rolls up to the stop sign, then disappears from my sight.

The unseasonably warm October temperatures are long gone and the chilly morning air has encapsulated every strand of grass in its crystal frost. I pull my thin coat tighter around my body and glance over at the Weixels' house. Luke's bedroom window is cracked open but his light is out. I wonder if he's staring at the ceiling, my betrayal playing over and over again in his mind like it is mine. I hope it's not. I hope he's asleep.

I run my hands through my messy hair and force my legs up the front walk until I reach the door. My stomach is throbbing as I say a silent, selfish prayer that Mom and Dad are asleep. I put my key in the door and quietly push it open. But there they are. Sitting in pajamas in the sunken living room we never use, loaded weapons resting at their sides. *Fuck.*

I close the door, lock it, and turn back to face them. They stare at me, their eyes wild with fury, their mouths pressed together into solid, thick lines. Their chests rise and fall in unplanned unison with heavy, enraged breaths. Their deafening silence is much worse than screaming. I walk across the foyer, throw my keys on the console table, and take a seat on one of the living room steps. Tension circles the room like a poisonous cloud. I pull my knees toward my chest and wait.

"What the hell is wrong with you?" my mother asks, her tongue slowly wrapping and pausing around each word. I stare into her sharp green eyes. They narrow as the seconds tick by without my answer.

"There are a lot of things wrong with me," I finally say. "Most of them have to do with being born to the two of you."

"Reagan, how the hell could you be so irresponsible?" my father explodes, ignoring my declaration. "You leave this house not only without telling us but without your gun to go get drunk at some stupid party. Are you trying to get us all killed? Do you even know what is happening right now?"

"I do but not because you had the courtesy of actually telling me," I say, my voice struggling to remain calm. "I had to go find out about Anna Taylor and Alejandro myself. You expect me to act like a Black Angel but yet you treat me like a child. So guess what. For one night of my life, I decided to act like that child."

"Don't you dare use that angry tone with us, young lady," Mom replies, her mouth twisting into an infuriated scowl.

"Do you have any idea what could have happened to you tonight?" Dad asks, his voice about five octaves louder than Mom's. "The watchers had to track you down at that party. We could have pulled you out right then and there, but we wanted to see how stupid you would be. And congratulations, you were horrifically stupid."

"So stupid in fact, I had to beg Sam not to report your actions to CORE," Mom adds, her voice now rising. "What are you trying to do? Get yourself killed? Or ruin your entire career?"

"See. That right there is the problem with the two of you," I reply, my hands at my side, my fingers digging into the hardwood steps. "You guys just assume this is what I want for my life but have you even bothered to ask me? No. Because you don't care. You just want what's best for the agency, right? The Black Angels come first."

Dad jumps up from the couch, his arm outstretched, his finger pointed at me, shaking. "Don't you dare talk to me like that. I'm absolutely done with this shit, Reagan." Dad grabs his gun off the couch and turns to Mom. "You deal with her."

Mom and I stare at each other as Dad stomps up the stairs and pounds down the hallway. He slams the bedroom door so hard I can feel the crack of the wood in my chest. The house is silent again.

"How could you say that, Reagan?" Mom says, furiously shaking her head. "When all we've ever done is protect you."

A laugh bursts from my throat, deep and angry. Mom's eyes narrow into slits.

"Why are you laughing?" she demands.

"All you've ever done is *protect* me?" I say, regaining my composure. "Are you kidding? All you've done is put me in harm's way. My whole life has just been one dangerous situation after another."

My words push Mom's back against the couch. Her narrowed eyes regain their shape.

"You don't mean that," Mom replies, slowly shaking her head. "You're just saying that because right now things are tense. But things will go back to normal—"

"Go back to normal? What normal?" I interrupt her. "Things have never been normal for me, and if I become a Black Angel, my life will never be normal. Ever. And you know what? I don't know if I want that."

My mother's head snaps up. Her shoulders fall and the surprise of my confession pushes the air from her lungs. She closes her eyes for a moment and regains her breath.

"Reagan, being a Black Angel is a privilege. To whom much is given—" she begins but I interrupt again.

"Yes, I know. Much is expected. I've only looked at that quote every day for my entire life."

Mom takes a breath, looking me up and down, her fingers wrapping around her Glock 22. "You are not a normal girl. Your talent . . . I've never seen anyone with your talent. Your name has been on the academy's list since you were ten years old. It's what we've been training you for. How can you just throw all our hard work away?"

"So it's about you, then? What *you've* done? Have you ever stopped to think about what's best for me? Don't you want me to be happy?"

Mom crosses her strong arms and bites at her full bottom lip. I can see her thinking behind those intense eyes, choosing each word carefully. "Some people aren't meant to be happy. Some are meant to change the world. *You* were meant to change the world. You think you'd be happy with the picket fence life?"

"Yes," I answer, my voice small.

"I'm your mother," she says, pointing at her chest. "I know you wouldn't."

I suck new air into my burning lungs. "Then you don't know me at all."

My eyes blur, my brain throbs as it fights to push tears back down. Mom opens her mouth to speak but I hold up my hand and stop her.

"I cannot do this," I say, my voice so quiet I'm not sure if she even heard me. But from the look on her face, I know she did. Those four words have been on repeat in my head for months, maybe even years. I've buried them, categorized them as nerves or anxiety. But

I know now they're the truth. "I've tried to do this for you, Mom. I felt like I owed it to you, to my country, but I cannot live like this. I cannot pull a trigger and hope it hits the right person. I cannot live a life where I'm constantly looking over my shoulder. I cannot walk around half dead. Numb. Because every other emotion I could possibly feel is too big and scary."

Mom slides her palm down the length of her face. Her lips form an exaggerated "O" as she slowly pushes out three dense breaths.

"I've seen real happiness, Mom. I've felt it. And I'm done living alone in the dark."

I stand up and walk across the living room toward the curved staircase.

"You're doing this because of Luke, aren't you?" Mom asks. His name and her accusation stop me cold.

Her words punch me in my gut and I have never been so insulted in my life. I grit my teeth, dig my nails into the soft wood of the stair rail, and try not to explode.

"Do you even know why I went out tonight, Mom?" I ask, turning around, my skin burning. "I went out to break Luke's heart. I knew we were one threat away from having to leave and I didn't want Luke to always wonder what happened to me. So I did what you taught me. I strategized. I screwed with people's minds. I created a game plan and it worked and now I feel awful. I just obliterated my chance with the only guy who might actually love me."

"Guys will come and go, Reagan—" Mom begins but I cut her off.

"Not this guy," I say, biting my teeth into my quivering bottom lip. "Guys like him don't come around every day."

"He's one boy," Mom replies, shrugging like I'm overreacting. "There will be others."

"How?" My voice shrieks, my face twisting with the implausibility. "You're basically destining me to a life of total, utter loneliness."

"Your father and I destined you for greatness," Mom replies. I tighten my grasp on the stair rail and listen, letting her words wash over me. "We've handed you a golden ticket and you're just going to throw it in the trash."

I grab ahold of the stair rail so tight, I'm surprised splinters don't cut into my skin.

"You know, I thought you were special, Reagan." Mom pushes herself off the couch to face me and continues. "But you're just going to blend in with everybody else. You'll become beige. And then you'll think back to this moment and you'll regret it."

My body is hot. The blood pulsing through my heart and into my veins feels like it's on fire. Mom stands frozen, her face defiant and the muscles of her arms twitching underneath her short-sleeved navy T-shirt.

"I won't regret a thing," I say and clench my teeth. "What kind of life did you dream for me when I was a little girl? One where I have to lie all the time? One where I have no one who really knows me? Where I am always waiting to feel the barrel of a gun pointed at my back? Is that the life you always wanted for me?"

"No, I'm not saying that, I'm just saying—" she starts, her voice calm and still.

"Yes, it is!" I scream and swallow the urge to sob. "Because if it

148

wasn't, then you'd actually let me choose. You wouldn't be standing here arguing with me."

The vein in Mom's neck is throbbing. Her chest rises higher with each breath. She's about a minute away from exploding. But I keep going.

"Why did you even have a child?" I cross my arms and tighten my lips. Mom's chest doesn't fall. She sucks in a breath and holds it in her lungs.

"Why did you even have me if you weren't going to be around to raise me?" I push harder. The words taste metallic and bitter as they roll off my tongue.

"I've been here to raise you, Reagan. Don't talk to me like I'm some deadbeat mother. Look at the house you live in," she yells and points around the room. "Look at the car you drive and the clothes we buy you and the schools you get to go to. A million girls would kill for your life."

Jesus Christ. I close my eyes and shake my head. She doesn't get it. Maybe she never will.

"What could you possibly want that I haven't given you?"

"Just you."

Mom's muscles release. She drops her arms to her sides, unsure what to do with them now. She looks away, runs her hand through her blond hair and then glances back at me. My hands, my feet, my legs are tingling again. I take a deep breath, trying to fill my body with new air to make it stop.

"You know, it really sucks when you realize just how selfish your parents are," I say, my voice barely audible. "You never should have become a mother if you wanted to be a Black Angel. And that's why I'm making this decision. I want a baby someday and, unlike you, I don't want her to ever be in danger. I'm walking away because, unlike you, I'll put her needs before mine. My love for her will never, and I mean never, feel like second place."

Mom's bottom lip trembles. She opens her mouth to speak, but the words won't come out. We stand there for a moment, just looking at each other. I watch her bite her lip, fighting the tears that lie on the rim of her eyes. She searches my face and for the first time in years, she *really* sees me. Every bad and broken part. She takes in all of me. And I don't think she likes what she sees.

She's still just staring, willing her mouth to move, for words to come when I turn on my heel and start climbing up the stairs. I leave her in the dark, our fight still bouncing off the uncomfortable fancy furniture and hardwood floors.

"I'm sorry, Reagan," Mom calls after me. I stop halfway up the stairs and turn around. A tear has broken free and is falling down her face. It rolls down her cheek and drips off her chin. She doesn't bother to wipe it away. It's strange to see her like that, frail and hurting. I've never seen her cry.

She sniffs back the tears and continues, "I'm so sorry I haven't been the mother you want me to be."

Her words punch me in the gut. And I almost give in. I almost take it all back so she can sleep tonight. But I just can't do it anymore.

"It's too late for sorry, Mom. It's just too late."

I head up the stairs. The smooth wood of the stair rail is cold and the chill I've been suppressing finally runs up my spine. Every step I take is heavy, every new breath hard, and this staircase has never felt so long.

It's only once I reach my bedroom door that I hear my mother break down and sob.

SIXTEEN

A GUST OF WIND WHIPS MY HAIR ACROSS MY FACE and rustles my book and papers on the table. I pull the dark strands back into place and tug my open black fleece jacket closer to my body. It's a few degrees too cold to be sitting outside, but I can't bring myself to go sit in the library or an empty classroom. With each class, the walls move closer and closer in on me.

The final warning bell rings and the quad quickly empties. A young guy in a vintage Ohio State hoodie sits at a picnic table on the opposite side. I've never seen him before, but today he's permanently in my peripheral vision. He's clearly my Black Angel watcher. I examine him with his dark features and muscular build. He definitely looks just young enough to be a student, but I know better. He's most likely a trainee at the academy. He feels me staring and looks up from the notebook he's writing in. I give him a knowing glance before he returns to his fake homework. The double doors next to him swing open and Luke walks through, the high winds ripping open his jacket. He tugs at his coat, looks across the quad, and spots me.

Damn. I've been hiding from him all day. He's supposed to be in the AP bio class I'm purposely skipping just so I don't have to see him. Luke stands frozen and stares at me for a second, unsure of what to do. *Go away. Go away.* But he doesn't listen. He shoves his hands into his pocket and begins walking toward me, tightening the anxious knot in my stomach that's gotten so big, I feel like I've swallowed forty pounds of lead.

I spent all of Sunday locked away in my room, unable to apologize or face my parents. This morning, I heard Mom getting ready in the bathroom. I stopped in the hall and listened to the low hum of the morning news and the buzz of Dad's razor, sounds I've become so accustomed to hearing, it's like they were built into the house between the brick and the drywall. I could have knocked on their door and kissed her good-bye or said I was sorry. But that angry burn in my veins was still there. So I turned my back, walked down the stairs and out the front door without saying a word.

My eyes stare back down at my books. I pretend to engross myself in King Henry VIII and all his lays. But Luke keeps coming. I take a deep breath. I don't want to do this.

"Why are you cutting?" Luke says, his voice accusing and angry.

I shrug and answer, "Just didn't feel like going, I guess."

"Avoiding me?" Luke asks, his eyes on the ground, his feet kicking at imaginary rocks.

A gust of wind shakes the red leaves on the trees next to us. I look up. Most of them hold on to their branches, but a few break free and float to the ground, adding to the carpet of colors. Reds and yellows and oranges and browns cover the grass and cement sidewalk. When I look back at Luke, his eyes are fixed on me, waiting for me to speak.

"What do you think?" I respond, my voice quiet, not the sharp, icy voice I was hoping to project.

Luke shoves his hands into his pockets and rocks back and forth on his toes. He shakes his head slightly and narrows his blue eyes. "Really? Some random Australian dude? Who's a sophomore by the way. Or did you not pick up on the fact that you were making out with an underclassman, Reagan?"

Reagan. My own name stings my skin. Luke never calls me anything but Mac.

"Never thought you'd do something like that to me," Luke continues to push. He stares at me, waiting for me to say something. Say I'm sorry. That I was drunk. That I never meant to hurt him. But I did.

As I look into his eyes, aching, anguished emptiness tears at the walls I've carefully constructed around my heart and slips inside. I want to crumble. To tell him the truth. But I can't. I'm shocked we're still here. It's only a matter of time until we disappear. So I'll continue to crush his soft heart until the thought of me, the memory of us, makes him sick.

"I guess you don't really know me as well as you think you do, Luke," I finally reply, each syllable wrapped in daggers.

Luke stares at me, long and hard. He opens his mouth to speak but the sound of squealing tires pulls our attention toward the parking lot. I can see the top of a gray van come to a stop behind a row of cars. And that's when I hear the scream. The piercing, heart-stopping scream of a young girl.

"No, please, no!" the voice screams. "Help me. Somebody help me!"

My training kicks in and I sprint across the quad. The screaming intensifies as I get closer to the parking lot. Fifty yards. Forty yards. Thirty yards. My Black Angel watcher is still twenty yards behind me, shouting my name.

"Reagan! No, stay back," he calls out but I keep running. The girl screams for help again and I push my legs to go faster.

"Shit," I say under my breath, my muscles in overdrive. As I reach the parking lot, a group of teachers and students have started streaming out of the buildings, still one hundred yards behind me. I'm twenty yards away when I lock eyes with him and those pins prick my spine. The janitor. He's inside the van, the side door swung open, a knife to the girl's throat. Her dark hair swings wildly away from her face and even with a blindfold over her eyes, I recognize her. Tess. Claire's bully. Her exposed arm is cut and bloodied but she's still fighting and screaming and pulling out of his grasp. As soon as he sees me, his dark eyes widen and his mouth drops open.

I sprint full speed for him. He immediately lets go of Tess and lunges for me, the knife outstretched in his hands. Before he can reach me, I grab his thick wrist, pushing his arm down and away from my body, then kick him square in the groin. The knife falls to the ground with a clang. I reach down to pick it up, ready to return it to the janitor's neck, but he's already back inside the van.

"¡Vamos!" he barks at the driver, sending the tires squealing. Tess is crumpled on the ground, grabbing her arm and crying in pain.

"Somebody call nine-one-one," I yell behind me as Luke and a group of teachers and students finally reach the parking lot. I run to her side and tear off the blindfold. She throws her arms around me, pulling my body closer to hers, her damp tears transferring onto my skin.

"Thank you," Tess cries into my shoulder. I position her on the ground, tear off my jacket, and tie a tight knot around her arm to stop the bleeding.

"You're going to be okay," I say and wipe her dark hair out of her eyes. I can already hear the sirens in the distance. "Help is coming."

"He called me Reagan," Tess says, grasping her bloody hands in mine. "Why did he keep calling me Reagan?"

I swear my heart pauses midbeat. By now, dozens of teachers and classmates have crowded around us and are shouting panicked questions. What happened? Who did this? Are you okay?

Every muscle in my body is buzzing. I stand up and look her up and down: same long, dark hair, same olive complexion, same gray T-shirt and same dark jeans. We could normally pass as sisters but today . . . we could pass for twins.

They came for me.

The sirens grow louder as I push my way out of the crowd and dial home. *Please pick up, please pick up*, my mind begs with each ring.

"Hello?" my mom answers after the third ring.

"Mom, get in the panic room right now," I yell into the phone as I run across the parking lot.

"Reagan, calm down for—" she answers, her voice tight.

"Just listen to me. Grab Dad and get in the panic room

immediately!" I am now screaming into the phone, my breath heavy from running.

"What's going—" she begins to say but I cut her off.

"There's no time to explain. You're not safe, someone is—" But before I can finish my sentence, the sound of shattering glass fills my ears.

"Reagan!" she screams but her voice already sounds muffled and far away.

"Mom!" I shriek, but the line goes dead. "Mom!" I scream one more time before I shove the phone back into my pocket.

I'm running faster than I ever have in my life but it feels like I'm wading through quicksand. Every step I take feels like I'm sinking further into the soft earth. But I keep pushing and running and breathing and begging. *Please, God. Please, God. Please, God.*

"I'm coming, Mom. I'm coming."

SEVENTEEN

I PLACE MY HAND, CAKED WITH BLOOD, ON THE METAL doorknob. It's black and gold and made to look antique even though the house is only a decade old. The metal is cold and soothes my fiery grip. I hold it there for one second. Two seconds. Three seconds. Contemplating what I'm going to do once I get inside. Wondering what kind of scene I'll find. I close my eyes. An image of our foyer flashes behind my eyelids. Blood is splashed on the white walls and bodies lie at the foot of the stairs. I shake my head and open my eyes before my brain shows me who the bodies belong to. *Stop thinking like that, you psycho,* I scold myself. *Pull yourself together.*

A rush of dread fills every inch of my body as I turn the knob, my finger wrapped around the trigger of the pistol. Part of me expects the door to be locked, but it's open. The foyer walls are still white. There are no bodies on the ground. I blow the air out through my lips and take a silent step inside, my arms outstretched and my gun pointed in front of me, ready to shoot.

I close the door as quietly as I can, but the click of the bolt brushing against metal fills the room. I stand in the foyer and listen. For footsteps, voices, fighting or screaming or gunshots. But I hear nothing.

The dining room and living room are untouched. The light from the kitchen pours from the doorway and streams down the hallway. I try to control the sound of my breath, the strike of my feet as I sidestep down the dim hallway, my back against the wall, gun pulled against my chest. I listen again. I'm straining to hear something, anything. The refrigerator kicks on in the kitchen. It hums and hums and hums and stops. I take a few more steps toward the kitchen, but Dad's half-open office door stops me.

Dad never leaves the door like that. It's either wide open when he's not using it or closed shut when he's inside. I listen for a second more, then kick the door open, sending it crashing against the wall. I point the gun in front of me, my finger gripping the trigger.

Dad's heavy desk is overturned, picture frames and lamps are shattered, and bullet holes dot his built-in shelves. "Holy shit," I whisper. I step across the splintered pieces of desk and run my fingers along the dark wood. The bullet holes are huge, made by a high-powered automatic weapon. My boot kicks a piece of glass. A silver frame with a picture of me as a little girl is on the ground. My face smiles wide for the camera. I have an ice-cream cone in my hand and chocolate smeared across my upper lip. I can't be more than five. My eyes are the same dark color as the ice cream and I've never looked so happy. I lean down and pick it up. The glass is cracked and a piece falls to the ground as I pull it toward me. Something red is smeared at the bottom. Blood. I look closer. A bloody fingerprint. But whose fingerprint? Whose blood? I place the frame on the shelf. My head is screaming. The muscles in my body feel like they're unraveling. But I won't scream. And I won't collapse. The training is taking over. I'm not scared anymore. I'm pissed. And the only thing I can think of is finding and stopping whoever is inside my house.

I step over the splintered desk, broken glass, and shell casings, making my way down the hall. I sidestep along the wall, my gun at my chest. My heel taps the woodwork along the kitchen door. My muscles tighten as I watch the light at my feet, waiting for a shadow to pass. Nothing happens. I whip my body around the doorframe and point my gun straight ahead. My eyes search the room for intruders but it's empty. Shards of glass are everywhere. I feel a cold breeze on my face. I point my gun to the left. The patio door is shattered and the glass that once stood there now glitters in a million little pieces on the floor.

The glass crunches under the weight of my feet as I sidestep toward the garage, my back pushed up against the wall of cabinets. On the other side of the island, a red brick lies on the ground. There's a deep gash in the wood above it where it first hit. The sound of it—the breaking glass, the pieces scattering across the kitchen, my mother crying out for me—floods my ears once again. There is a coffee cup on the counter; Mom's creamy pink lipstick hugs the white rim. Today's mail is spread out on the island and the portable phone is smashed to pieces next to unopened letters and unread magazines.

Wind passes through the kitchen and something flapping near the brick catches my eye. I step carefully across the kitchen, lean down and pick it up. My hands are trembling as I pull at the rubber band wrapped around it. It snaps against a coarse edge, coming undone, and the sound makes my muscles jump. I unfold the piece of paper. The word *VENGANZA* is written in all caps followed by a drawing of a hammer. *REVENGE*, the thick black ink screams at me. The fumes are still fresh and make me dizzy.

"No," I say to myself, crumbling the piece of paper in my hand. "No!"

If someone is still here, they certainly know by now I'm inside. But I want them to know. I want them to come after me. I run out of the kitchen and into the den. My breath is short. My pulse is panicked. I point the gun into the room. My arms outstretched. Searching. No one.

I run through the hallway. The sound of my pounding feet echo and fill the silent two-story foyer. I sprint up the stairs, two, three at a time. My legs are moving without me even telling them what to do. Without me even thinking. The hall is empty. I shove open the guest bedroom door and point my gun inside. Nothing. I move down to the next and the next and the next. Still nothing.

I sprint down the hall toward my parents' room. The door is closed. I stand and listen. I hear my breath going in and out of my lungs. I push open the door and point my gun inside. I step onto their plush carpet. Slivers of glass stuck in my boots catch on their floor. But the room is empty. The house is silent.

The panic room. Maybe they made it downstairs in time to the panic room.

My body flings down the stairs so quickly I almost fall. I catch myself with the railing and keep going. The glass flies in the air as

I sprint across the kitchen but before I can open the garage door, a thud stops me cold.

I stop and listen. I hear the thud again. I raise my gun to my chest and sidestep along the cabinets of the kitchen, careful not to disturb the shattered glass and give away my location. Footsteps walk quietly down the hallway. My body presses against the side of the door frame as the footsteps get closer and closer. They're heading right for me. My heart pounds, matching the thud of the footsteps. I take a breath and whip my body around the door frame, my gun raised and pointed at the temple of Luke.

His eyes widen to the point that I can see all the white around his blue irises. Staring into the barrel of my pistol, Luke instinctively raises his hands into the air.

"What are you doing here?" I whisper as I lower my weapon.

"What the hell is going on?" Luke replies, his voice a low and unsteady gravel. He peers into Dad's trashed office and the sight unhinges his jaw. "Oh my God . . ."

"Quiet," I whisper, cutting him off. I grab his wrist and pull him into the kitchen.

"Mac, we need to call the cops," Luke whispers, his shoes crunching against the broken glass.

"Luke, quiet, I'm better trained than any cop," I say and look up into his stunned eyes. "Just stay close to me and don't say another word."

Luke stares at me, momentarily frozen, then nods and takes a step closer.

I open the garage door. He follows me inside. I punch the code into the basement. Luke's mouth drops again as the doors open and the stairs appear.

"Let's go," I whisper and pound down the stairs.

I reach the gun range. I scan the room with my eyes and my weapon. I pray to see someone. Anybody. Even if it's a Colombian. If someone is down here, then I know I'm not too late. My finger tightens around the trigger. My heart sinks. There is no one. I run to the weapons room, Luke on my heels. Nothing. I turn toward the martial arts room and inch my way toward the closed panic room door.

Maybe they're in there. Maybe they made it, my brain repeats over and over again. But somewhere inside, I know they haven't. I feel tiny pieces of me start to break apart. Like my soul is being slashed one square inch by one square inch and thrown into the air like confetti. Mocking me. I try to breathe the pieces back in. I try to collect them. But they float away. And I feel emptier and emptier with each step I take.

I reach the door. I close my eyes. I beg. *Please, God. Please, God.*

I open my eyes. I open the door. It's empty.

My knees are shaking. I swallow the scream inside my throat. The adrenaline drains from my body and it begins to ache. I grip the handle of the panic room door. My knuckles are white and every time I breathe, I feel like a knife is being plunged deeper and deeper into my spine.

There is a crack in the weapons room followed by the sound of metal scraping against metal.

My muscles twitch and tighten back into place. I pull Luke by the collar and we duck behind the wall, my gun at my chest. The sound of scraping metal stops. I hear footsteps on the cement floor. I watch as two shadows move closer.

"Anything?" I hear a male voice whisper. The footsteps are now only a few feet away. I take a breath, whip my body around the door frame, and point the gun into the room.

The escape door is open and standing inside the weapons room are two faces I recognize. Aunt Samantha and the young Black Angel watcher from school, both with Glock pistols pointed at my head. I lower my gun. They lower theirs. We stare at each other.

"They're gone, aren't they?" Sam finally asks, her voice calm and quiet, her gun hanging at her side.

I bite my lip and slowly nod. Their faces become a blur. They're gone. My parents are gone.

EIGHTEEN

"REAGAN, COME ON. LET'S GET YOU SOMEWHERE safe," Sam says, but I don't move. My jaw, my eyes, my arms, and my legs are locked and feel like they weigh about a thousand pounds. Her eyes are kind and wide and blue. They stare at me, waiting for me to follow her. The axons and synapses in my brain fire, telling my body to take a step forward, but I can't. I don't shake or cry or speak. I am stone.

My brain repeats two words over and over again. *They're gone. They're gone. They're gone.* The words rattle back and forth in my skull and I want to scream, but my mouth stays tight. My tongue doesn't move.

"Reagan," she repeats softly.

They're gone. They're gone. They're gone.

She waits another beat for me to move on my own. She looks into my eyes, presses her thin lips together, then grabs me gently by the wrist and pulls me toward the weapons room. The tug on my arm forces one foot to step in front of the other, and I let her guide me up the stairs.

I begin to feel little things. Her thin fingers around my wrist and the stairs beneath my feet. My boots echo. I concentrate on the sound of my steps and the breath in my chest to drown out the screaming in my head. I focus on moving forward so I won't crumble into a ball on the floor. I just move where she pulls me.

Sam guides me into the garage and through the glass-shattered kitchen. The crack and pop sounds under my feet hurt my spine. I want to throw my hands over my ears and rock back and forth on the floor. Luke steps on a large chunk of glass behind me. It shatters into pieces, forcing my body to flinch. Sam feels my body tighten; her hand slides down my wrist and laces my fingers with hers. She squeezes my hand firmly. I squeeze back and the nostalgia of that feeling crushes me.

When I was eleven, Mom grabbed my hand in a grocery store parking lot and squeezed it three times, which meant *I love you*. We had our own secret language with hand squeezes but this time, I didn't squeeze back. I was embarrassed. I tried to pull my hand away, but she held on to me. She squeezed my hand three times again. A boy from my class walked out of the automatic sliding glass doors with his mom and I ripped my hand away. She looked down at me, hurt and confusion in her green eyes. The boy said hello to me as we passed and then she understood. I wasn't a little girl anymore. I didn't need, nor did I want, to hold her hand. I remember that moment so clearly. The way she looked down at the ground and laced her hands together, filling the empty space where my palm used to be. She never tried to hold my hand again. Never. Not in public.

Not even at home. But I'd do just about anything to hold her hand now.

"Why don't you sit down," Sam says, pulling me over to the deep gray linen couch in the den. I obey and take a seat. I stare at the dark grooves and slashes in the hand-scraped hardwood floor, still unable to speak, as Luke sits down next to me.

"What is going on, Sam?" Luke asks, his worried eyes still on me. He's met Aunt Sam a half dozen times at my house or at a backyard barbecue. He was told she was Mom's college roommate and best friend.

"Luke, I think it's best if you leave right now," Sam says.

"No way, I'm not leaving her until someone tells me what's going on," Luke replies, his voice frantic. He gently places a hand on the small of my back. "We need to call the cops, the FBI, something."

"She's not asking you to leave. She's telling you to leave," the Black Angel watcher says.

"Who are you, anyways?" Luke asks.

"I'm Cooper," he answers, arms folded across his muscular chest, gun in his hand. "Look, everything is fine. We don't need cops. We just need you to go."

"Everything is not fine," Luke says, raising his voice and motioning down the hall. "There are bullet holes the size of bazookas in the office, there is shattered glass all over the kitchen, and the MacMillans are clearly gone. Things couldn't be further from fine."

"Luke, it's complicated and now a matter of national security. I think it's best if—" Sam begins but I cut her off.

"He needs to stay," I say. The words feel thick and heavy as they fall off my tongue. "They saw him with me at the school. He's in danger now too."

Sam looks over at Cooper. He nods. She lets out a long breath. "Fine, he can stay for now. Until we assess the situation and confirm he's safe. Luke, I know your background. You want to be a cadet, right?"

"Yes, ma'am," Luke says, nodding.

"Well, your first code of silence starts this second," Sam replies, her voice stern and serious.

"Okay. But what . . . how . . . who are you guys?" Luke stammers. He blinks wildly and shakes his head. His eyes search my face, my body, and linger on my right hand. I look down to see my pistol in my grip, my finger still wrapped around the trigger. I didn't even realize I was still holding my gun.

The door to my secret life is swinging open. Part of me wants to run through it, embrace it, and be happy that Luke finally knows. The other part wants to slam the door shut, walk away, and pretend this never happened.

I tell my mouth to open and say something, but I'm still paralyzed. The only movements I seem to be able to master are blinking and breathing, and even those require some serious effort.

I feel Sam's eyes on me. She's waiting for me to speak. To answer Luke's questions. But I can't. So she begins.

Sam tells Luke about the Black Angels. That I've been training my entire life to be one of them. She tells him the basics about my parents and the double lives and the cover stories and the missions. But I'm only half listening. I fade in and out of the conversation as I stare at the corner of the ceiling. I let my body, my mind float there.

Hide there. I hear Luke ask more questions. I hear bits and pieces of the answers. Danger. Protection. Secrecy. Code. I hear Luke ask how many people know about the Black Angels. My family. My mind comes back to my body, my eyes focus, and I speak.

"No one," I say, my voice fighting to lift out of its fog. "No one in my life knows who I really am. If anyone knew, it would put my life at risk. Their lives at risk."

"So the van, the guy at school . . ." Luke says, starting to put the pieces together.

"They were coming for me," I answer and finally look up into his eyes.

"The last mission went badly," Sam continues to fill him in. "Really bad. Revenge was promised and we think it was their mission to kidnap Reagan today."

"I think they've been watching us for a while," I say and stare at the ground.

"It looks like they've been monitoring you guys for the last month," Cooper trumpets from the other side of the room. "Since your parents locked up Torres's brother. How did you know that?"

"I saw the man who tried to take the girl at school last week dressed as a janitor and watching me. I tried to run after him but he disappeared. I saw the gray van near our street a couple times, but I told myself it was nothing. I thought I was just being paranoid."

"Your first rule as a trainee is to trust your instincts," Sam says, her voice growing tight. "Why didn't you say anything?"

"I thought my mind was just playing tricks on me again," I answer and shake my head. "You know it's happened before. I've been wrong before."

"You should have told your parents," Cooper replies.

"I know I should have," I say, my voice hard and defensive. I swallow the lump that is rising in my throat. "Because maybe if I did, I wouldn't have had to hear my mother scream my name as they threw a brick through the back door and dragged her away."

"Jesus Christ," Luke replies softly. He shakes his head slowly. "Mac, I'm so sorry."

"Don't call me that. You don't even know my name," I snap. The moment the words escape my lips I regret them. Luke's face tightens from the sting. I love it when he calls me Mac. But now, it just feels like a lie.

Luke's Adam's apple bobs as he swallows hard at something in his throat. He nods. "Okay. I won't. What's your real name?"

"Reagan Elizabeth Hillis," I say. It sounds so foreign to me, like I'm talking about somebody else, a childhood friend or distant relative, someone only in my memory.

"Okay, Reagan Elizabeth Hillis," Luke repeats the name. It sounds warmer in his voice than my own. Luke turns to Sam. "So what's next?"

"Intel analysts at headquarters have been tracking them," Sam says, holding up her phone. "They are trigger happy right now, waiting for us to pounce on them, so we're going to hang back. Let them think they've evaded us so that when we do make contact they're caught off guard. We think they're heading to a private airport somewhere in southern Ohio or Kentucky. We've got crews already on their way. And headquarters has already intercepted a message from Torres with his demands."

"What are they?" I ask. The numbness is starting to wear off.

I can feel my heart beating like a hummingbird in my chest again and the feeling in my arms and legs is starting to come back.

Sam looks at me and shakes her head.

"You don't need to know the details, Reagan," she says and looks away, hoping I won't ask any more questions. She continues talking to Luke. "We're assembling a team to intercept them at the airport and we're hoping that we—"

"Why won't you tell me?" I interrupt her. Sam pretends like she hasn't heard me and continues talking to Luke, refusing to look at me.

"—have enough information to find them," Sam continues, her voice steady. "We believe Torres is moving them—"

"Tell me!" I raise my voice, my tone startling Sam.

Sam finally looks back at me. She tightens the grasp of her gun. She looks down at the ground and then up at me.

"Please," I beg. "No more secrets. I need to know."

"Torres wants you, okay?" Sam says, throwing her hands up in the air with equal parts fear and frustration. "That's why they tried to grab you at school. The plan was to take you back to your house and kill you in front of your parents, but they grabbed the wrong girl and now everything has changed."

"Why do they want me?" I ask, but as soon as the question rolls off my heavy tongue, the pieces of Torres's psychotic puzzle snap horrifically into place. "Because of what happened to Torres's son?"

Sam and Cooper stare blankly at me, afraid to confirm my suspicion.

"An eye for an eye, right?" I say, my voice shrinking into a whisper.

"Much worse. He'd probably beat you. Torture you for days. Kill

171

you and then kill your parents too," Sam explains, the words getting tangled in her throat. "I've been intercepting and analyzing data from this guy since I was at the National Security Agency. Over the last seventeen years, he's been responsible for over two hundred and fifty deaths. Pulled the trigger or twisted the knife in half of those. He is a merciless, psychotic serial killer and whether it was our guns or not, his son is dead and he won't stop until somebody pays."

My lungs stop working midway through my last breath. Luke's hand reaches out for me, his fingertips lingering on my forearm. As he presses down, I can feel that my clothing is damp with sweat.

"We should have made you guys leave after the mission," Cooper says and shakes his head. "But we thought we had a few days to track Torres and his team. See if you guys were in real danger."

My mouth whispers, "This is my fault."

"No. Don't say that," Sam says, shaking her head. Luke tightens his grip around my arm.

"No, it's my fault. I didn't tell them about the janitor and the van. And we got into the biggest fight this weekend, Sam," I say, my hands balled into stinging fists. "I made Mom feel guilty about all the times they took me away. I clouded her judgment. This is my fault."

"Stop it, Reagan," Sam demands and crosses the room. She puts her hand on both shoulders. "Listen to me. We need to get you guys to the safe house immediately. You need to pull yourself together and grab everyone's go-bags. You probably won't be coming back here again."

I stare at the ground, clenching my fists so hard my nails are one tight squeeze away from drawing blood. I knew it was coming.

But I certainly didn't think I'd be forced to slip away from New Albany, my house, my life, like this.

"Okay," I say with a nod. I clear away the fog and will my body to move. It obeys. I rise and take the first step toward bringing my parents home.

NINETEEN

BANG. BANG. BANG. HAMMERING ECHOES THROUGH-
out the house. Sam and Cooper are cleaning up the glass in the
kitchen and nailing a board they found in the garage against the
shattered patio door.

"They're just behind this wall," I say to Luke as I slide my hand
along the smooth surface of the bookshelf in the bonus room.
There's the spot. I push and the bookshelf swings open to reveal
our small emergency closet.

"Whoa," Luke says as we step inside. The closet is wrapped in
steel and weapons line nearly every square inch of its walls.

"This is in case we can't make it to the basement," I answer, still
moderately numb and focused. I spot our three black go-bags in
the corner and begin to haul them out of the closet.

"What's in them?" Luke asks, helping me with the last one.

"Things we can't live without," I answer, laying my go-bag down
on the ground. I unzip it and begin picking out different items. "My
doll, Mimi. I used to drag her around everywhere with me when I

was a kid. Letters and cards from my parents. Photographs. Jewelry. Stuff like that. We have to leave so fast most of the time, we don't really get to pack. We have just enough time to grab our go-bags and get the hell out of here. We leave everything else behind."

"How many times have you had to do this?" Luke asks, his hands reaching out to touch the fabric of Mimi's fading yellow flowered dress.

"Too many," I answer and move to zip up the bag, forcing Luke to pull his hand away from Mimi. He looks up at me and I finally meet his gaze. His eyes are wide, wild with confusion, but the corners of his mouth turn down.

"I just...I can't believe you've had to live like this," Luke says, shaking his head, scared and sorry for me.

I shrug, my eyes cast down as I finish zipping the bag. "I don't know any different. This was the life I was born into."

Flashes of the fight play back, jumpy and distorted, like a 1920s movie reel. Her tear-stung eyes. My fuming words. I shake my head, rattling my brain, trying to clear away the memory and say, "I got in an enormous fight with them about it this weekend. I told them that I couldn't do this anymore. That I didn't want to be a Black Angel. I said some terrible—"

"Reagan," Sam's voice interrupts from the doorway. "You've got five minutes to get the rest of your stuff together. Luke, can you come help me with something?"

"Sure," Luke says, then glances back at me to make sure I'm okay. I give a small nod, a silent promise that I won't fall apart in the next five minutes.

I grab the go-bags and run down the hall to my room. My body

175

is still wet with sweat and freezing. I tear off my sweater and pull on a clean, warm sweatshirt. I close my dresser drawer with so much force, my mirror shakes. Jewelry and an envelope slide off the top of my messy dresser and onto the floor.

I lean down and pick up the envelope. My name is written in blue ink in my mother's beautiful cursive handwriting. Mom is old-fashioned like that. While the rest of the world prints or emails or sends texts or Facebook messages, Mom insists on writing in the cursive she learned in third grade at her all-girls Catholic school. She says she's afraid Sister Roberta will hunt her down and throw erasers at her head if she starts printing.

Is this letter old or new? Mom sometimes writes me notes about missing me when she's out on a mission. I find them on my bed or on my dresser when she gets home. I flip the envelope and see the back is still sealed. New. I rip it open and unfold the single sheet of paper inside. Today's date is written in the top left-hand corner. I sink onto the ground, my back leaning against my dresser, and begin to read.

Reagan,

I meant what I said the other night. I'm sorry that I haven't always been the mother you wanted me to be. I have dreamt of having a daughter just like you since I was little. When I found out I was pregnant, it was one of the best days of my entire life. You moved around all the time. Kicking me, punching me right in the ribs. Everyone was convinced you were a little boy, even your dad. But I knew you were my Reagan. I knew you were a little fighter. I could feel your strength every day and, watching you grow up, I see it in your actions. Not just your physical strength, but the way you fight for people and help them. The way you stand up for what you believe in, no matter what anybody else may think. You are the strongest woman I've ever met.

You were right. This life is a selfish one and I haven't always put your needs first. Maybe I should have chosen when you were just a hope and a prayer in my heart. I didn't anticipate how being a mother and a Black Angel would affect you and for that I'm so sorry. But just know if I had to go back and choose, every single time, I would choose you.

I want you to live your life for you. So if being a Black Angel is not what you want, then please, find your dream. If your dream is to be a doctor, then go be the best doctor in the world. If your dream is to get married and have children, go be the best wife and mother in the world. I have no doubt that you will be.

I'm sorry that your life has never been normal and we've put you in so much danger. I wish I could go back in time and redo my life so that you never had to feel scared. Not for a single second.

Always know how much I love you and how

proud I am of the young woman you are. The world is expecting some big things from you, Reagan Elizabeth Hillis.

Love you always,
Mom

A tear runs down my cheek and splatters on her signature, making the ink expand. I quickly wipe it away so the ink won't run and ruin the letter but it's too late. The word *Mom* smears across the page, leaving a trail of hazy blue rivers.

My eyes stare blankly at random words in the letter. *Life. Danger. Love. Mom.* The adrenaline that's been pumping through my body for the last hour begins to fade and the guilty knot in the pit of my stomach pulses. The guilt and pain and fear I've been trying to ignore radiates through my body and every muscle, every bone begins to splinter.

"Reagan?" Luke says from the door. I open my eyes and look up at him, my knees still to my chest, the letter still in my hand. When he sees my red eyes, his face drops. "What is it?"

"My mother left this in my room." I fight to stand up and hand him the letter. He takes it from me and reads as I rip the knife from behind my headboard and stuff it into my go-bag.

I stare out the window at the Weixels' tire swing spinning gently in the wind. My fingers instinctively reach for the charm on my left wrist. Her bracelet. I press down on the sterling silver, wishing the double hearts held magic powers.

"I never got to say it," I say without turning around. I look down into my bag, repositioning my Glock pistol and bulletproof vest.

"Say what?" His voice drops, the way it always does when he knows exactly what I'm talking about.

"I never got to say I'm sorry," I answer and stuff an extra sweatshirt into my bag with so much force, the bed bounces beneath my weight. "I said some horrible things to her. Just horrible. I basically told her she was a bad mother. That she was selfish and should never have even had me. And you know what. She's not the selfish one. I am."

"You are the furthest thing from selfish," Luke replies. I feel the heat of his body as he inches toward me. "That is the last word I would ever use to describe you."

"If I wasn't selfish, I would want to do this job. I'd just deal with all the bad stuff that comes with it."

"Reagan, this is an incredibly dangerous life. Look at what's happening right now. You have the right to choose."

"I just want them back, Luke," I say, my voice on the edge of trembling. "This is my fault and I'll do anything to . . ."

"Listen to me," Luke says, grabbing my shoulders and slowly turning me around. "This is not your fault. You've got to stop doing this to yourself because you'll be no good to anyone."

A cold sigh presses through my even colder lips and I nod to appease him. But I don't know how I'm going to stop blaming myself. A silver sterling picture frame on my nightstand catches my eye. Mom has her arms around my shoulders and is smiling for the camera. I'm looking up at her and laughing. Dad snapped the picture out on our back patio this summer. We built a fire in the fire pit, roasted marshmallows, and stayed up late, just talking about nothing. It was a perfect night.

"Luke, what if we're already too late?" I say, still staring at the photograph.

"They are going to find them, okay?" Luke says, his voice as strong as his grip on my shoulders. "They are going to bring them home and you are going to get to say you're sorry and whatever else you want to say to her."

I love you. You're my hero, my mind whispers. I dig my teeth into my bottom lip and nod.

"Reagan? It's time," Sam's echoed voice calls from the foyer. My body buzzes and the adrenaline returns. I fill my lungs with new air and quickly wipe both cheeks with the back of my hands. Black Angels don't cry. Black Angels fight. And I'm going to fight.

"Come on. Let's go," I say, handing Luke Mom's and Dad's go-bags. He walks out the door as I grab the sterling silver picture frame off the nightstand and shove it into my bag. I throw the straps over my shoulder, take one last look around my room, shut off the lights, and silently say good-bye to my life on Landon Lane.

TWENTY

"WE ARE FIVE MILES OUT FROM THE AIRPORT, FIVE miles out, copy?" A voice, mangled by static, comes through one of the speakers in the safe house's situation room.

"Copy. We've got you," Sam says into the microphone on the steel weapons table turned makeshift desk. The basement of the safe house looks a lot like ours on Landon Lane. Same weapons room, shooting range, and panic room. But instead of a martial arts studio filled with mats, dummies, and punching bags, the room here is packed with enormous monitors, microphones, computers, and other intel equipment that helps us communicate with CORE and Black Angels in the field.

"We still think they're going to that private airfield in Kentucky?" I ask, my hot hands grasping onto Sam's cool metal chair. I'm watching over her left shoulder as the SUV's thermal camera travels down a dark two-lane road. As the SUV rounds the curve, a truck passes in the opposite direction, its heat transmitting infrared energy that's converted into an electronic signal. The haunting black-and-white images that show up on our monitors have so much detail, I can tell the driver's smoking.

"The analysts at CORE seem pretty confident that's where they're going," Sam says, pulling up the airport's coordinates on her laptop. "There's a private plane waiting there and when we ran the tail number, it came back as being registered to some bullshit corporation in South America that we know doesn't exist. Has Torres's fingerprints all over it."

I look up at the other six monitors. Two Black Angels are already stationed at the airport, waiting to intercept the kidnappers and rescue my parents. The thermal cameras attached to their helmets show their movements as they position themselves out of sight near a private hangar, but still in view of the Gulfstream. Looks like a G650. The most expensive one on the market and probably paid for in money covered in blood and cocaine.

"Three miles out, three miles out," the scratchy voice blares again through the speakers in the monitor.

"Copy," reply the two men in the field.

"Do we still have eyes in the sky on Torres's SUV?" Sam says, pressing the talk button in her microphone with one hand and hitting a crackling monitor with the other. "We keep losing the feed."

"Yeah, we're on them, Sam," says the Black Angel pilot.

"Is everybody ready on the ground?" Cooper asks, standing behind Sam's right shoulder. "This is still a civilian airport, so we need to be really careful."

"I'm keenly aware, Cooper," Sam replies, annoyed, never taking her eyes off the screens.

"Why haven't we cleared out the airport?" I ask, arching my eyebrows at Cooper. "There's no way these guys are going to just lie on the ground during a take-down. We need to disarm them before they even know we're there."

"We would clear out the airport but someone inside might tip off Torres," Sam replies, switching on another monitor screen. "We cannot take that chance."

"Then clear it two minutes before the car gets there," I reply, my eyes fixated on the monitor that travels along the two-lane, wooded road, my parents just a mile in front of them in the darkness. "That way, no one has time to warn Torres or his guys on the ground."

"There's no way we can clear an entire civilian airport in two minutes," Cooper answers, his voice smug, like I don't know what I'm talking about. "We've got to do it this way."

"This is a huge mistake," I say, my voice tightening with every word. "There's no way they're going down without some type of gun battle, which means injured Black Angels on the ground. My parents included."

"Reagan, we have taken down Torres's guys before," Sam answers, clacking away at her keyboard. "If we rush them, we think they'll go down peacefully."

"Thinking isn't good enough—" I start but Sam cuts me off.

"We don't have a choice." Sam whips her head around, her long blond ponytail smacking her in the face. "I know you don't want to hear this, but this is our best shot at getting them back. We don't want Torres to have even the slightest idea that we know where they're taking them. Who the hell knows if we'll get another chance?"

As Sam turns back to the monitors, fear tangles through my body, its long, dark fingers gripping my lungs and forcing out an anxious breath.

"Reagan, maybe it's best you don't watch the take-down," Sam says, her eyes jumping from monitor to monitor.

"Yeah, why don't we go in the other room?" Luke adds, warily placing his hand on my shoulder.

"No. I'm fine," I answer and cross my arms, forcing Luke's hand to slide down my back.

"Look, I appreciate your help," Sam replies, typing another message to the analysts at CORE. "We all know you have a gifted mind when it comes to strategy. This is just too much to take in."

"Come on, Reagan," Luke says, pulling again slightly on my shoulder.

"No! I'm staying," I answer, my voice defiant. "I've trained for this stuff all over the world, haven't I? Don't freaking ask me to leave again."

For a moment, there is no sound in the room. Sam stops typing at her computer. Cooper stops rocking back and forth on his toes. Even though no one can hear us on the other side of the microphone, the radios are momentarily silent. It's so quiet, you can hear us not breathing, the emptiness created by shocked, breath-held lungs.

"The target's SUV is one mile out, copy, one mile out to the airport," a voice crackles, forcing our bodies out of their motionless state. Luke gently peels his fingers off my shoulder and sidesteps away.

Sam clears her throat before pressing down on the microphone and says, "Copy."

The lower-right monitor with our view from the air cuts out again, black-and-white confetti taking over the screen and distorting our clear picture of the kidnappers' SUV. Sam hits the monitor in frustration. "Dammit," she hisses under her breath then pushes down on her microphone. "Todd, I keep losing your visual."

"We've got 'em here at headquarters, Sam," another male voice answers.

"Thanks, Thomas," Sam replies, her voice calming down. My eyes widen. I've never met Thomas, never even talked to him. But I've heard my parents mention his name at least a thousand times. He's their main contact at CORE, the one who gives them directions on where to go, who to rescue. He's their eyes and ears as they head into a danger zone. Thomas does his best to keep them alive. "I just don't like doing this blind," Sam adds.

"Me either. But we don't have much choice," Thomas answers back. "All right, units on the ground, stand by. The target's SUV is pulling up to the gate at the airport right now. They'll be to you in sixty seconds. But stay out of sight. We need you to wait for the second Black Angel team. Stand down until backup reaches you."

"We've got two guys on the ground," I say and point to the monitors. "They need to go as soon as Torres's guys get out of the car."

"It's too dangerous," Sam replies, keeping her eyes glued to the monitors. "We need to wait for backup."

"But if they see the SUV, they're going to know we're coming for them and they'll open fire," I protest. "They're already on edge. They're waiting for us. The only chance we have is to ambush them about five seconds after the kidnappers get out of the car. They'll be momentarily preoccupied with getting my parents out. That's the moment we have to go. Not a second before. Not a second after."

"This is the plan, okay?" Sam replies, raising her voice. "This isn't our first rodeo, Reagan. We need more manpower or we're going to lose your parents. We *have* to keep them in the country."

The nerves in my brain fire a dozen embattled emotions: terror and strength, agony and hope. My lungs swell with voluptuous panic and I swear I can actually feel my adrenal glands pumping adrenaline and cortisol into my body.

"We've got a visual," a Black Angel on the ground speaks into his radio as the SUV comes into view on one of our many monitors. My hot fingers grip the sides of the metal chair and I have to tell myself to breathe.

"All right, guys, this is it," Thomas's voice comes through the monitor. I bite down on my lip as I watch the SUV come to a stop next to the jet. The back doors fly open and there they are, the thermal cameras giving away details I don't want to see. My parents' mouths are gagged, their wrists tied tightly behind their backs. Guards armed with semiautomatics grab them roughly at their biceps and push them toward the plane, guns pointed at their backs, one pull of the trigger away from death.

The guards push them quickly up the plane steps and panic rises, barbed and scalding on my skin.

"Sam, we need to go right *now*," I say and grab her strong bicep. "Torres's guys are going to get away!"

"No, we have to wait," Sam replies, ignoring my firming grip and watching as Mom and Dad are forced farther up the plane steps. "Shit. Gavin, where are you?"

"I'm here. I'm pulling into the airport right now," the voice answers back. My eyes are no longer locked on my parents. They are fixed on the armed kidnappers at the bottom of the plane's steps. *No, no, no,* my mind is screaming as I wait for the inevitable to happen. Every muscle in my body ignites as I watch the guards' heads whip around, turning toward the sound of the approaching SUV. I open my mouth to warn Sam but before I can formulate a single word, they open fire.

Bang. Bang. Bang. The sound of squealing tires is drowned out by a steady stream of gunfire.

The Black Angels on the ground immediately pop up from their hiding spots. *"Baje al suelo,"* they scream in Spanish. Get down on the ground. The video bounces violently as they sprint toward the jet.

The staccato hammer from the kidnappers' automatic machine guns answers their commands.

"Shit, where are they? Where are they?" Sam yells, standing up from her chair and searching for my parents on the monitors. The view of the plane, my parents, and the kidnappers wildly rises and falls as the Black Angels on the ground duck for cover. Sam grabs the microphone and with a shaking voice demands, "Where's my god damn eye in the sky, Todd?"

Bang. Bang. Bang. Bang.

"Man down, man down," a voice cries out from somewhere in Kentucky. My eyes dart from one monitor to the next. *Who's down?*

Who's down? One of the helmet cameras is pointed sideways on the ground; its only view is of a few stands of grass rising defiantly out of the cracked asphalt. I wait for the camera, for his body to move. It doesn't.

"I told you!" I scream, taking a step toward the monitors, but Sam pushes me away.

"Shit," Sam says, raising her outstretched fingers to her forehead. She regains control and turns on the microphone. "Gavin, where are you?"

"I'm chasing them but the plane is already on the runway," the voice answers back.

"Well, STOP them!" Sam roars into the microphone before throwing it down onto the steel table, the clash of metal on metal shattering my spine.

Oh God, please no, my mind whispers, my head inflamed, as I watch the SUV race past the two injured Black Angels and toward the tarmac. It turns wildly onto the runway and speeds after the Gulfstream.

"Go, Gavin, go," Thomas's voice breaks in over our monitors. "Shoot out the wheels."

Bang. Bang. Bang.

The Black Angel in the passenger seat of the speeding SUV opens fire, trying to hit the wheels of the Gulfstream. But the plane is unmoved.

Bang. Bang. Bang.

The Black Angel shoots again but the jet only picks up speed, its lights growing more distant.

"Come on, Gavin. Go. Cut him off!" Sam screams into the

microphone but it's too late. There's no way he can match the Gulf-stream's speed.

"Shit," Cooper says under his breath. My knees begin to buckle and a million pins prick my skin. We watch in helpless silence as the Gulfstream gains speed and momentum. The monitor with our faltering eye-in-the-sky visual finally flickers on in time to see the Gulfstream's nose lift into the air and escape into a starless sky.

TWENTY-ONE

MY MUSCLES ARE SORE FROM LEANING AGAINST THE
gun range's cold, concrete walls, and the adrenaline that kept me
going over the last few hours is slowly seeping from my chilling
blood. But I don't move. I physically can't get off this floor. I stare
straight ahead, each breath more shallow and excruciating than
the last. A shiver pricks at the lower part of my back. My sore arm
reaches in what feels like slow motion for the sweatshirt in front of me.
I pull it over my head, using it as a buffer between my back and this
seemingly impenetrable steel-and-concrete fortress. Much better.

I can hear Sam and Cooper in the situation room on the phone
with CORE. They won't let me talk to anyone. They don't want to
hear any of my ideas. They didn't listen to me the first time and now
a Black Angel is dead and my parents are handcuffed at thirty thousand feet somewhere over Middle America. After my tenth strategi-
cally sound recommendation, Sam reminded me that I'm not a Black
Angel agent yet and as much as I love her, I kind of wanted to punch
her in her cute little button nose. So I've shut down. I've sat with

my legs pulled to my chest for the last half hour and haven't spoken a word.

Luke walks through the open doorway and into the dimly lit gun range, steam rising from the cup in his hand. He offers it to me.

"Tea," he says as I accept it and stare into the hot caramel liquid. "Splash of cream. Four Splendas."

"Thanks," I say and take a sip. I let the warm liquid coat my tongue and run down the back of my throat.

Luke slides his back along the wall until he reaches the spot on the ground next to me. His position matches mine. Knees up, head back, forearms draped over the tops of his kneecaps. "I know this is a stupid question, but how are you doing?"

"Best I can," I say and attempt to shrug my shoulders but they don't really move. More like a flinch than a shrug. "I just had to walk away. Sam isn't listening to me at all even though I was completely right about the airport take-down. She doesn't want to hear it. She probably thinks I'm too emotionally compromised or some bullshit."

"Do you think you are?" Luke asks, his eyes fixed on my face as I continue to stare straight ahead.

"Noooo." I let the answer slowly leak out of my mouth with extra o's for emphasis. "I think I was the only one thinking clearly during that blown mission. I knew we should have rushed them and opened fire as soon as Torres's guys got there. I knew exactly what would happen if we waited or tried to take them peacefully. They've been watching my family for too long. They already lost me. No way were they going to return to Colombia without my parents."

"You were right," Luke says with a sigh.

My lungs take a breath, but the air down here is heavy and thick and makes me feel like I'm drowning. "I wish they would have just taken me," I say, my voice gravelly, like I've swallowed a fistful of broken glass. "Then none of this would be happening."

"But you'd be dead."

"I'd be dead but everyone else would be safe."

"Don't say that," Luke says, grabbing my arm, turning my face toward his. "Don't even think it."

I nod in forced agreement. But it's hard not to. The butterfly effect. Had I done one tiny thing differently, I wouldn't be sitting here.

"We'll find them, Mac," Luke says, his face falling as soon as the nickname escapes his lips. Cooper's and Sam's muffled voices just beyond the wall fills the sudden space between us. He looks down at the ground, digging the heels of his sneakers into the cement floor, then looks back up at me. "Sorry."

"I actually really like that nickname. I've never told you that before. But now it just feels strange, like Mac is part of another life, another Reagan, and you know the real one now."

"How many Reagans have you been?" Luke asks, his blue eyes still sad.

"So many," I say and tuck a strand of my dark hair behind my ear. "Seven or eight. At least that's the number of covers I remember. I've created a lot of lives and told a lot of lies. Honestly, it's been hard to keep them straight. That's one of the reasons why I didn't want to do it anymore. I know the good I could do as a Black Angel. It's just..."

"So hard," Luke says, finishing my thought, and I nod. Luke opens his mouth to speak, then changes his mind and stops.

"What?"

"Nothing."

"No, tell me."

"I don't know," Luke says, rubbing the palms of his hands over the top of his jeans. "I feel in this weird way sort of envious of the training you've had. I want to be in the military more than anything. Maybe even become a Black Angel one day now that I know the group exists. But at the same time, I feel like you've been cheated somehow. I can't really imagine what it's like to feel like you're in constant danger while also trying to pass geometry."

I look down at my hands and examine my almost nonexistent fingernails. I tuck them into the sleeves of my sweatshirt and hug them to my chest. "I've gotten so used to it—to the fear—that it's sort of become my normal. I feel so guilty about not wanting to go to the training academy. I was planning on it all my life. I didn't have a question in my mind. That was just what I was meant to do. But in the last year things have just . . . shifted."

"You got a taste of normal life," Luke says. It's incredible how that boy can read my mind.

"Yeah. I mean, I feel like I made real friends and created a real life. I met you," I reply, and shrug. "And when I was with you guys, there was sort of this lightness I never felt before. I guess I'm scared of losing that feeling."

"Well, I support your decision." Luke reaches out and touches my arm with the tips of his fingers. I look down at his hand. He pulls it away and runs it through his hair. "I want you to be happy."

"Me too." I turn my body toward him and lean my head against the concrete wall. "You know, the danger and all that stuff . . . I could live with it. I mean, I really like the idea of helping people. Like saving that girl today, I wasn't remotely scared when I was doing it. I think I just hate that I can never have a real life. I can never get close to anybody. I hate having to leave with the clothes on my back in the middle of the night and never see the people I care about ever again. That's the part of this job I have a hard time dealing with. I don't ever want to disappear and have someone wonder what happened to me for the rest of their life."

Luke's eyes widen as my words answer the question that has been spinning on repeat in his head for days. "So that's why," he finally says, his voice barely audible.

"I'm so sorry, Luke," I say and look into his eyes so he knows I mean it.

"I knew there had to be a reason," Luke says, his voice soft and still, his eyes dropping to the floor, hiding what's written inside. "I just never thought you'd hurt me like that. Even under these absurd circumstances."

I reach out and place my hand on his wrist. "After Templeton, I found out how bad the mission went and I could feel it. That threat of having to leave again. I needed you to hate me. I thought kissing that guy would make you never want to talk to me again."

"It almost worked," he says, pulling his hand away. His face scrunches as the night comes back to him.

That's the part that has haunted me: the broken look on his face after he saw me kiss Oliver. The hurt behind his eyes crushed me then and crushes me now.

"I wish I could tell you I didn't mean to hurt you, but I did. I figured it'd be less painful than finding out that I just disappeared.

I didn't want you to come knock on my door and have no one answer or for my phone to ring straight to some automated voice saying my number was no longer in service. For you to search for me. I know you. I know you'd worry about me forever."

We hold each other's stare for a second. I want to ask him what happens now. What happens to us? Could he still love me? I open my mouth to speak, then close it. Afraid of the answer. Maybe I'm too late. Maybe he doesn't feel that way about me anymore. And if he doesn't, I don't think I want to know.

"Luke," Sam's voice says from the doorway. We turn to look at her. "We need to start preparing for the mission so we need to get you home."

"Has someone done a sweep of the area?" I ask, my heart compressing anxious beats in my heavy chest.

"We've done a complete check," Sam replies, nodding. "He's safe."

"Okay, great," I say and rock myself off the floor, my legs carrying me quickly into the weapons room, where I grab my Glock pistol. "Just let me take him home with Cooper or something and I'll come back and we can go over the mission with CORE."

"Reagan," Sam says softly. And just by the way she says my name I already know the words that linger on the other side of her turned-down lips.

"Do you want me to drive or do you want to drive?" I ask, looking around for the keys, stalling the inevitable. My pulse pounding against my neck, fluttering beats of hope and fear.

"Reagan," Sam says again, now at my side, but I avoid looking at her, rationalizing that maybe if I don't stare directly at her, she won't say it. She does anyway. "There's no way you can be involved with the mission."

"Why not?" I ask coolly, loading rounds of ammunition into my clip and avoiding her eyes.

"Sweetie, there's about a dozen reasons why," Sam replies and I have to suppress the instantaneous urge to remind her how much I hate being called sweetie. Starting a sentence with "sweetie" is like immediately telling someone they're dumb or wrong. Or both.

"Well, there are about one hundred reasons why I *should* be involved," I answer, tucking my gun into the back of my pants.

"Reagan, be reasonable here," Sam replies, firmly grabbing my arm. "As much as I want you there, even think we need you there, you are not a full agent. You're emotionally compromised. And on top of that, you are the original target. We need to get you out of Ohio and to Langley tonight. If you were in my shoes, you know you'd make the same exact call."

My eyes stare hard at the sharp blades lined up on the metal counter, waiting to be packed and put on board a jet bound for Colombia. With my free hand, I reach out and touch one of the serrated edges. I run my finger carefully along each bump and imagine plunging it into Torres's neck. I have to get down there. I have to at least be in the country. And if Sam won't take me, I'll get there myself.

"I understand," I lie, my voice shrinking.

Sam looks over her shoulder at Luke standing in the doorway then turns back to me. "Take a minute to say good-bye," she says, her voice low. "You'll probably never see him again."

The weapons room's dense air burns my lungs as I take in a deep, noisy breath. Sam pats my arm, giving me a weak, closed-mouth smile before walking back into the situation room.

Luke stares at me, his pale eyes tired and worried. I press my lips in a thin line and move toward him, taking him by the wrist and leading him into the darkest corner of the gun range, out of Sam's earshot.

"They're taking you home," I tell him, my voice low and my heart pounding painfully beneath my breastbone, each beat begging: *Don't go. Don't go. Don't go.*

"What about you?"

"They're taking me to Langley tonight."

"What happens from there?"

I shrug. "I don't know. New name, new life. The way it's always been."

"So . . . will I ever see you again? Is this good-bye?" Luke asks, his eyes glassy and searching my face.

"We're leaving in one minute, Luke." Sam pokes her head into the room then disappears.

My arms wrap around Luke's neck and pull him toward me. "I don't want to say good-bye to you," I whisper, tears stinging the back of my throat and muting my voice.

Luke puts his arms around my waist and pulls me closer to him. I take a mental note of the way his body feels against mine: strong and warm and safe. I bury my face in his shoulder and take in his scent. Soap and cinnamon and something metallic I don't recognize.

"I can't imagine not seeing you again," Luke says into my ear, his hands running up my spine, rubbing a smooth spot on the back of my neck with his fingertips.

"Reagan," Sam says from the doorway. "I'm sorry. But it's time."

I rise on my toes and brush my lips against his smooth cheek. Luke's arms tighten around my waist, and my body tingles and aches all at once.

"Stay by your phone," I whisper in Luke's ear. "I'm going to need you."

I squeeze Luke's neck hard for one more second and then let him free. I watch in silence as Luke follows Cooper up the steps. When they reach the top, Luke turns around and looks down at me, his right hand rising in a silent good-bye. His lips turn up into a small, sad smile. I take in the way his long lashes frame his kind eyes. The way his dimples crease into his creamy cheeks. I file him away as he turns around, walks through the door, and disappears.

TWENTY-TWO

"OKAY, IS EVERYONE DIALED IN WHO NEEDS TO BE?"
I can hear Thomas's muffled voice on the other side of the situation
room door. As soon as Cooper got back, they closed the door, refusing to let me in to hear any part of the plan. It's classified. Even though
it's *my* parents.

I shrugged, acted like I understood. But here I am, my face
pressed to the cold door as I rack my brain trying to figure out how
to get all the intel I need.

I imagine Thomas standing in the situation room at Langley,
the live feed of CORE's bunkered conference room broadcasting
onto one of the large monitors in front of Cooper and Sam. I know
I've seen inside CORE's headquarters before. I know exactly what
it looks like. Where have I seen it? I rub my hands over my scrunched
forehead as my brain scrolls through years of training. I close my
eyes as jagged half memories pulse into my mind, a half a second at
a time. Then my brain lands on a memory from a year ago. Mom
on her tablet during our middle of the night ride from Philadelphia

to DC. She had pulled up the situation room at Langley and was listening to a briefing on the hitman in our house.

How did she get there? *Think, Reagan, think.* I draw a deep breath through my pursed lips, almost hoping to hypnotize myself and pull out a long-buried memory.

My brain focuses on the moments before she pulled out her tablet. She told Dad she needed coffee. He said he'd pick up some once they crossed out of Pennsylvania. She pulled the tablet out of her go-bag, typed in a series of numbers, and pulled up the conference.

The Black Angel code.

I tear across the room and open Mom's go-bag. I rifle through her stuff. Her favorite sweater, pictures of me as a kid, letters from Dad, and I find it. Her Black Angel–issued tablet. It's not like anything you can buy at Apple.

I turn on the screen. It commands a six-digit passcode. My fingers type in the Black Angel number I memorized. 1-7-8-2-2-9.

As soon as I break in, a message pops up on the screen:

CORE Conference In Session.

Below that message bubble, there are two options.

Join as Elizabeth. Join Anonymously.

Join Anonymously. Duh.

Thomas and the situation room at Langley take over my screen. I'm in.

"According to the flight plan, they are landing at a small private airport near Tumaco." Thomas touches a screen built into the conference room table and a map of Colombia takes over my tablet. He circles a tiny town on the Colombian coast near Ecuador. I pull out my phone and take a photo of the map. "Torres has a large ranch outside of town so we believe Jonathan and Elizabeth will be taken there."

"So, what's the next step?" I hear Sam ask. I imagine her on the other side of the wall, biting down on her right thumbnail.

"The Columbus team will fly down to Ecuador immediately," Thomas answers. "There will be a foreign Black Angel agent waiting for you at the private airport in Quito. He'll get you to San Lorenzo, where we'll put you in the bed of one of our trucks and get you across."

"What about the rest of the team?" Sam asks.

"DC is unfortunately having huge storms right now," Thomas answers with a heavy sigh. "Our pilot won't take off. Says it's not safe for a plane that small, so we've had to book a commercial flight for Meredith and PJ. Flight leaves in two hours. Eduardo, a Black Angel transporter, will be waiting for them at El Jefe Café in the commercial airport in Quito."

Thomas pulls up a picture of Eduardo and circles the location of El Jefe Café in the airport. I snap another photo on my phone.

"Eduardo doesn't have a high-security clearance," Thomas continues. "So keep the discussion of the mission to a minimum until he gets you to the official team in Colombia."

"Can we trust him?" a young woman, who I can only assume is Meredith, asks from inside the conference room at Langley.

"Yes, we've worked with him many times," Thomas's voice answers and pulls up the route the teams will take once they land. I snap another photo of the blue squiggly line that leads from Quito to San Lorenzo, a beach town just outside the Colombian border where Thomas explains each team will be smuggled separately across the border.

"Don't wait in San Lorenzo for the DC team," Thomas reminds Sam. "You guys need to get across the border first so we don't attract attention."

"All right," Sam agrees.

"Get ready for the codes. Here we go. Columbus team, 220394. DC team, your code is 392043," Thomas says and the screen switches back to the conference room at Langley.

220394. 220394. 392043 392043. I repeat the numbers over and over again until they lock into place.

"Plane is on its way to you guys in Columbus," Thomas says and glances at his watch. "Should be there in less than fifteen."

"Got it," I hear Sam reply. "We'll get our gear and get out of here."

"All right. Radio contact can be spotty down in Ecuador but the team you're meeting in Colombia will have full satellite capabilities," Thomas replies. "Good luck, everyone."

The screen goes black. I hear the scrape of metal chairs on the other side of the wall as Cooper and Sam stand up. I fly off the floor and silently run to the opposite side of the room, hiding Mom's tablet in my go-bag.

I slink back down onto the ground, my back up against the wall, my lips pushed into a disinterested pout as Sam opens the door.

"Reagan, you can come in now," she says, waving me through. I stand up, steadying myself against the wall to catch my breath from that too-close-for-comfort maneuver.

I follow Sam into the weapons room where Cooper is hurriedly packing M4 carbines, pistols, knives, and ammunition into steel weapons cases.

"We need to get you to Langley as soon as possible but we've got to get down to South America," Sam states, running her hands through her hair and fixing her falling ponytail. "Cooper, you've got to stay with her until Brian gets here to take her to CORE."

Cooper stops dead in his tracks, his strong arms crossing over his body. "No way. I'm going on this mission with you. You cannot go alone. What happens if the DC team can't make it? We need fire-power."

"We can't just leave her. Brian is still two hours away—" Sam begins.

"I'll be fine," I interrupt, my voice strong and confident. I need them to leave me alone.

"We cannot leave you by yourself," Sam says, shaking her head and putting her hands squarely on her hips. "We need someone to protect you and get you to Langley safely."

"Sam, just go. Look at where we're at," I say and motion around the weapons room. "I'll grab some weapons, I'll lock myself into the panic room, and I'll wait for the watcher to come pick me up."

"I don't know," Sam says with her face cocked to one side. I grab her by her shoulders.

"Don't worry about me," I say and give her a reassuring squeeze. "You know I can handle myself. Just please, go get my parents."

"Sam, we've got to get to the airport," Cooper interjects, click-ing closed the last packed weapons case. "We don't have time to waste here."

Sam looks up into my eyes and presses her lips together. I know she's weighing the pros and cons of delaying the trip down to Ecuador or leaving Cooper behind. She glances at her watch and finally nods. "Okay. Brian will be here in less than two hours. Grab some guns and get into the panic room."

I walk over to the first cabinet door and pull a loaded Glock 22 pistol and M4 carbine off the shelf. Sam hands me a bottle of water and wraps her arm around my shoulder as we walk in silence toward the open panic room door.

I step inside the seven foot by seven foot steel-and-concrete box and turn to face Sam, her eyes suddenly glassy. She takes my hands into her own, opens her mouth to speak, but words don't come out. I don't know what's making her so emotional. Visions of me as a little girl. The thought of my parents gagged and beaten. The mission to rescue them resting heavy on her shoulders. Probably a combination of all three.

"Bring them back to me," I whisper and she nods, kissing me on my cheek.

"I will," she whispers back, running the back of her fingers against the apple of my cheek. She lowers her eyes, unhinges the panic room door from the wall, and pushes it with a noisy creak until the door is closed. I punch in the six-digit code and my body suppresses a shiver as the weighty bolts shift into place and lock me inside.

TWENTY-THREE

JUST LEAVE. JUST LEAVE. I WATCH THE BUILT-IN monitors from inside the panic room as Sam and Cooper throw the last of the aluminum weapons cases inside the black SUV. Sam slams the trunk, grabs the keys out of Cooper's hands, and makes her way to the front seat. I hold my breath as she turns on the car, pulls out of the driveway, and disappears from the camera's view.

My body stands motionless, staring up at the camera for sixty long seconds, waiting for their headlights to return. They don't. I punch in the six-digit code. The metal bolts clank out of place and the door hisses back into its unlocked state. With guns still in my hands, my shoulder pushes open the heavy door and I run back into the situation room.

I place my weapons on the desk, pull out my phone, and immediately begin capturing photos of everything and anything related to the mission. Routes, flight schedules, code names, coordinates, a map of Torres's ranch near Tumaco.

On a slip of paper, the word Brian and a phone number is

scrawled out in Sam's messy handwriting. I need more time. I pick up the satellite phone and dial Brian's number.

"This is Brian," a deep voice says on the other end of the phone.

"Brian, hey, it's Sam," I reply, lowering my voice two octaves to try to match Sam's natural vocal range. "We are on our way out the door but stand down on coming to the safe house. We're actually going to move Reagan to another safe house on our way."

"You sure?" Brian asks.

"Yeah, this area is compromised," I answer, pinpricks of sweat threatening as the lies roll off my tongue. "We need to get Reagan out of New Albany. So we'll take care of it."

"But the direct orders to move her came straight from CORE," Brian says, his voice questioning.

"Look, what do you want from me, my codes?" I reply, trying to pull off my best annoyed and in charge Sam. "BA 178229, code name Beacon, mission code 220394. Seriously, Brian, I don't have time for your questions. Just stand down and I'll talk to you after I'm back stateside."

"Okay. My apologies," Brian answers, finally satisfied. "Be careful out there."

"We will," I answer and hang up without saying good-bye.

I stare down at the guns on the desk. I can't take any of these with me on the plane but I grab the small pistol and tuck it into the back of my jeans. I look around the situation room one more time for any detail of the mission I may have missed. The walls of the basement are starting to inch their way closer with every shallow breath and despite the cool temperature, my body is burning. I need to get out of here. I run into the weapons room, grab my go-bag, sprint up the stairs, and head out the door.

The freezing night air encases my scorching body and burns the delicate membranes inside my nose. An old-model Jeep is still in the driveway. I try the door. It's unlocked but no keys. I flip down both sun visors and pull open the glove compartment. Nothing. I do a mental scan of the situation room. There were no keys down there. Cooper must still have them in his pocket.

I sprint back inside the house and tear open the cabinets under the kitchen sink. Yes. Toolbox. I grab a flathead screwdriver and hammer and run back outside. This better work. I know how to hot-wire a car the hard way but that takes too much time. I jam the screwdriver into the ignition and pound it with the hammer.

Please work. Please work. After one more tap, I turn the screw-driver and the car comes to life.

"Yes," I whisper to no one. I back out of the driveway, pull out my phone, and call Luke.

"Hey, you okay?" he answers after a half ring.

"Yes, I'm fine. Look, I need you to book me a flight to Quito right now," I reply and wind down the two-lane country road on the outskirts of the country club neighborhood.

"Absolutely not. You need to turn around and go back to the safe house immediately," Luke insists.

"No way," I snap. "I need to get down there."

"This is so dangerous, you're going to get yourself killed and . . ." Luke begins.

"Luke, I can't sit at Langley and watch another failed mission over the monitors," I answer, frustrated tears burning my exhausted eyes. I take a deep breath, forcing them to retreat.

"Reagan, this could be suicide," Luke says again.

"I know," I answer. "But if I don't go, my parents will die. I can feel it, Luke. They are going to die."

My gut wrenches as the words tumble out of my mouth. This isn't a scare tactic, a ploy to get Luke to buy me the ticket. Throughout my years of training, I've developed a sixth sense, that know-it-in-your gut feeling that so many agents develop over time. And I know the words I'm saying are true.

"Please," I beg and suddenly feel disconnected from my body; like I'm watching this conversation instead of having it. "Help me, Luke."

Luke lets out a long sigh. I can hear him typing at his computer.

"Two flights. One leaves in ninety minutes at ten p.m. The other leaves tomorrow morning," Luke answers, his voice tight with what-am-I-doing worry.

"Book tonight," I answer. "I need to get down there before the DC team so I can swipe their ride."

"Done," Luke answers. "Got to love that Platinum AmEx."

"Thank you. Be right there," I say and hang up.

My car turns down New Albany Country Club Drive and races toward the Weixels'. I glance at my clock just before I turn down Landon Lane: eighty-five minutes and counting. I pull into their driveway but before I can put the car in park, Luke is running down their front path, a backpack strapped to his back. He pops open the car door and climbs in.

"Okay, we better get going if we're going to make that flight," he says, slinging his backpack off his shoulder and throwing it with my stuff in the backseat.

"What do you mean *we?*" I ask.

"I bought two tickets to Quito," Luke replies and fastens his seat belt.

"No way, Luke," I say, shaking my head with ferocity. "No. Way. I'm not letting you come with me."

"Well, I'm not letting you do this alone," he answers, shaking his head back at me.

"It's way too dangerous," I reply, throwing my hands in the air. "I've been training for this since before I lost my baby teeth."

"So have I," Luke insists. "I may not have been trained as a Black Angel, but I've been training my entire life to be in the military. Look, I know I don't know as much as you, but Reagan, it's suicide to try and do this by yourself. I'm not going to let you. And if you make me get out of this car, I'll call Sam and tell her what you're doing."

"You wouldn't do that to me."

"Yes I would. To keep you safe, I would."

"Luke, I have to do this," I say, my voice rising. "You don't understand what it's like to sit in a room completely helpless and wait to hear if the people you love are dead or alive."

"Of course I do." Luke's voice surges to match mine. "How do you think I'd feel if I stayed here and let you go?"

His words knock out the last thread of air I'm so desperately trying to keep in my lungs. We stare at each other for a second, but the gravity of the moment pulls our eyes to the floor.

"Look . . ." Luke says, his voice now calm. "If you're going to take the DC team's truck, then we better look like a team. Otherwise, you'll be put right back on the next plane to Dulles Airport with a half-dozen bodyguards around you."

My lips are throbbing, pressed tightly together between my teeth. He's right. I can't just show up in Quito and expect to get across the border. They're expecting a team.

"What about your parents?" I ask, looking over his shoulder to his front door. "Won't they freak out if you're gone?"

"They're in DC until Sunday," Luke answers. "I told them I had JROTC training and overnights the rest of the week and would be hard to reach."

"Okay," I finally reply, a heavy sigh passing through my sore lips. "You can come but you have to follow my every order, do you understand?"

"Promise," Luke answers. I throw him my phone.

"Okay, first thing. I have photos of all the plans on there," I say and back out of his driveway. "Text every photo to your phone, then delete them off mine. I'm dropping my phone off at Harper's. Then we'll go to the airport."

"Why are we going to Harper's?" Luke asks as he texts all the photos to his number.

"Because it's two minutes from the safe house," I answer and pull out onto New Albany Country Club Drive. "If they try to track my phone, maybe it will confuse them once they find out I'm not at the safe house. Buy us a little more time."

We drive in silence the three minutes to Harper's, Luke transferring over my files and deleting any trace of who I really am. When we pull into Harper's driveway, she's climbing out of her Range

210

Rover in yoga pants and an oversize sweatshirt. I glance at the clock: 8:48. Seventy-two minutes.

"My two favorite people," Harper says, her smile wide, as we hop out of the still-running car. "What are you guys doing here?"

"Taking a drive," I say with a casual shrug.

"Wanted to come and say a quick hi," Luke says and wraps an arm around Harper. She returns his half hug and gives his waist a squeeze.

"I'm so glad you did," Harper says, pulling her enormous tote over her shoulder. "I just got back from the club. Tried that new yoga class with the superhot teacher. Don't know if the gorgeous face and Australian accent was worth the pain. I think he broke my hymen and not in the fun way."

"Too much, Harper," Luke responds, shaking his head as a laugh bubbles up my throat with tears close behind. She's in front of me, so close I could touch her, and yet my heart already misses every piece of her.

"Still RGFs?" Harper asks, giving me a wink. I shrug while Luke looks back and forth at us, confused.

"You two," Luke says, shaking his head and letting go of his hold on Harper. "I'll never figure your little language out."

"You guys want to come inside?" Harper asks.

"No, no, we've got to get going. I just wanted to see you," I say and wrap my arms around her neck as Luke starts walking toward the car.

"Are you okay?" Harper asks as I hold her tighter than normal.

"Yup. NBB," I reply. Never been better.

Before I pull out of our embrace, I gently drop my phone into her wide-open tote and pray it sinks to the bottom. She can never find anything in that bag.

I squeeze Harper one last time and whisper in her ear, "Thanks for always being such a good friend."

"Of course," she whispers back.

I pull away from her and quickly walk toward the car, afraid of the tears that lie at the base of my throat.

"Love you," she calls after me. I turn around, thankful for the darkness that hides my tear-stung eyes. I put my hand to my lips and blow her a kiss.

"Love you too," I say and know it's the last thing I'll ever say to her beautiful face. I open the car door and take her in. The way she wraps her wavy hair into a wild bun. Her full, pink cheeks. The way she smiles, first sluggishly then bright and wide all at once. I file every piece of my dear, sweet friend away and that pain pierces even deeper into my heart.

I pull out of her driveway, my face catching the dim glow of the streetlight, giving me away.

"You okay?" Luke asks, reading my face.

"Yeah," I say, swallowing hard and forcing any remaining tears back down. "That's the first time I've actually gotten to say good-bye."

Luke doesn't say anything. He just reaches out, his fingers dancing on the top of my hand for a moment before he returns them to his lap. I glance at the clock: 8:55. I press on the gas and we race in anxious silence to the airport.

TWENTY-FOUR

"SO ONCE WE FLY INTO QUITO . . ." I SAY QUIETLY, pointing to Ecuador's capital on my tablet. I tap my finger on the screen, zooming in tighter on Quito. I trace the route to Colombia with my index finger, creating a squiggly blue line. "The Black Angel transporter will get us to a meeting point somewhere near San Lorenzo and then we'll travel to Colombia through our channels. We'll meet up with the team in Tumaco and make our way to Torres's ranch by tomorrow night."

"How are we all going to make it across the border?" Luke asks, staring at the digital map.

"Foreign Black Angel agents have connections at the border, so we're just going to have to hope they will be on duty," I answer, tapping on the map again. It zooms in tighter on the border. Luke squints his eyes, studying the route. "But most important, CORE has already arranged for two trucks with hollow beds. They use them all the time on missions to cross dangerous borders without being detected. We will hide in there until we get outside of Tumaco."

"And if anyone spots the trucks, the agents just will look like your average farmers, carrying their load," Luke interjects, nodding.

"Exactly," I say, pushing my hair off my face. "Believe me. My parents have done this like a hundred times. Probably hidden in the exact trucks we're going to take. I've practiced it a few times during my training at some of the different international camps. It's uncomfortable and hot in there, but they've all been intricately designed so no one ever suspects there are people inside."

"International camps? Where have you trained?" Luke asks, his voice soft even though there's no one else seated within ten rows of us. Late-night flights to Quito in the middle of the week aren't exactly an in-demand ticket.

"All over," I say and do a mental scan. "Israel one summer to learn from the best Krav Maga experts in the entire world. Russia another summer for weaponry training. China for hacking and digital training. I've trained in Mexico and the Middle East. I did some training one summer with MI-6 in England. They have a group there that's connected to the Black Angels. Very secret, very underground. Children of agents are born into that life and are trained their entire lives to become the next generation of agents. Just like me."

"That's amazing," Luke says, shifting in his seat, his leg brushing against mine. "You've gotten to do so much."

I nod in quiet, conflicted agreement and stare blankly at the tablet, my eyes pausing on different Colombian towns. Florencia. Mocoa. Montería. Cali. Bogotá. Such beautiful names for a country filled with so much violence. They sound more like the names of resorts or spas, not cities where shootings are an everyday, every-hour occurrence and the streets run red with blood.

My ears pop. I didn't realize how muffled everything had sounded since takeoff. The noises around me amplify. The roar of the plane's engine fills my head and pulls me away from the map, hushing my racing mind.

I press my forehead against the plastic window and feel it give under the weight of my skull. I stare past the wing and wispy clouds. The lights of small towns twinkle back at me. We pass over fields and two-lane country roads, pockets of subdivisions. I stare down at the strip malls and the grocery stores, dark office buildings and lit empty parking lots, warm homes with smoke rising from their chimneys and cars parked in the driveway. I count the houses on the streets and wonder what their lives are like.

I imagine women washing dishes in the kitchen, scraping food off white plates and staring out their windows at dark backyards, still swing sets, or their own distorted reflections. Their children sit at the kitchen table doing homework while their husbands read newspapers or fiddle on laptops in the family room. They all wait for dishes to be put away, for sink tops to be dried, and showers to be had so they can spend time together. Watch TV, read a book, get ready for bed. Go to sleep and start the routine all over again. That may sound like a boring existence to some. But right now it sounds perfect.

The cabin lights above us dim. I stare up as the bright white darkens to a warm orange. Luke pulls out his phone and glances at the time.

"I think you better try to get some sleep," Luke says, tucking his phone back into his pocket.

"What about all the tactics and strategy?" I ask, my voice catching in my throat, giving away my emotional and physical drain.

"We've been going over it for hours. We know it," Luke says, looking up at me for a moment. "And besides, we're only going to be there as backup, right?"

"Right," I answer even though the thought of sitting in the truck sounds just as awful as sitting at Langley.

"Come on. It's been a long day," Luke replies and touches my hand. His fingers are warm on my cold skin.

"I'm almost too tired to sleep," I say, tucking my leg beneath me.

"How about I tell you a story?" Luke asks. No one's told me a story since I was little. I nod and Luke pulls a blanket off the empty row across from us.

"Come here," he says, patting his lap. "Lie down."

"What about you?" I ask. "You need to sleep."

"I'll be fine." I curl up my legs and lie down, my head resting in his lap. Luke drapes the blanket over my body, pulling it up around my shoulders. "What kind of story do you want to hear?"

"Tell me about your favorite vacation." I snuggle up to him.

"Okay. When I was a little boy, we'd take a trip to North Carolina every summer," Luke begins. "We'd stay at a condo on the beach and every morning Claire and I would eat mini chocolate Entenmann's donuts on our balcony and count the number of waves that crashed on the sand. Claire hated getting all sandy and spent half of the trip running her little legs under the faucet on the boardwalk,

Every day we'd get our little buckets and collect seashells. Starfish, sand dollars, and clamshells and . . ."

The sound of Luke's voice lulls me to sleep. My breathing slows. And just before I drift into darkness, I feel his hand sweep a piece of hair off my face and gently tuck it behind my ear. My body, my mind let go and I fade into black.

TWENTY-FIVE

"THERE IT IS. EL JEFE CAFÉ," I SAY, PULLING AT LUKE'S arm. "Follow my lead. We have no Black Angel ID. Just the codes. We need to look like we've been here before and know what we're doing. Got it?"

"Got it," Luke replies with a confident nod.

I scan the café and spot Eduardo. His dark hair is longer than his picture, the ends brushing against his shoulders every time he moves. Dressed in dirty jeans and a plaid shirt, Eduardo is pretending to read a newspaper but his eyes search every passenger. He needs more training. A real Black Angel would never look so obvious.

"Eduardo," I say as I reach his table. His brown eyes look up at me, his thick eyebrows arching with surprise. *The code*, my mind screams before he could question me. "392043."

"You're both younger than I thought you'd be," Eduardo says, putting his coffee-stained newspaper down on the cheap ceramic table.

"*¿El Martillo sabe que estamos veniendo?*" I ask. Does the

Hammer know we're coming? I stare down at the cracked lino-leum floor as we make our way out of the airport and to a waiting black Jeep.

"*No tiene ninguna idea. Están seguro. Por ahora,*" Eduardo says, pausing and dropping his voice on the last two words. *You're safe. For now.* The way he says it with that heavy pause in between sentences means we won't be safe for long.

The Jeep bumps down a two-lane dirt road, the sound of the tires hitting the uneven mounds of dirt and rocks filling the silent car. As my shoulder slams into the side of the door, I long for the smoother, paved roads of Quito, four hours behind us. Eduardo is doing his best to keep the Jeep steady while Luke and I study the layout of Torres's house and grounds on our tablet.

I catch the transparent ghost of my reflection in the glass. My eyes look bloodshot and my skin is an oily gray. I only slept two hours on the plane. But I'm thankful for even just a couple hours of rest. At least then I was able to push away the panic and bury the image of my parents bound and gagged somewhere. But I woke up sweating, terror inflaming every muscle. *They're gone. They're gone,* I remembered, my heart straining under the shifting weight of so many unknowns. *Where are they? What has Torres done to them? Are they even still alive?*

Luke tried to calm me down and lull me back to sleep. I closed my eyes and lay back down on his lap. I pretended to be asleep. But really, I just spent those hours trying to swallow the screams creep-ing up my throat.

My training kicked in the moment we touched down in Quito. I'm quiet again, focused. My muscles are tight and my jaw is clenched. I try to relax, but I can't. It's physically impossible. I just want the moment to come. The moment where I see Mom's face and hear Dad's voice. When we're all on a plane back to the United States and this nightmare is over.

"Hey," Luke says, careful not to use my name in front of Eduardo. We don't know if he knows the names of the DC agents he was supposed to pick up, but we're not interested in tipping him off this far into the journey. I turn to see him rummaging through his backpack on the ground. He pulls out a packet of cheese and crackers. "How about some food?"

"I'm not really hungry," I say and turn away, looking back out the window.

"You need energy," Luke replies, pushing the package toward me. I reluctantly take it and rip open the cellophane. I bite down on the crackers. Luke's still looking at me. "You doing okay?"

"I'm fine," I answer without looking at him. I brush a crumb off my sweatshirt and shove another cracker in my mouth. I'm not lying. I am fine. If you consider numb fine. All those years of psychological training that my parents drilled into my head are working. If I actually let myself feel anything, I'd be having a daymare or panic attack right about now. I don't have that luxury. For once, I welcome the feeling of being half dead.

As we bounce over a big bump, my muscles tense and I grab the bottom of my seat with both hands. The mountains of Quito are long gone and the huts are getting closer together, so we must be getting closer to San Lorenzo. A group of seagulls stands in the middle of the road and scatters as the Jeep passes. The ocean is near.

These lightly traveled two-lane roads we've been using to stay under the radar are known for robberies. I drag my fingers along the leather seat and feel the pistol resting between us. An Ecuadorian robber would be dead before he could even comprehend just who he was dealing with.

"Do you feel like you have the floor plan down?" I ask quietly. "Because once you get inside the beds of those trucks, you'll be lying down in total darkness."

"I've got it," Luke says, looking back at the tablet. He taps the screen, zooming in on the exterior grounds.

"Good," I say. Eduardo's extra tablet is already at my side. My mother is convinced I have a photographic memory, and I'm beginning to think she's right. It took me a matter of minutes to get the layout of the entire property down, but I studied and studied the floor plans, just to be sure.

"We're almost there," Eduardo says, turning onto a paved road. The houses on this road are becoming bigger. Two donkeys stand together in an empty lot. We pass a cemetery with white gravestones and colorful flowers. A man walks down the street, his skin a shade darker than mine, a fishing pole over his right shoulder and a bucket in his left hand. Children kick a soccer ball just down the street. Eduardo takes another left. A green-covered mountain juts out in front of us and beyond that is the sea.

A man stands in front of an industrial building, dressed in a dirty flannel shirt and mud-covered jeans. I wait for the Jeep to pass him, but our speed slows. The man gives Eduardo a little wave and lifts up a large metal door. We pull the Jeep into a dark and empty warehouse.

"*Un minuto,*" Eduardo says, pulling our bags out of the back of the Jeep.

Eduardo and the other man load our bags, along with extra weapons the team in Colombia is expecting, into a rickety, dented farm truck. I step behind the Jeep to change into my gear. I strip down to my bra and underwear and throw on the Black Angel uniform. Black pants, a black tank top, black shoes, black socks, black, black, black. The black will help us hide in the shadows once darkness falls in Tumaco.

"*¿Estás listo?*" I ask, pulling my bag over my shoulder and walking toward Eduardo. The closer I get to him, the more it smells. What the hell is that? I look down and see a shovel and what looks like mulch. The stench gets stronger and as I get closer I see it's not mulch. It's manure.

"What are you doing with that pile of manure?" I ask, pulling my dark hair into a low ponytail. I grab the red rubber band around my wrist and loop my hair through it one, two, three times.

"Putting it on top of you," Eduardo answers casually in English, his accent heavy. I'm supposed to have done this before so I force myself to recover from the shock of all that . . . well . . . shit . . . on my head. "Once inside, we'll put the boards back down. But we have to stop the guards from inspecting the truck at the border. They will not want to stick their hands in horse manure. They'll let us through."

"That's right. Genius."

"We ready?" Luke appears at my side, dressed in dark jeans and a black shirt, a black sweatshirt wrapped around his waist. His military training must have kicked in the moment he bought two tickets to Quito to even have the foresight to shove dark clothing into a bag. It's not Black Angels gear but it will do.

"Let's load up," Eduardo says, shoving two loaded Glock 9s into our hands. "One weapon each. There's not room down there for more than that."

"Go ahead," Luke says, placing a hand on the small of my back. I hand my bag to Eduardo and jump up into the bed of the truck, my pistol at my side. I lie down, the cold metal soaking into my warm, exposed skin. Luke jumps up and lies down beside me.

"*¿Bien?*" Eduardo asks, a long board in his hand. We both nod. "Here goes."

Eduardo puts the first board over my face. Then another and another and another. The boards are only a few inches away from my nose. Tiny, enclosed spaces and I are not friends. I'm totally claustrophobic but through my training, I've had to learn how to deal with it. I close my eyes, breathe in through my nose and out through my mouth as the final board locks into place and the rush of panic subsides.

Thump. Thump. I open my eyes as pile after pile of manure is thrown onto the bed. The small slivers of light between each board disappear.

"Eduardo, not near our faces, please," I holler through the boards as Eduardo buries us alive.

"I got it," Eduardo's hollow voice answers from the other side. *Thump. Thump.* The trickle of light near our faces remains, but the rest of the truck is covered, the slivers of light almost entirely gone.

"*¿Listo?*" the second man in the warehouse yells. I hear the metal garage door roll up.

"*Vamos*," Eduardo answers. I hear his footsteps on the concrete floor circle the truck. The cab creaks as he climbs inside. The engine starts and the truck jumps as he pulls out of the warehouse and down the bumpy streets of San Lorenzo.

I stare straight ahead at the remaining splinter of light inches from my eyes. I wish I could see the blue sky, the clouds, the mountains, the sea.

"You okay?" Luke asks. I hear his feet shifting at the bottom of the truck, banging against the metal.

"I'm okay, are you?" I ask.

"Yeah."

We fall silent. I listen to the sound of the tires on the road. The bump of the rocks, the sputtering engine and squeaky cab. I try to concentrate on the little things around me. But my parents keep creeping into my mind. I picture them tied up, scared. I wonder if they're being tortured. The thought of those animals hurting them makes my bones ache. I wonder if Torres's plan is to kill them or just use them as bait to lure us there. Lure me there. I picture my mother's face, her green eyes defiant, her body strong. She won't break down. I may not know everything about her, I don't know her fears or the secrets she carries in the corners of her soul, but this, I know. She'll go kicking and screaming, not sobbing and begging.

"Reagan?" Luke speaks. His head is turned toward me and I can feel his warm breath on my cheek.

"Yes?"

"Are you scared?" Luke asks in a small voice, somewhere next to me in the darkness. I let the question soak into my skin.

"No," I say after a beat. "Not for me. But I'm scared for them."

Just saying those words out loud triggers the panic I've been suppressing to rise up my chest. I swallow it hard, trapping it in my throat. I won't allow myself to be afraid.

"I just want to bring them home," I whisper. He doesn't say anything, but I know he hears me. I feel his hand run along the bed of the truck and reach for me in the darkness. I open my palm to him and take his hand in mine. He squeezes my hand three times. I squeeze three times back. And we ride just like that, our fingers laced together, in total darkness and silence, all the way across the Colombian border.

TWENTY-SIX

"YOU GUYS ARE ALMOST OUT," EDUARDO'S HOLLOW
voice calls to us below the boards of the beaten-up truck. A shovel
scrapes above me as he scoops up manure and dumps it over the side.

"God, it's hot in here," Luke says. I cannot see him, but I hear
him tapping against the boards. "And smelly."

"You'd better get down on your knees and kiss that manure
when we get out of here," I say, my voice scratchy from not speaking. "Without it, they would have found us for sure."

"First of all, that's gross," Luke says, the volume of his voice
changing. He has turned his head toward mine. "Second of all, what
do you mean?"

"They wanted to search the truck when we got to the border," I
say and drum my fingertips along the bed of the truck, the metal
beat bouncing around the hollowed space.

"Your Spanish must be fluent, right?" he asks.

"Of course," I answer.

"How many languages do you speak?"

"Seven. Well, eight if you count English."

"Whoa. I speak like two and a half counting English. The half is Spanish so I didn't really understand what they were saying."

"Just glad we got through," I say, drumming my fingers faster on the steel bed, its metallic ting a perfect anxious soundtrack.

I couldn't hear everything they were saying, but I could hear key words like *busca*, which means "search." *Caja* means "bed." At one point I heard a deep voice say *"retira las tablas."* Retrieve the boards. That's when I couldn't breathe. I squeezed Luke's hand so hard. He clearly didn't feel the fear in my grip because he answered me with a few short squeezes. *"Retira las tablas,"* they said again. I don't even want to think about what they would have done if they found us hiding below. Arrested us? Maybe killed us? I will never look at manure the same way. I want to hug it right now. Eduardo too. He was right. As soon as they saw the manure in the bed of the truck, they were no longer interested in searching beneath the boards. They let us through.

Bump. Bump. Eduardo's feet walk over the boards. The truck creaks as he jumps off the back and then, light. I squint and shield my eyes as the light hits my face for the first time in hours.

"Get ready to get screamed at," I say to Luke, the knot compressing in my stomach.

Eduardo removes the boards one by one, throwing them in a pile on the floor. Each board lands with a crack louder than the one before. I open my eyes wider and see we're inside another warehouse. The late afternoon sun shines through dust-covered windows near the ceiling. Even through its layer of filth, I'm grateful to see the orange glow.

"You guys are free," Eduardo says, removing the last of the boards. I push my hands against the metal bed and lift myself up. I push out my chest and lean my body to the right, then the left, working out the tiny knots that have formed in my lower spine.

"What. The. Fuck?" Sam's voice pierces the air. I turn around to see Sam standing near a second beat-up truck, her mouth open, her hands pressed tightly to her hips.

"Hi, Sam," I say, swinging my legs around toward the back of the truck. I let my feet dangle for a second before sliding my body onto the cement floor. My limbs are heavy and tight.

"Reagan . . . and Luke! You too? Seriously, what the FUCK?" She's now screaming, the word *fuck* bouncing off the warehouse walls and wrapping itself around my already-constricted chest. She points her finger at my face, waving it with a fury I've never seen from her before. "You're supposed to be at Langley right now. What the hell are you doing here? Have you completely lost your fucking mind?"

"Sam, calm down for one second," I say, putting my hand up in the air.

"Calm down? Don't ask me to fucking calm down," Sam says, her normally pale cheeks streaked crimson. "Do you have any idea how many Black Angel Directives you've broken? Let alone just throwing your training and good old-fashioned common sense to the wind? I can't even begin to piece together how the two of you got down here, but you stole DC's truck. They are waiting on that truck."

"Not anymore," a tall man with dark, sun-kissed skin, a black beard, and a long black braided ponytail says as he hangs up the satellite phone. "Finally got a hold of the DC team. Their plane had to make an emergency landing in Costa Rica. There's no way they're going to make it down here."

Sam puts her hands on the top of her head and blows air in and out of her body. I look back at the stranger. His body is terrifyingly strong, but his eyes, chocolate brown with flecks of gold, are warm. On either side of his thick lips are deep, half-circle creases that make him look like he's smiling even when he's not. He walks toward me.

"You're Elizabeth's daughter," he says, his accent slightly less thick than Eduardo's. I nod and he smiles. "I can tell."

"You can?" I ask. "People say we look nothing alike."

"It's not your face," he says and takes a step closer to me. "It's the way you move. Graceful. Like her."

For the first time in the last twenty-four hours, I smile. No one's ever called me graceful or compared me to my mother like that. It's something I've always admired about her. Funny to describe someone who kicks people in the face for a living as graceful, but she is. She sort of just floats. Even the way she fights, her Krav Maga moves are fluid and beautiful. They can do so much harm but look like they take no effort at all. She's sneaky like that and underestimating her strength has gotten people killed.

"I'm Lazaro," he says, taking my hand in his, gripping it hard. "But your parents just call me Laz."

"You know them well?" I ask, trying to place any mention of his name. I've definitely heard it before.

"Very well," he says, placing his second hand on top of mine. "I've always wanted to meet you. Heard so much about you. From your parents. From CORE. It's an honor."

"Yeah, we'll see how much of an honor it is when Thomas finds out about this," Sam says then turns to Eduardo, who is unpacking our bags from the truck. "Eduardo, what is wrong with you? How could you transport these two?"

"It's not his fault," I interject and walk closer to Sam. I can feel her burning blood from several feet away. "I knew the codes. I knew the plan. He thought we were the DC team."

Sam turns slowly to me, her hands now balled into fists, her blue eyes dark and narrowed. "Why did you do this? Do you know how much trouble you're going to get in? How much trouble you're going to get me in? Let alone the fact that this is just about the most dangerous city in the world you can be in right now."

"I couldn't go to Langley," I say, trying to keep my voice calm. "I couldn't just listen. That's not what I'm wired to do. But more important, I was the original target. People are *dying* because of me. I need to be here and you know it."

Sam shakes her head, her eyes fixated on the dirty cement floor. She inhales deeply and quietly says, "If it wasn't more dangerous to put you two on a plane back to the United States, I'd be doing it in one second. But it's too late."

"Plus, we need them," Cooper says, walking closer to us, a satellite phone in his hand. "The DC team is not going to make it in time. We can't get Elizabeth and Jonathan off that ranch with just me, you, Laz, and Eduardo. I'm not happy they're here. Thomas

230

isn't happy they're here. But at least it gives us two other bodies that can run intel from the truck. Help us in the field."

"I'm trained for that," I say and nod. "And Luke has had military training his entire life. He will do anything and everything you ask of him."

"Fine," Sam says, lowering her hunched, tight shoulders. She pulls at a clump of her blond hair before pointing her finger back in my face. "But you will do exactly what I say, do you understand me?"

"Sam, I—" I begin but she cuts me off.

"*Exactly* what I say," she says again, her voice ballooning around the first word.

"Yes," I reply with a small nod, and then look over my shoulder to where I know Luke is quietly watching. "We'll do whatever you say, right, Luke?"

"Of course," Luke answers and walks closer to us.

"This is all fucking ridiculous but I don't have time to yell at the two of you anymore. We've got work to do," Sam says, crossing her arms and walking back toward a black moving truck parked in the corner of the warehouse. The back door of the moving truck has been rolled open and satellite phones, laptops, monitors, and other equipment have been positioned at the end of the bed, setting up a makeshift intel center.

Luke and Eduardo begin unloading weapons and extra satellite equipment from the backs of the two beat-up trucks, transferring them to the moving van. Cooper stands and types at his laptop while Sam gets back on one of the satellite phones. She's shaking her head, I'm sure talking about me.

Laz puts his hand on my shoulder and leans in. "I think you need to be here," he says quietly in my ear.

"You do?" I ask, raising my eyebrows. He seems to be the only one.

"Por supuesto," Lazaro says and nods. His dark ponytail swings between his shoulder blades. "Your parents would be very proud of you. This is all they've ever wanted for you, *mi querido."*

Laz wraps his arm around my shoulder and gives it a squeeze. I nod, hoping his words are true and that I am doing the right thing.

Eduardo drops my bag from the back of the truck at my feet. I lean down and sling it over my shoulder.

"We'll find them," Laz says softly as I head for the moving truck. I turn around, my eyes meeting his. His eyes are sad but determined. He nods, his hands tightening around an assault rifle.

We'll find them. I let his words puncture my skin, sink into my veins, and pump through my body. I hold on to the promise of a complete stranger as I grip the worn straps of my go-bag and walk across the warehouse to the waiting truck.

Sam is on one of the satellite phones. She pulls it from her ear and cups her hand over the mouthpiece.

"Hey, guys, can we all huddle up for a second?" Sam calls out to Eduardo and Luke, reassembling the hollow trucks. They throw down the boards and jog across the warehouse. Sam pushes a button and puts the phone down on the edge of the truck.

"All right, Thomas, we're all here," she says, pulling out her tablet and turning it on.

"Okay, here is the latest," a thin voice says on the other side of the phone. The connection is hollow and the line is scratchy. These

232

phones are untraceable, so it's a sacrifice the Black Angels are always willing to make. "We've gotten satellite images of Elizabeth and Jonathan being led into the back barn, about five hundred yards away from the main house," Thomas says and my tense shoulders drop, a cold breath passing through my lips. They're alive. "They were handcuffed and had bags over their heads when they were pulled off the truck. But we have every reason to believe it was them."

My jaw clenches and my teeth bite down so hard I'm afraid they'll break at the thought of my parents handcuffed and blindfolded, treated like criminals.

"An important note. Elizabeth was limping very badly when they pulled her off the truck. We don't know if she was injured during the gunfight at the airport or on the plane down to Colombia, but . . ." Thomas takes a breath and sighs into the phone. "We have reason to believe that she is gravely injured."

I lower my eyelids and stare at the ground so no one can see my reaction; a flood of rage cripples my veins and I swear it's turned the whites of my eyes devil red. I dig my nails into the flesh of my hips and concentrate on the sting. What have they done to her? I've seen my mother bruised, cut up, stitched up, and sprained, but never truly injured. The image of her limping across a field, her foot dragging across the dirt, makes the knot in my stomach feel like a knife wound. I know my mother. She would never limp, never, ever, unless she was truly unable to put one foot in front of the other. She'd gather every ounce of strength, grind her teeth, and endure the worst pain possible before showing her enemies that she was anything less than superhuman.

"We will need to make sure we get all the guards down before we grab her because she cannot run. She will need to be carried," Thomas continues. I don't know if I'm allowed to speak, but right now, I don't really care.

"I can carry her," I volunteer. My voice is louder than I expected it to be and it echoes in the open space. Cooper flicks his glaring eyes up at me as the satellite phone cracks and squeaks.

"Reagan, is that you?" Thomas asks after a beat.

"Yes, it's me," I say, shifting my weight and hugging my arms to my body. The entire group has turned their heads. Their eyes are on me. "I can carry her out of there while the rest of the team secures the guards."

"Absolutely not, Reagan," Thomas answers, the harshness in his voice impaling my skin. "You were the original target. In fact, he's contacted us twice now, saying he wants you in exchange for their lives. We at CORE are all obviously pretty enraged about you breaking multiple layers of protocol to get down to Colombia. You've broken pretty much every Black Angel Directive we have so far and you're not even a full Black Angel agent."

"I know," I say, pushing my voice forward, stopping it from shrinking into my body, accepting defeat. "I just can't sit by and watch. I need to be here to help."

"Sit by and watch you still will, Miss Hillis," Thomas says, his voice stern and angry. "I have half my mind to put you on the next flight back but we can't risk tipping off Torres. So you will help. But you will absolutely stay in that truck and help run intel, do you understand me?"

"I understand but I am a trained fighter and I—" I protest but he cuts me off.

"Reagan, do not question me," Thomas pushes back. "Half the Black Angel tribunal wants to pull Eduardo off this mission so he can guard you in that warehouse. And then we'll have an even smaller team in the field to rescue your parents. Do you want that?"

"Of course not," I answer.

"I respect the fact that you want to help save your parents," Thomas continues. "But this is extremely dangerous. It's pretty much guaranteed that if they capture you, you will die. There will be no amount of negotiating or promising to release a prisoner in the United States for your life. Are you sure you want to play a part in this mission?"

"The risk is enormous," Cooper adds with a nod.

"If they grab you, they won't hold you like they're holding your parents," Sam says, turning around and facing me. "They've made that extremely clear. You are their revenge killing. It's not enough for Torres just to kill your parents. He wants to kill their spirits. So you have to understand that if something happens to you, we won't be able to get you back. Just think about that, Reagan."

My fingers are pressing down so hard on my charm, I'm shocked the hearts aren't bending in the heat. I swallow the fury and fear that has broken out of its box and crawled, like black poison, through my veins, polluting my lungs, my heart, my mind. I breathe in, push it back down, and let the numbness take over my body.

"I understand the risk," I say, my voice tangled in my throat. I clear it and press my lips together. "I'm done with the questions.

Don't ask me if I'm sure I'm doing the right thing. Don't ask me if my parents would want me to do this or if I realize the risk I'm taking, because right now, I do not care. I'll do whatever it takes to get them back home safe, and if that means that I might get hurt or die, then so be it. You can't change my mind, so save your breath."

Sam's and Cooper's eyes widen. Luke has taken a step back from me. Eduardo's mouth comes unhinged and Laz... Laz is smiling.

"All right, Reagan." Thomas finally breaks the heavy silence. I feel my hands begin to tingle. I shake them out as Thomas breaks down the positions of the guards, the guns they're carrying, the time we'll hit the compound.

I search the faces of the rest of the team. They are nodding, listening intently to CORE's instructions. Cooper and Eduardo are crouched down in the truck. Laz and Luke stand side by side, their arms crossed, their muscles rigid. Sam stands with her hands confidently pressed to her hips. No one looks afraid. And I realize just how powerful and amazing the Black Angels are, how impressive their network is, to be able to pull something as complicated and dangerous as this in under twenty-four hours. I see now why my parents love being a part of this team.

"Thomas, the sun is beginning to set here and we've got at least an hour's drive to the ranch," Sam says, turning around to look out the windows. "We'd better get loaded up. Anything else we need to know?"

"Yes, one more crucial bit of information," Thomas says. The line crackles, then comes back. "We've intercepted a message between Torres and his team about a half hour ago. We are under a definite time crunch. Torres is planning on leaving the ranch sometime tonight with Jonathan and Elizabeth and moving them to another location. We have no idea where. He hasn't given up that information, and you all know that moving victims is usually a bad sign. We do not have time to waste here. It looks like we've only got one shot to get this right."

"Shit," I hear Laz say under his breath.

One shot. I watch as the team's determined, hard faces squirm with worry, their steady breaths deepen. On missions, it's about watching and waiting for that perfect moment, calculating the right time to attack. Rush a compound too soon or too late and Black Angels come home in body bags. I look out the warehouse windows. The sky is streaked pink as the sun dips into the west; the world is darkening, and with it, our chances of bringing my mom and dad home alive.

TWENTY-SEVEN

ICY GOOSE BUMPS PRICK MY SKIN. THE TRUCK'S walls are cold and hard but I refuse to dig into my bag to find a sweatshirt. It's a waste of time to do anything but study these files as we drive to the ranch.

I pull up the map of the property. The red dots represent a guard. One on each side of the barn, eight guards around the house, one patrolling the guest house and pool house. The plan is to hit at 8:30 when most of the guards will have gone inside for dinner. The barn will still be surrounded and the guards will eat with their weapons on their laps, ready for any sign of trouble. If we have any chance of getting everyone out of there alive, we have to be quick and we have to be quiet.

My fingers swipe right across the tablet and into the weaponry file. The guards are carrying Heckler & Koch MP5s. My mind quickly flips through its mental database of guns. MP5...German, developed in the sixties, the most widely used submachine gun in the world, powerful, but not as accurate as the M4 carbines we carry.

I flip through to Torres's file; his cold, dark eyes stare back at me and a shiver runs through my freezing body. I scan his profile. Fifty-two years old. Four children. One wife. One mistress. Three brothers. One in jail, one overseeing cartel operations in South America, and one stationed in Central America. Five suspected residences. Billion-dollar drug enterprise. Twenty bodyguards. Six years in the Colombian army.

The next stat stops me cold. I pull the tablet closer to my face and read it over and over again. Am I hallucinating? Every muscle in my body tightens and my head throbs with the implausibility of what I'm reading. But I read it again. Foreign Black Angel agent. Five years.

"What the hell is this?" I ask, my voice on the verge of shaking. I look up from my tablet. Luke and Sam continue working behind their monitors. Laz and Cooper are inspecting each weapon, snapping magazines and ammunition into place.

"What the hell is what?" Sam asks without stopping her typing.

"Foreign Black Angel agent," I spit out. "Torres was a foreign Black Angel agent? This is a typo, right?"

Cooper and Laz look up from the weapons. Sam and Luke stop typing. Silence expands in huge rings around us until it fills the entire truck. Everyone stares at me, their mouths tight, waiting for someone to explain.

"Someone tell me this is a mistake," I say, my eyes bouncing from one tense face to the next.

Laz clears his throat and runs his right hand along his long, smooth braid. "It's true. Seventeen years ago, Torres was a foreign Black Angel agent. Like me. He was one of us."

His confirmation knocks every last molecule of oxygen from my lungs and sends my entire body backward. I hit my head against the steel wall, shake it out, and breathe again. "Are you serious?" I ask, even though it's clear from their anxious eyes, they are telling the truth.

Laz slowly nods. "Santino and I were from the same town. Knew each other in school. Rose up the ranks of the Colombian military and were both recruited by the Black Angels in our twenties to be foreign agents. He was my partner for five years. I went on more missions with him than I can count. He was an amazing fighter. One of the best foreign agents they'd ever had. And then one day after a big mission in South America, he just disappeared. Took about half a million dollars' worth of guns and ammunition and equipment from the agency and went rogue."

"He went completely underground and didn't surface for another three years," Sam continues, biting at her thumbnail between thoughts. "We knew about a rising drug lord in Colombia known as the Hammer, but we had no idea it was him until the National Security Agency put two and two together. We should have killed him then when we still had the chance but he grew too powerful. Took everything he knew from the Black Angels and applied it to his criminal enterprise. He even calls his guards the White Angels, just to rub it in our faces."

"I don't understand," I reply, my voice fighting to rise out of its stunned fog. "How could he have spent all that time as a Black Angel and then turn on everyone?"

"He became a Black Angel knowing he was going to turn on us," Cooper replies and looks back down at his M4 carbine. "He is a master manipulator. The only reason he joined the Colombian military was to learn how to fight and use weapons. How to run an army for the drug kingdom he wanted to build."

"He used us," Laz says, his eyes narrowing with anger. "He used every single last one of us. The Black Angels turned him into one of the best fighters and shooters in the world. He's been able to train his teams to be exactly like us. And the scariest part is he knows all of our secrets."

"That's how he was able to get to your parents, Reagan," Sam speaks. "He knows how the Black Angels operate. We've tried to change our security since he went rogue but he's still figured out how we arm our homes. He knows about the alarms on every property, about the security cameras. . . ."

"He knows about the basements . . ." I say, my voice trailing off, my mind flashing back to last year. The young hitman, pulling at our metal tool chest. That's how he knew a secret door was there. Torres told him where we'd be hiding.

Sam nods. "That was one of Torres's men. Your parents were part of a raid in Ecuador that killed his cousin. Santino wanted everyone involved dead, including your parents. He sent that hitman to your house with orders to kill them. And to kidnap you."

"Did he know my parents?" I ask, grasping the gun at my side so hard, my hand is beginning to cramp. I shake it out and tuck it into the long sleeve of my oversize sweatshirt.

"Yeah, he knew them," Laz replies. "They had only been Black Angels a short time when he went rogue, but he knew them well enough to stay under their skin."

"To stay under all our skin," Sam replies, her voice so soft, I think I'm the only one who heard her.

I shake my head, stretch my legs out in front of me, and cross my arms over my chest. "I thought this was supposed to be the best agency in the world. I just don't understand how he could get inside this group and fool all of you."

"He's the only one who's ever done it," Laz says, memories of betrayal changing the tone of his voice, the expression on his face. "He was just that good."

Silence envelops the back of the truck. There is nothing more to say. Eventually everyone returns to their work. I stare blankly at my tablet, Torres's face gaping back at me. I knew Torres was evil, but this takes it to an entirely new level. How he could go through all the strenuous training, pass all the psychological tests, and not get red flagged is beyond me. But I guess it takes a real sociopath to fake his way through five years of being a Black Angel. To go on missions and save people's lives, to befriend his colleagues, to always have their backs and then turn around and stab them there.

I used to believe that every person was good or at least started out good. It's people like Torres who have forced me to lose that innocence. Some people are just born evil. They are born with that bad seed. And it just grows and becomes bigger and all-consuming until it manifests into hate and then harm and then torture and then murder. Humans are capable of stuff that scares the shit out of me. I just hope we get to the ranch before my parents become two more bodies on Torres's very long kill list.

TWENTY-EIGHT

"TWO MILES OUT," I HEAR EDUARDO'S SCRATCHY voice say over the radio from the front seat. "Two miles until we reach our location."

Everyone is gearing up, strapping on black boots and their black bulletproof vests, double-checking their guns and tucking away their knives, ammunition, and zip ties. Luke struggles with the Velcro on his vest.

"Here, let me help you," I say as I tighten his strap, looking into Luke's eyes for the first time in an hour. His lips curl up into a small, relieved smile. I've felt his eyes on me, desperate for me to give him some sort of sign of how I'm feeling and what I'm thinking. I've been seesawing between moments of numbness and moments of panic. I haven't wanted him to look at me and see vapid emptiness or hysterical fear. The truth is I don't know how I should feel. There isn't exactly a guidebook on how to feel when you're on your way to rescue your kidnapped parents from their psychotic colleague turned traitor.

I know Luke. He's been watching me, trying to figure out what to do, what to say. But there's nothing to say. Just being here is more than enough because he doesn't have to do this. He doesn't need to put his life on the line to save my parents. But he has, and I know he would even if I begged him to stay.

I move my hand along Luke's strong shoulder, adjusting the vest so it sits evenly on his body.

"Thanks," he says as I pull one last piece of Velcro across his stomach and memories of my dad helping me with my own vest come flooding back to me. Once a month, Dad would run one of his drills with me in the basement using different situations. Hostage standoffs, bomb threats, terrorist take-downs, just to see how I'd react, what guns I would take, what martial arts skills I would use. All those Saturdays strapping on a vest I didn't really need, loading a gun I wasn't even going to shoot, sidestepping quietly through a house with no one inside, has all led to this moment. And now I'm ready for the real thing.

Luke, Eduardo, and I are suited up even though we're staying in the truck. Eduardo behind the wheel, Luke and I monitoring the satellites and intel from CORE. We're *extreme* backup. Sam actually used the word *extreme* like seventeen times when referring to us as backup. Sam, Laz, and Cooper will take down the guards and storm the barn.

"One mile from the field," Eduardo's voice comes over the computer monitors. "One mile."

"All right, everyone have their earpieces in?" Sam asks from the back of the truck. She's surrounded by monitors, watching the satellites, intercepting last-minute data, and talking directly with CORE.

The tiny blue light of my earpiece shines up at me from the palm of my hand. I slip it into my right ear so we can all hear one another.

"Thomas, are you online? What's the latest?" Laz asks into his earpiece. There's a small crack on the other end.

"Yes, I'm here," Thomas answers. "From our satellite images, Torres went out to the barn around eight o'clock and stayed there for sixteen minutes before returning to the main house. It's dark now so the images aren't as clear, but it looks like several of the guards from around the house have started to make their way in for dinner. There should still be four guards around the barn. I don't think Torres will let those guards leave their position for anything."

"So all sources point to them still being inside the barn?" I ask, my voice carrying up to the tiny black microphone built into my earpiece.

"Affirmative," Thomas replies. "And a word of caution; even if you disarm these guards, they most likely are concealing weapons too. With what happened at the airport in Kentucky, I've gotten full clearance from the higher-ups to shoot to kill."

Shoot to kill, I repeat in my head. In just a few minutes, the team has full permission to take a life. I have never wanted to kill anyone. It's the part of the job I've hated, the idea of being the hand that forces someone's last breath. But tonight's different. If it's a choice between them or us—if it means my parents can go free— then let there be bodies and blood on the ground.

My pulse throbs anxious beats against my neck. My thigh and calf muscles begin to twitch and tingle and I have to stop myself from sprinting out the door of the moving truck. I lean my head against the metal wall and close my eyes. I breathe and try to focus on something to calm me down. Moments of my life filter through my brain. They're not full memories, just flashes—Mom dressed in her cream robe, the squeak of Dad's office chair, the clink of coffee cups on the kitchen counter, Mom's biscuits in the oven, Dad's paper on the island. They're meaningless, mundane moments that now mean everything to me.

"Half a mile from target," Eduardo updates us in our ears, flicking my eyes open.

"Everybody locked and loaded?" Sam asks, standing from behind the mountain of monitors.

Team members nod or answer, "Ready."

"Luke, Reagan," Sam says, stepping closer to us. "As soon as we're out those doors, you guys are on. We'll have cameras strapped to our helmets so you'll be able to see. Do you remember how to work everything? Have any questions on what I've showed you?"

"No. We've got it," I confirm.

"Silencers on?" Laz asks, twisting a silencer on his M4.

"All set," Cooper answers, running his fingers along the smooth metal of his silencer. Everyone around me nods.

"Two hundred yards from target," Eduardo says in my ear and I can feel the truck beginning to decrease its speed.

My lungs feel like they're collapsing. I breathe in, but the air in this truck is metallic and suffocating. After hours of talking and planning and replanning, no one speaks. The only sounds I hear are the tap, tap, tap of Luke at the keyboard, Velcro ripping apart as Sam adjusts her vest, and Cooper's fingers drumming nervously on the metal wall of the truck.

Soft whispers break up the quiet. I look up at Laz. His hands are collapsed together, his eyes are closed, his mouth moves quickly. I catch snippets of what he's saying. *Dios mio. Seguridad. Jesus Cristo.* He's praying. I watch him as he carefully crosses himself in the name of the Father and of the Son and of the Holy Spirit. He raises his hand to his lips and gently kisses his fingertips. He opens his brown eyes and they immediately meet mine.

"Who were you praying for, Laz?" I ask, my voice quiet.

"For your parents. For you. For all of us," Laz answers and nods.

"Thank you." I lean my shoulders against the truck. "I hope God hears you."

"Have you asked God to protect you?" Laz asks, taking a step closer to me.

"I haven't really prayed in a long time," I say and shake my head. "It feels selfish to ask for help now."

"Dios te escucha," Laz says, his index finger pointing up toward the heavens and then down to his right ear. He nods slowly, his brown eyes glistening. There's a flash of sadness in them. Maybe the sorrow is for me. That I walk through life without God in my heart and prayers on my lips. I study his face: He blinks and the sadness is gone. He looks peaceful, envy crushing my already-aching

heart. I wish I believed God would always protect me or that prayers carry power or that good really does conquer evil. Life would be easier that way.

"God hears you," Laz repeats, this time in English. "God hears you always."

I want to believe that if I pray hard enough for strength, protection, and the lives of my parents, that God will hear me and make it so. But I don't think it works that way. God doesn't choose who gets to live and who has to die. And if he does, he's a God I don't think I want to know.

The truck's heavy tires squeal as the truck comes to a complete stop.

"Go time," Sam says, clutching her gun to her chest.

"Let's bring them home," Thomas says. I push my earpiece deeper into my eardrum.

Cooper unlocks the back door of the truck and it swings open with a screaming creak. One by one, they jump the five feet down to the ground, their boots scraping against the gravel road.

"Are you sitting down with me?" Luke asks from behind the monitors.

"Yes, just one second," I say and walk toward the back of the truck. "I can't breathe in here."

I jump quietly off the back of the truck and onto the gravel road. I take in a breath. The air outside is humid and salty and sweet. The shore is only two miles away and Colombia's fragrant flowers are in full bloom.

I watch as Sam, Laz, and Cooper walk into darkness, their calves and lower thighs disappearing in the field's high grass and weeds.

A half mile is what separates me from my parents. A half mile until they come face-to-face with some of the most ruthless assassins in the world.

With each breath, my racing heart slows. Something resembling peace washes over me. Maybe it's my training or the smell of seawater. Maybe it's Laz's prayer. Whatever it is, my heart isn't filled with fear. It's filled with something I've never felt before. Whatever it is, I need it to stay with me. I breathe in the Colombian air and hold it in my lungs. *Stay with me, please. Dear God, please stay with me.*

TWENTY-NINE

"THERE ARE FOUR GUARDS AROUND THE PERIMETER of the barn, do you copy?" Sam's voice whispers in my ear. I take my right hand off the keyboard and touch my ear.

"Copy," I say and hear the rest of the team repeat "copy" after me. Luke and I are seated on the floor of the truck, watching the team's cameras on our monitors. The team is one hundred yards away from the barn, crouched in the grass, watching the guards. One guard is at the front of the barn standing stationary, the MP5 machine gun cradled in his arms. The guard on the side facing the field paces back and forth. Like a good soldier. Torres probably loves this kid. He's tall and muscular and incredibly alert.

"Are you guys seeing this?" I warn, my voice carrying up to my mouthpiece. "The guard on the south side of the barn is super intense. We have to wait for him to calm down a bit if we even want a chance in hell."

"We see him," Sam answers me. "Good eye."

"Thomas, any indication they'll change guards soon?" Cooper asks. I hold my breath, hoping he'll say yes. We need a lazy guard, one that's more concerned with cigarette smoking than gun holding.

"No. They just changed guards an hour ago," Thomas answers. His voice in my ear sounds hollow and reminds me just how far away I am from home. "They probably won't change again for another hour and a half, and by then it might be too late."

"All right," I hear Cooper say on the other end. "We have to move in now. This is the only chance we've got."

"Wait one more minute," Laz's voice enters my ear. Hearing his calm, deep voice helps me breathe. "The right time will come."

"We don't have time to sit and wait," Cooper hisses.

"*Un minuto,*" Laz repeats. "*Un minuto.*"

Cooper sighs in my ear as we watch the guard pace. After a minute, his steps slow, his stride narrows, and his weapon looks heavier in his hands. When he reaches the front of the barn, his hand wraps around the wall. He peers at the guard on the other side, then ducks back around. My eyes stay glued to him. *Put it down. Put it down. Put it down,* I silently beg. The faithful soldier looks around once more before his shoulders slump and his puffed-out chest caves in. I release the breath I've been holding as he leans his weapon against his leg, digs into his pocket, and pulls out a cigarette. The light from a match flickers around his face, smoke rises from his lips, and just like that, the good soldier lets down his guard.

"Yes," I whisper.

"Move in. Now," Cooper says into my earpiece.

The cameras on their helmets bounce ever so slightly as they creep toward the barn. Each step they take is delicate, careful not to crack a stick or rustle the weeds and grass. The light positioned at each side of the barn plays to our advantage. The guards can only see directly in front of them. They're practically blind to the team hiding in the field.

Luke and I watch the team move quickly and quietly, one right behind the other, crouched low to the ground, the weeds still covering most of their bodies. My heart picks up speed with each yard they cover. Forty yards away. Thirty yards away. At twenty yards away they pause. I turn my attention back to the guard. He lifts his cigarette to his mouth and sucks in the tobacco. He holds the smoke in his lungs and tilts his head toward the sky. A line of smoke billows from his lips and rises in the air, separating and then dissipating a few feet above his head.

"Hurry, he's almost done with that cigarette," I say as I watch him pull the cigarette back up to his lips. A puff more and he'll be at the filter. Then the gun will be back in his hand and our one shot of taking him down without a fight will be lost.

"We see, Reagan," Laz's voice says in my ears. My shot of the bodyguard disappears. I hear the grass rustle in my ear. They're on their stomachs, watching their prey, waiting to strike.

"This is still not a good angle," Sam whispers and my earpiece cracks and pops. "He's going to see us coming, cigarette or gun in hand. We have to take him down from here."

"Sam's right," Luke says next to me. "He's going to see you guys coming no matter what."

"Take him down, Cooper. Let's hope he falls to the right and not the left," I say. I study the guard's position. If he's shot in the head and falls to the right, the other guards will have no idea. If he falls to the left, he's close enough to the front of the barn that the other guard may see him fall forward and know we're here. But it's a risk we have to take.

"Do it," I say and reach for the M4 at my side. "Now."

The grass rustles in my ear as Cooper rises from his hiding spot and lifts the gun to his shoulder. I turn my attention back to the guard. *Please fall to the right. Please fall to the right.* He takes one last drag of his cigarette, flicks the last bit of burning ash onto the ground, and leans down to his right to pick up his gun. Then I hear it. The stifled pop of a M4 carbine. The bullet whizzes through the air and strikes the guard square in the temple. Blood rushes out of his ear and pours down his face as he falls to the ground. To the right, thank God.

I press my lips into a relieved "O" and allow the breath I've been holding to escape.

"Three guards to go," Sam says, her voice hushed and steady. "Cooper, you take the back. Laz and I will take the front and then the three of us will attack from both sides on the north side of the barn. We go on my count. Ready?"

"Let's do this," Laz says. I can hear small metallic pops and cracks through my earpiece as they all ready their weapons to shoot.

"Eduardo, Luke, Reagan, we'll give you a signal when we've got Jonathan and Elizabeth," Sam whispers. "Then you come immediately to us, but not a minute before that, you got me?"

"Got it," I say, my mouth struggling to push out the words,

adrenaline strangling my vocal cords. I climb onto my knees and stare at the dead guard on my monitor. Even through the thermal cameras, I can make out the bloodstains on the ground beneath him. His gun is still in his hand.

"On my count," Sam says, her voice heavy, carrying the weight of the danger that's in front of her. In front of us. "In five, four, three, two, one."

Their bodies rise from the grass. They dart to the side of the barn, their breaths heavier in my earpiece with each yard. I feel Luke shift with anxiety next to me but I don't take my eyes off our guys. Their backs against the wall, Sam stretches out her arm, nods, and points to the back of the barn. Cooper crouches down, his weapons pointed in front of him. He steps quickly toward the back side of the barn. Laz and Sam point their weapons in the opposite direction, step over the guard's dead body, and make their way to the front of the barn.

Please, God, please, God, I repeat over and over again in my head. I'm gripping the gun at my side so hard my hands are becoming cramped and sore. *Please, God, please, God.*

"On my count," Sam whispers again in the earpiece. "Five, four, three, two, one."

With that, all three swing around the sides of the barn and pull their triggers at the exact same time, the power from their shots forcing them back. I watch as the guard in Sam's monitor falls to the ground. But just as I'm about to breathe a sigh of relief, the bright, pulsating flashes of a gun light up Cooper's monitor. *Pow. Pow. Pow.*

"Shit," Laz says in my ears, his normally calm voice now panicked. I watch Cooper's camera bounce as he races around the back side of the barn, seeking refuge from the gunfire. He missed. He fucking missed.

Pow. Pow. Pow. Pow. Pow. More gunfire from the back of the barn. From Laz's camera, I see lights turn on inside the house and within seconds I know every guard on this property will be sprinting toward the barn.

Without a word, I rise and grab my M4 off the ground.

"Reagan, wait," Luke says, pulling himself up, but I'm already jumping off the bed of the truck and sprinting through the high grass.

"We're going in," Luke yells somewhere behind me as we sprint toward the barn.

"No, go back!" Cooper booms in my ear. "The mission is blown. We're aborting. We have to get out of here or we're all going to die."

"I'm not leaving without them," I scream into my ear, tightening my grip on my weapon.

"Go, go, go. They'll be here any second," Sam yells back and I don't know if she means to go back to the truck or get to the barn. But it doesn't matter. I'd be sprinting into the line of fire either way.

I run so fast, my feet feel like they're not even touching the ground. *Please, God. Please, God,* I plead with each step. *Please let us make it to the barn before the guards.* I scan the grounds as I sprint. I see them. Their flashlights dot their positions in the distance, bobbing with every strike of their heel. We're one hundred yards. Now seventy-five. Now fifty. Now twenty-five. Now ten. I reach the barn first and jump over the dead body that lies in front of the door. I yank at the heavy barn door. The curved metal of a lock pulls the door back.

"Damn it, it's locked," I say and pull the door again out of frustration.

"He's probably got the key." Luke kneels down at the dead guard's feet. I look over my shoulder. The group of guards is only two hundred yards away.

"There's no time," I yell over the gunfire and screaming in my ear. Luke rises to his feet but I push his body out of the way. "Stand back."

I point my pistol up at the lock and pull the trigger. *Bang*. It slices through the metal and the lock falls to the ground. I pull at the barn door again and it slides open.

"Go, go, go," I yell to Luke and push him inside. He enters, his weapon stretched in front of him, and I walk into the darkness, pulling the barn door shut behind me.

"Do you think they saw us come in here?" Luke whispers to me, his breath heavy.

"I don't know but let's move," I say, still trying to catch my own breath. Luke and I take another step into the barn, our weapons still in front of us. "Do you see them?"

"I can't see anything," Luke says and looks from left to right in the almost pitch-black barn. Dark shadows resembling hay and shovels and rakes are the only things we see.

"Mom, Dad?" I call out, my voice beginning to shake. What if they're not here? What if they're already dead? Panicked, I yell again, "Mom?!"

"Reagan?" I hear my father's gravelly voice say from somewhere in the darkness. A lump lodges in my throat at the sound of his voice.

"Dad, where are you?" I ask, pushing back stacks of hay and

sheets and garbage. As my eyes adjust to the black, Luke pulls out a flashlight the size of a pen.

"Back corner," Dad says, his voice almost a whisper. I can barely hear him over the eruption of gunfire. The other armed guards have arrived.

Luke's light scans the barn and finally I see him, crouched behind a stack of hay.

"Oh my God," Luke says, and as I run closer, I see why. Dad's face is bruised and crusted with old and new blood. His left eye is purple and swollen shut. His lip has been split and his right cheek is slashed. I push my way through the barn, not even sure what I'm shoving out of the way. As I reach him, tears swim in the only eye he's able to open.

"What on earth are you doing here?" he asks, pressing his swollen lips together. A tear falls from his right eye and is caught by the open wound on his cheek.

"I couldn't stand by and watch another mission get blown," I say and touch the only remaining unbruised spot of his cheek.

Dad moves his arm toward me but something holds him back. Metal scrapes against metal and I can see his right hand is handcuffed to a metal pipe against the wall. On the other side of the pipe is an empty set of handcuffs. My heart drops.

"Wait, where's Mom?" I ask, staring at the empty space next to him.

"Torres took her inside a little bit ago," Dad says, following my stare. His body begins to shake. He sucks in his swollen lip, trying to control his tears. "I'm afraid of what he'll do to her before . . . before he . . ."

"I'm not going to let anything happen to her." I shake my head, the lump thickening in my throat. I try to swallow it away but can't. I can't bury the emotions. Not now.

I pull my Glock 22 pistol out from the back of my pants. "Pull your chain as tight as you can."

I can see the metal digging into his skin and the pain on his face. I point my pistol at the exposed links and pull the trigger. Without a silencer on my pistol, the pop of the gun fills the barn and rattles against my chest. The bullet rips through the link, slicing the handcuffs in half. Dad pulls his free hand away as the other cuff scrapes down the pipe and hits the dirty, hay-covered ground.

Dad cradles his sore hand to his stomach and reaches up to me with his left hand. I kneel on the ground and let him pull me into his body. I wrap my arms around him and bury my face in his chest. He's lost his scent of aftershave and fresh linen and smells of sweat and blood and dirt. As much as I thought this moment would be filled with love and relief, I just can't get there. I'm filled with rage. His swollen eye and bloodied face, my father, beaten and broken down.

Bang. A bullet rips through the barn wall, twenty feet behind us. I break free of Dad's embrace and pull him off the ground.

"We have to get him out of here," I say, draping Dad's arm around my shoulder. "Where's the truck?"

"I'm pulling into the field now," Eduardo says in my ear. "I'm fifty yards away from the barn."

"Can you walk that far?" I ask as Dad limps toward the barn door, half of his body weight on my shoulders and back.

"I can make it," Dad says, clutching his left knee, his face wincing, his breaths short and shallow.

"Laz, Sam, we've got Dad, but Mom's in the house. What's going on out there?" I say, holding my hand up to my earpiece. Another shot rings out from somewhere outside and I can hear grunts and heavy breathing, the telltale signs of hand-to-hand combat. No one answers me.

"Thomas, what's going on outside?" Luke says, taking Dad's other arm and draping it around his shoulder.

"Stand by, we're looking," Thomas says. "The images are coming in on a delay."

Come on, come on. I press my lips together and stare out the tiny window at the front of the barn. The field in front of me is clear and the house lights are all on. *Mom, where are you?*

"Looks like all the activity is in the back of the barn," Thomas finally answers. "Our guys are still up but six guards are down. Two are still fighting off our guys, but everything is happening twenty yards behind you. You're fine to exit the barn, but go now."

I shift Dad's weight onto Luke, pull open the barn door, and point my gun outside. I inch my way out, scanning the grounds for guards or any other shooters. Another bullet cracks through the air behind me and the hairs on the back of my neck stand up.

"Another guard down," I hear Laz yell in my ear.

I wave Luke back outside and into the moonlight. Eduardo flashes the headlights in the truck. "Take Dad to the truck," I say to Luke and kiss my father on his swollen cheek. "I'm going to get Mom."

"Reagan, don't. Torres will kill you the second you step foot in that house," Dad protests.

"Reagan, get in the truck with your father," Thomas says in my ear. "That's a direct order."

"No, Thomas. I'm not taking orders from you right now," I say and grab my father's hand. "I'm going to find her. I promise."

"Reagan, don't," Dad begs, tears welling up in his eyes. "I cannot lose you both."

But there's nothing he can do to stop me. There's nothing he can say to get me on that truck.

"Reagan, no . . ." Luke yells after me.

But I'm already running toward the house. The anger that started in my heart has pumped through my veins and circulated through my entire body. A fire burns with every step, growing with each stride, until I cannot feel the strike of my heel or the wind on my face. All I feel is heat.

"She's entering the house to find Elizabeth. Someone stop her," I hear Thomas say in my ear.

"Reagan, get back here," Sam pleads.

"Reagan, get in the truck, please," Cooper says, his voice harsh. "This is what Torres wants. He wants . . ."

"Goddammit," my mouth hisses as I yank out my earpiece and shove it in my pocket, quieting their protests.

My blood is hot and my muscles feel like they're being pulled apart. I dig my heels into the ground. *Run faster, run faster, run faster.* My legs stretch out further, pulling me closer and closer to the house. Two hundred yards. One hundred yards. Fifty yards. Twenty yards. I grip my weapon as I reach the back patio. No one is around. My fingers grasp the cool metal handle of the guest room door.

"I'm coming, Mom," I whisper. I pull down on the handle and swing the door open. I point my gun into the guest room. It's dark and empty. I listen for footsteps, for gunshots. I hear nothing. "I'm coming."

THIRTY

I STEP INSIDE THE DARK ROOM. A KING-SIZE FOUR-poster bed is against the wall to the right. A fireplace and sitting area with two chairs and a small table is to my left. *Where is the freaking door?* I step quietly across the plush carpet, my gun still pointed in front of me. I see a thin line of pale light on the floor straight ahead. *There it is.* I cross the room and put my ear to the door, listening for what may be happening on the other side. I listen for footsteps or voices or screaming, but I hear nothing, just an eerie stillness. I stay there for another moment just to be sure, my hand on the doorknob, when I hear the tap, tap, tap of someone's feet. But it's not coming from the other side of the door, it's coming from outside. Someone has followed me. I let go of the door handle and dive to my knees behind the bed.

The footsteps slow. I look through my scope and point the gun straight at the open door that leads to the brick patio. I see a long, thick shadow on the ground in the moonlight moving toward me. I tighten my grip on the gun and brace my finger to pull the trigger.

A man's silhouette steps through the doorway, his gun pointed into the room. "Reagan?"

"Jesus Christ, Luke," I whisper and lower my weapon. "You almost just got a bullet to the temple."

"Sorry, I called for you the entire time I was running," he says, lowering his weapon. "Why didn't you answer?"

"I took out my earpiece," I whisper and step around the bed toward him.

"Reagan, you can't do that," Luke says, grabbing me gently by the shoulder. "That's like the number one thing Sam said. You need to stay in contact with everyone."

"I can't find her with everyone screaming in my ear to stop," I whisper and search for his eyes in the darkness. The dim moonlight hides their color but I can still make out his long lashes. "What are you doing here? I told you to go to the truck with Dad."

"I got him in the truck but then I came after you. There's no way I'm going to let you do this by yourself," he whispers. I should have known he'd never let me do something so dangerous alone. As much as I love him for it, I don't think I can live with myself if he gets hurt.

"Please. Can I convince you to go back?" I whisper and grab his arm.

"Not a chance," he says, putting his hand back on his weapon. "Where do you think they are?"

"I don't know," I say and do a mental scan of the house blueprint. Would he take her to a bedroom? No. The library? No. The garage? No. I put mental Xs on every room until I get to the basement. And then I remember the unfinished space down there.

They've been torturing her. And as much as Torres loves to hurt people, the thick, rich carpet at my feet tells me he likes nice things. He wouldn't want to get blood on his expensive furniture and floors. He needs a cold, dark, filthy room for his dirty work. "Let's start in the basement."

I press my ear to the door again and listen. Still nothing. I grip the door handle, pulling it all the way down so the metal doesn't scrape against the doorjamb. Light from the hallway spills into the room as I lower my stance and peer into the hall. I look left, I look right. No one. I step into the hallway, my gun pointed in front of me. I motion for Luke to follow me into Santino Torres's elaborate home.

The hallway to the right leads toward a large living room. I can see portions of an enormous gray sofa and a glass coffee table. Tall ornate lamps anchor both sides of the sofa and a vase holding a large purple orchid sits at the center of an antique trunk that's being used as a side table.

To the left is another hallway. It's dark and uninviting, but I know this is the way to the basement. With our backs up against the wall, we sidestep our way down the hallway, our heavy boots scraping against the dark woodwork. I lift each foot and set it down like a ballet dancer, touching down my toe, then the ball of my foot, then the heel, doing my best to not make a sound against the hardwood floors.

Black-and-white photographs cover the cream-colored walls. Beautiful pictures of the ocean, clouds, mountains, Colombia's famous Cattleya orchid. Each photograph is matted against a white background and hangs in a simple, elegant black frame. There's a certain softness to the pictures, the angles and the focus, something I wouldn't expect a killer like Torres to collect.

We get to the end of the hallway. I bend my knees, lowering my stance, and peer around to the next hall. It's empty. About fifty feet away is a dark wood door that I know leads to the basement stairs.

I hold up my hand, motioning for Luke to stop while I listen for creaking doors, even the sound of someone breathing. Still nothing. I raise my thumb, giving Luke the "all clear" sign. I whip my body around the wall, stretch out my arms, and point my gun down the empty hall. I wait another moment before taking the first step, my fingers tingling.

We press our backs up against the wall and sidestep our way toward the basement door. I hold my breath as we get closer. Forty more feet. Thirty more feet. Twenty more feet. Ten more feet.

Bang. The tip of Luke's gun hits the side of the bookshelf and before I can even turn around, a guard has swung around the corner, his strong arm wrapped around Luke's throat.

"Luke," I say, raising my gun to fire at the guard, but before I can get my finger around the trigger, I feel myself fall backward. *What the hell?* I reach for the bookshelf along the wall to brace myself, but it's disappeared. Suddenly, my breath is gone. I try to lean forward, but someone has grabbed me by the throat from behind. *Holy shit,* my head is screaming as a man pulls me away from Luke and into the hidden, pitch-black room with so much force, the heels of my boots drag against the hardwood floor.

I try to scream, but every wisp of air has been forced out of my lungs. I cannot breathe. The man's grip tightens, crushing the bones in my neck. I flail my body and try to suck in new air but nothing comes. Sixty seconds more, I'll be dead. *Don't let me die this way,* my mind cries. *God, don't let me die this way.*

I drop my weapon on the floor to free my hands. It lands with a blustering bang. I grab the man's large right arm with both hands, grind my teeth, and pull down with all my strength. I feel him weaken, the tightness of his grip loosening so I can suck in a new breath.

"*Puta, puta,*" the man yells at me. *Bitch, bitch.* He tries to tighten the choke hold but I've already pulled his arm too far down. I feel his body weight to my right. I jut my left leg behind his, forcing him to lower his stance. I yank down on his arm and jerk my head out of his grasp. He yelps as I pull his right arm behind his body and across his muscular back.

"*Mierda,*" the man hollers as I pull his arm even tighter. *Come on, come on, come on,* I scream in my head. His arm fights back, pulling me forward, but I won't let go. With his body off balance, I kick in the back of his knee with my left foot. He buckles under the force of my strike and falls to the ground. I pull away and try to run for the door, but he still has me by the wrist and yanks me down on top of him.

My elbow strikes the ground first and my body lands beside his with a thud. Pain rushes up my arm and through my entire body, but I push it away. He holds my left hand down on the ground and struggles to get on top of me. I knee him in the stomach and swing my free arm to punch him in the face. My fist strikes his nose. I hear a pop and feel his bones shatter against the back of my fist.

"*Puta,*" he screams, letting go of the tight grip on my arm and raising both hands to his bleeding face. This is my chance. With nothing holding me back, I rise to my knees and put out one foot to stand up. He leans forward and grabs me by my thick ponytail. I scream as he yanks me back onto the ground, my head slamming against the hardwood floor.

Now he's really pissed. "Bitch," he thunders in English. He climbs on top of me, his legs straddled on either side of my stomach. Before I can throw another punch, his hands are wrapped around my neck.

I cough and try to breathe. I bring my hands up to pry his fingers away from me, but I can't loosen his grip. I twist and kick my legs, but he's too heavy. His hands push down even harder on my neck. My lungs are screaming for new air that doesn't come and I feel like I'm drowning.

"You shouldn't have come here," the man says to me, his mouth spitting every word. The blood from his broken nose drips down onto my face and inside my mouth. It tastes metallic and bitter and dirty. I shake my head. I try to spit it out but can't find the air. "Your parents killed my nephew. I had to watch him die. I hoped you would come so I could look in your eyes while I kill you."

I turn my face toward him. My eyes adjust to the darkness as my mind registers that he's not just another one of Torres's White Angels. I'm looking into the face of his brother and partner, a man as notorious a killer as Torres himself. His eyes are filled with so much hate, so much anger and rage. I panic as I realize his dark eyes may be the last thing I ever see.

My hands pull again at his fingers while I kick and twist and dig my feet into the ground to lift him, but he's two hundred and fifty pounds. He pushes down even harder on my neck.

"Die, *puta*," he hisses, his face inching closer to mine. "Die."

His eyes flash with frustration. I twist once more and slide my hand along the hardwood floor. I feel the top of my pants. My fingers crawl further down my side. *Please, God. Please, God. Please, God.* And then I feel it, the metal handle of my knife.

"Die, *puta*." He's now screaming in my face. I can feel my body fading. Shiny silver sparks are in my peripheral vision. They creep closer into my eye line, and behind it is nothing. Black. Death.

No. No. No. My head is screaming. *Not like this. Not this way.*

With every ounce of strength I can find in my dying body, I drag the knife from its hiding place in the side of my pants.

"Die, *puta*," he shouts again. He's so close to my face, he doesn't see the knife in the air. I hold the knife above his head, then with a last burst of dying strength, I slam it into the side of his neck. His eyes widen and his mouth drops as the metal penetrates his skin. He finally loosens the grip on my neck.

I gasp new air into my scorching lungs. The anger in his eyes is now replaced with shock and pain. Blood pours from his neck and drips down onto my face. His hands leave my neck and slowly lift up to his own. He touches the serrated blade in his throat. I push him off my stomach and his heavy body rolls onto the floor.

I jump to my feet and stand over him. His body has started to convulse and his limbs are shaking. His chest rises and falls with quick, panicked breaths. I watch as crimson blood pours down the side of his neck, soaking the white area rug.

As he looks up at me, his eyes fill with the type of fear you must feel when you know you're about to die, when you know there is no way you can possibly fight back or live through this. A tear runs down his cheek and his mouth trembles. The shaking grows more violent. The blood pours faster, heavier. His eyes stay locked on mine, glassy and pleading for help.

I thought I'd feel some sort of pleasure as I watched a man who wanted to murder my parents die in front of me. I thought I'd get some sort of satisfaction watching the light fade from his eyes. But I don't. I don't feel pity or sadness either. I feel nothing, and as I watch him shake, I just want it to be over. I just want this to end. I reach around my waist and pull my pistol out from the back of my pants. I wrap my finger around the metal. I've held this type of gun a thousand times, but it somehow seems heavier in my hands now. Maybe because I'm light-headed—weakened from the fight— or maybe it's because I know that once I pull the trigger, I will always be a killer. I will always have someone else's blood on my hands.

Bang. The shot forces my body back. The bullet strikes him in the temple. The shaking stops. The hand he held at his neck falls to the ground. I stand there, my arms stretched in front of my body, my pistol still pointed straight ahead. I watch as blood streaks down his cheek from the bullet hole in his skull. His shallow breaths have ceased and I know he is dead.

My fingertips cautiously reach for the skin on my neck where his strong hands used to be. It stings. I pull my hands away, tuck my pistol into the back of my pants, step over the dead body, and pick my M4 up off the floor. I stand at the open door, lean my body against the door frame and listen.

I hear a struggle down the hall, and then someone yelling in pain.

Luke. I sidestep down the hall, my gun pointed in front of me, and follow the sound. Another grunt, a strike, someone loses their breath, a body falls.

I peer around the wall and Luke is down on the ground, a man straddling him on either side. Luke's fist makes contact with the man's jaw. Tiny droplets of blood splatter from his busted lip, dotting the cream walls.

"Te voy a matar, hijo de puta," he yells in Spanish. *I'll kill you, bastard.* He pulls a gun out of his pocket and unlocks the safety. Without even thinking, I raise my gun and fire.

The stifled pop of my M4 fills the hallway. My bullet strikes him in the back of his head. The gun in his hand drops to the ground as his body falls forward, on top of Luke.

My feet pound down the hallway. No need to be quiet anymore. They know we're here.

Luke pushes the man off of him, rolling him onto his back. The man's mouth is open. His eyes stare. Blank. Dead. I reach for Luke's hand, pulling him off the floor.

"Are you okay?" I brush Luke's bruised cheek with my fingertips. He winces and pulls away. Embarrassed, I return my hand to my side. "Sorry."

"No, it's all right. I'm okay," he says, taking my face in his hands and pulling it toward his until our foreheads touch. "Thank you for saving me."

"You would have done the same," I say and break out of our embrace. "Come on. They know we're here. We don't have much time."

Broken glass from fallen picture frames crunches under our feet. The only bit of color in the entire hallway hangs at the other end.

The sight of it makes my chest tighten. A large ornate cross covered in gold with large gemstones and diamonds in the center. Inscribed in a gold plate above the cross are the words *Sigue a Dios*. The fire inside me rages hotter. Beat, torture, murder . . . then hide behind the cross.

Luke stops and stares at the plaque next to me. "Follow God," I say, reading the inscription again. I grab the cross off the wall and slam it down with so much force, it shatters. Pieces of gold and rubies and diamonds scatter across the hardwood floor. I tear the plaque off the wall and throw it as far as I can. It lands near the guest room with a clang and slides toward the pool of blood near the dead guard's head.

I point my gun down the dark hallway toward the basement door. The hairs stand up on the back of my neck. I can feel his presence, sense his evil. I know he's on the other side of that door. I just pray my mother is with him and still alive.

THIRTY-ONE

THE BASEMENT IS DARK AND QUIET. IT FEELS FIFTEEN degrees colder than the rest of the house and the sudden change in temperature makes my skin throb.

Luke and I creep through the massive media room with plush leather chairs, a popcorn machine in the corner, and movie posters on the wall. *Scarface* hangs in the center. *Way to be a walking cliché, Torres.*

Luke points to an open door ahead. We both push our backs up against the wall and the textured gray wallpaper rubs against our gear with each step. We pause once our feet touch the door frame and listen for any sound on the other side. Nothing. I whip my body around the door and point my gun inside. A wine cellar. Thousands of bottles line the walls and a large table sits in the center with three wineglasses at every seat. This man lives very well. Running a drug enterprise is certainly more lucrative than being a Black Angel.

I give Luke the all clear and wave him forward, and that's when I see it. A closed door at the south end of the basement. According to the house plans, this is an unfinished storage space. A million pins prick my skin. I know she's in there, I can feel her. I nod toward the door and Luke's blue eyes widen.

The door feels cold and thick as I press my ear to it, hoping to hear something on the other side. There's a rustling and the clanging of metal, then a man speaking in Spanish followed by a woman's voice.

"Stop," she says. "Please, stop."

My heart is beating so loud now it drowns out the sounds on the other side. But I know that voice.

"It's her," I mouth to Luke. I gently test the doorknob. Locked. "Kick it in."

He takes two steps back as I ready my weapon, waiting to fire at Torres on the other side.

Luke counts down with his fingers. Five, four, three, two, one. I suck in a breath.

Boom. The door frame cracks as Luke smashes his foot against it, sending it crashing against the storage room wall.

I run into the room, my gun pointed in front of me, my trigger finger ready to shoot. And there in the corner, with a long, rusty chain wrapped around her wrist, is my nearly unrecognizable mother. Her cheek is purple, her arms slashed, blood dripping from her broken nose. Her white tank top and underwear are crusted with old blood as she lies on a dirty mattress on the floor. Behind her, with his back pressed up against the cinder-block wall is Torres, salt-and-pepper goatee, dark eyes, and thick, graying hair, holding a shiny pistol to my mother's head.

Mom looks at me, half terrified and half numb as she yanks at the choke hold Torres has on her neck. I point my weapon straight at his head. I want to pull the trigger but I don't have a clear shot. He's so close to Mom and they're both thrashing around. A half an inch off, and she'll meet the end of my bullet. It's too risky.

"It's over, Torres," I say, my voice fighting to stay steady. "Let her go."

"No, Reagan, don't," my mother pleads, her voice thin and her eyes panicked, screaming at me to run.

"I finally get to meet the famous Reagan Hillis," Torres says, his voice low and husky, his accent thick. "The chosen one, yes? So glad you could join us."

"Reagan, no! Leave now," Mom begs, her feet scraping against the gray concrete floor just beyond the mattress. She moves her body left, then right, trying to twist out of Torres's grasp. The metal chains around her arm clang against the wall as he pulls her body tighter.

"Where do you think you're going?" Torres hisses in her ear. Mom closes her eyes and pulls down on his arm. He doesn't budge. "I'm not done with you."

"All your men are dead," I say, my voice rising. "And I'll kill you too if you don't drop your weapon and let her go."

Torres throws his head back, a laugh bubbling up his throat. I shiver at the sound of it. "I'm not stupid. I was trained by the best too, you know. You don't have a good shot. You don't want to be responsible for killing your own mother. So I'll make it easy on you. I'll kill her for you."

Torres clicks the safety off of his pistol and points it at my mother's head, pushing the barrel into her temple.

"Reagan, run. Get out of here," she screams. My entire body

274

stings. I cannot feel my legs or hands or feet. I try to control the shaking that I know will soon follow, but my fingers have already started to tremble. I couldn't get a good shot off now even if I tried.

"Don't hurt her," I yell and lower my weapon. I take my finger off the trigger and hold the gun at my waist. "Take me instead."

"Reagan, don't," Luke says, keeping his weapon pointed squarely on Torres.

Torres's eyes turn away from my mother and focus on me. "Lay your weapon down and I'll think about it."

I bend my knees and place the gun on the ground. With my foot, I slide it toward him and his lips curl into a malicious grin.

"Reagan, no," my mother pleads. "Please, don't do this."

But it's too late. I raise my arms in the air.

"You wanted me, right?" I say, my voice stronger than I thought it would be. "I'm your revenge killing. So take me. Let her go."

"We tried to grab you at school," Torres says, licking his bottom lip. "But you were too smart for us. But your parents ... your parents were stupid. Stupid and slow. They always were that way. When they were trainees, I could take them down with one move. But you ... you are the strong one."

"Please, baby. Don't trade your life for mine," my mother whispers, her voice shaking, her hands still pulling down on Torres's arm. The long chains clang against the wall they are attached to, but she's too weak, too beaten and broken to fight him off. I look down at Mom's exposed legs. Black-and-blue swollen welts run across her shins as if someone had beaten her with a baseball bat. And all the emotions I've been fighting to keep in their little box start to spill out.

275

"What a beautiful daughter you have." Torres speaks slowly into my mother's ear and laughs again. His words are thick and sticky and make me nauseous. He looks back up at me. "What a lovely gesture, trading your life for hers."

"Don't you touch my daughter," my mother screams and thrashes with the most strength I've seen since walking into the room. She pushes her feet against the ground and throws their bodies backward, slamming Torres's head into the cinder-block wall behind him.

"You little bitch," Torres booms, lifting his pistol into the air and striking her across the face with so much force, her lip splits open. Dazed, she lowers her head and blood spills from her full bottom lip.

"Mom," I wail and take another step closer to them. Luke puts his arm out in front of me, holding me back. Hot tears sting my eyes, blurring my vision. I bite my tongue and push them away. I will not let him see me weak. "Leave her alone. You've got what you wanted. Let her go."

Bright red blood drips down my mother's chin, dotting her white tank top. Her blond hair, matted with sweat, hangs over her left eye. Torres takes the barrel of his gun and slides it across her forehead. Her body shakes as Torres uses the tip of his pistol to move her hair away from her eye.

"There, there, my princess," Torres says, kissing her forehead, watching my expression with each move he makes. I trap the scream in my throat. "You never expected to see your mother so weak, did you?"

"She's a strong woman," I say as I watch my mother trying to regain her sense of focus and control. Her hands slowly creep back up to Torres's left arm, still wrapped tightly around her neck. "You haven't fought fair, Torres. You've tied her up and let your hired hitmen beat the hell out of her. If you actually let her fight you, you know she'd break your neck in ten seconds."

"I find that hard to believe," Torres says, returning the barrel of the gun to the right side of Mom's head.

"Let her go. Unchain her and let her walk out the door with him," I say and nod toward Luke. "Then you can have me, the one you came for. Then you get even."

I take another step and hold out my hands. My legs are shaking, but my mind is clear. She could save more people than I ever could. She'll do more good in the world than me. This is the way it should be.

"No!" my mother cries as I step closer. Tiny pellets of blood shoot from her mouth with every word. "Reagan, I love you. I won't let you die for me."

"Let her go, Torres," I say, taking another step. His cold eyes lock with mine. I hold out my hands and feel calm, at peace. Ready to die in her place. Tears stream down her face and I know she's not crying for herself, but for me, for the choice I'm making. "My life for her life. Let my mother go."

"It's an intriguing offer," Torres says and tightens his grip on my mother's neck. "But you see, my only son is dead. He was four years old, killed by your mother. And a year ago, your parents killed my cousin. He was like a brother to me. So as much as I appreciate your offer, it's not enough."

"What more do you want?"

Please let her go. Please let her go. Dear God, help me. Please let her go.

But God doesn't hear me. God won't answer my prayer. I know it the second Torres's crooked smile rises up his face, buckling my knees.

"She has the blood of two of my loved ones on her hands. I want an eye for an eye."

"What does that mean?" I ask, my voice barely audible.

Torres stares at me and digs the gun deeper into my mother's temple. "That means . . . I kill you both."

My heart stops beating. I lock eyes with Mom just before he pulls the trigger. There's terror and regret and love. I squeeze my eyes shut and try to stop time. But the clock still ticks. The world still spins.

Bang. The sound of the shot rattles off the cinder-block walls and concrete floors. When I open my eyes, everything is blurry around the edges, like the world has fallen off of its axis. I look at my mother, blood pouring from her head, eyes closed. Her hair falls over her face as her body slumps and tumbles onto the dirty, stained mattress.

"No!" someone yells. A bloodcurdling scream follows and rings in my ears. It consumes the room and knocks any trace of air that remains in my lungs. It takes me a moment to realize the person screaming is me.

Pop. Pop. Pop. Luke opens fire on Torres, striking him in the shoulder. Torres takes a shot at me. It hits my bulletproof vest, knocking me backward. *Pop. Pop. Pop. Pop.* Luke fires from his M4 again, hitting Torres in the right side of his chest. Torres grabs his wound, takes one more shot, misses, and runs for a door in the back of the room. He slips through and disappears.

"Mom," I scream and sprint toward her. She's not moving. *Please, God. Please, God. Please, God.* It takes forever to reach her, the seconds feel like hours. I drop to my knees next to her, flip her onto her back, and grab her face, the blood from the bullet wound soaking into my hands. "Mom, please! Mommy!"

Pow. Pow. Pow. There are gunshots from somewhere else in the house. I don't care. I hold my mother's face, pull it toward me, and cradle her in my arms. "Mommy, I've got you. I've got you. Please wake up. Mommy, please wake up!"

"Reagan, we have to go," Luke says, grabbing me by the arm. "I hear more guards."

"We have to help her, Luke," I shriek and push him away. I kiss the top of her forehead. "She's hurt. She's really hurt. We have to stay and help her."

"We stay and we'll be dead too—come on," Luke says, pulling me up off the ground. I watch as my mother's head slips out of my hands and down onto the blood-soaked mattress.

"No! I won't leave her," I shout and try to kneel back down. My fingertips touch her cheek for a second before Luke picks me up by my waist and drags me toward the door.

"Let me go," I cry, trying to twist out of Luke's grip. "I have to help her."

"We have to get out of here or everyone is going to die," Luke yells at me, pulling me out of the storage room.

"No, Luke, no," I scream. I stare at my mother's face as he lifts me up and pulls me out of the room. She gets smaller and smaller and smaller. And then, she's gone.

"Reagan, stop," Luke yells as I flail in his arms.

"Put me down," I scream and pull at his fingers, struggling to get out of his firm grip.

"No, I won't let you die. We have to get back to the truck," Luke says and pulls me into the media room. He unlocks the door to the walk-out lower level and we're back outside.

Bang. Bang. Bang. Bang. Shots ring out from somewhere in the field.

"There they are," Luke says and points to the waiting truck, one hundred yards away. "Come on, Reagan. Run."

Bang. Bang. Bang. Bang. Luke pushes me up the hill from the basement and the two of us sprint to the truck. *Maybe the others can help my mother,* I think. *They'll come inside and save her.*

"Go, go, go," Luke yells to Eduardo and bangs on the side of the truck as we reach the back. Cooper and Laz grab my arms and pull me inside. Sam grabs ahold of Luke and pulls him in.

"We're in," Luke says into his earpiece and slams the truck door. The crashing metal makes me jump. "Go, Eduardo. Go."

"No, we can't go," I wail. I feel the truck move. I slam my hand on the side of the truck with all the strength I have, trying to get Eduardo to stop. "We have to go back for Mom."

"We can't, Reagan." Luke grabs me by the shoulders. "There's nothing to go back for."

"We have to help her." My voice is strained from screaming.

"What happened?" Dad asks from the other side of the truck, tears welling up in his eyes. His voice drops to a whisper. "Where's Elizabeth?"

"She's chained to the wall in the storage room." The truck makes a wild left turn. I grab on to the side to stop myself from falling over. "We have to go back there. We can't just leave her."

"Reagan, she's dead," Luke screams. He grabs me by the shoulders and shakes me, tears swimming in his blue eyes. "I'm sorry. She's dead."

"She's not dead," I shout and push him away.

"You saw her get shot," he says and grabs on to me again. "You saw the same thing I did. Torres shot her in the head."

"She's dead?" Dad asks, his voice shaking. He looks up at Luke, his lower lip trembling. "Is she really dead?"

"I'm so sorry, sir," Luke says and shakes his head. "There's no way she survived that gunshot wound."

"But we can't just leave her. We have to go back. We have to go back," I scream and reach for the truck's back door. Luke pulls me away by my waist and holds down my hands and my arms.

"Reagan, we can't," Luke says, his voice hushed and breaking in his throat. "She's gone."

And that's when I break down. Every part of me, my skin, my blood, my heart, my lungs, feels like they're being stabbed by a hundred knives. Pierced by a thousand bullets. Set on fire by a million matches.

"We have to go back," my voice squeaks as the pain doubles me over, racking my body with sobs. I search for new air but it doesn't come quickly enough. "We have to go back."

"Shhh. Shhh. Shhhh," Luke whispers in my ears, his arms holding me from behind. "Shhh. It's going to be all right."

"No, it won't," I scream. My legs are trembling. I fall to my knees. "It will never be all right again."

My body crumbles into a ball. Luke kneels next to me and puts his arms around my shoulders. I raise my hand to the center of his chest and push him away. I don't want him to touch me. I don't want anyone to touch me. *God, take me, take me, take me.* I hug my body to my knees. And I scream. And I scream. And I scream.

EPILOGUE

THE PLANE'S ENGINE ROARS, FILLING THE DEAFENING
silence in the cabin of the CIA's jet. After forty-eight hours of hiding
in Ecuador, CORE has finally given us clearance to return to DC.

Torres is alive. And looking for me.

The AC blasts from the vent above my head and a shiver con-
vulses my body. Luke feels my body twitch next to him. He carefully places his warm fingertips on top of my icy hand. For the first
time in days, I don't pull away. But I don't grab for him either.

I pull my burgundy cardigan tighter around me; Mom's favorite sweater from her go-bag. It still smells like her, a mixture of her
face cream and the Givenchy perfume Dad bought her every Christmas. I lift a corner of the fabric to my face and take her in. How
long can her smell linger? A month? Two months? By Christmas,
she'll be gone.

I haven't cried today. I feel strangely guilty about that but I think
I'm cried out. My body aches from hours of heavy sobs. The excruciating pain I've felt the last two days in the safe house has been

replaced by numbness. I don't feel anything, not the heartbeat in my chest, not the warmth of my blood, not the air in my lungs. I'm way past half dead. I know exactly what will happen once the numbness fades so I hold on to it for as long as I can. The pain will be replaced by rage, at myself, at Santino Torres, and I don't know if I'm ready to feel that yet.

We've already gotten instructions from CORE on Mom's cover story: a horrible car accident while overseas on an assignment. The car crash is just another lie I'll have to repeat over and over again for the rest of my life. I don't know what happened to her body. I get nauseous every time I think about her rotting away in some shallow grave on Torres's property or decaying at the bottom of the sea or reduced to ashes in a fire pit. That's the part that will keep me up at night.

Mom's not the first Black Angel they've lost. She won't be the last. I know CORE and the other operatives are doing everything they can to find Torres, but as each day passes, I already feel their intensity, their determination to find him and bring him to justice starting to fade. I'm not naive. This won't always be their top priority. Soon there will be new missions to complete, new hostages to rescue, new terrorists to take down. Elizabeth Hillis, her strength and kindness and bravery, will be talked about in hushed tones. When people speak of her, they'll call her a hero. But eventually, people will forget and her death won't be remembered as a horrible tragedy, a great loss for the agency and for the country, but just another casualty of the business.

But I won't forget. I won't forget the look of horror in her eyes as Torres pulled the trigger. I won't forget the blood and the tears and the lashings and the beatings I know she endured. I won't forget the love she gave me every day, the good she could have done in the world if he just would have let her walk away.

I close my eyes, flashes of her flood my mind. Mom in her robe the night before the last mission. Mom kissing my cheek as I finish the last bite of my breakfast. Mom pulling me on her lap as she braids my hair into two long pigtails. I think about Mom's favorite picture of us that she kept on her nightstand. I'm about five years old, sitting on Mom's lap, my hair freshly braided. My mouth is open and my almond eyes are so squinty, they're almost closed shut. I'm laughing like a maniac. Mom has her arms wrapped around me, her cheek pressed up against mine. She's smiling so big in that picture. I wonder what we were laughing about. And I wonder if I'll ever feel that happy again.

My mind pushes away each memory, knowing I never will. A tear slides down my cheek as that missing piece of me surpasses throbbing and crosses over into piercing pain. For me, the world will never look as colorful. The moon will never seem as bright. My laugh will never be as loud. My smile will never be as wide. Santino Torres took away the most important person in my life. And without her, he's stripped away every piece of me that was good.

But there's one thing he can't take away. He can't take my anger. He can't steal the rage that's beginning to flicker at my core. For now, it's just a spark, but soon it will be a flame, then a fire, then an uncontrollable inferno. Torres doesn't know it yet, but when he pulled that trigger, he signed his own death certificate.

I'm coming for you, Torres, my mind whispers. *I'm coming.*

TO BE CONTINUED . . .

ACKNOWLEDGMENTS

First and foremost, thank you to Jean Feiwel, Holly West, Lauren Scobell, and the entire Swoon Reads/Macmillan team. You've changed my life. Words cannot truly describe how grateful I am. I couldn't dream of a more brilliant, insightful, and enthusiastic team. You guys are total rock stars and I've loved every single minute of working on this book with you.

To Merrilee Heifetz: The day you called to offer me representation, I couldn't feel my face for two hours. And I still feel like I won the lottery. Thank you for your incredible guidance and support. To Allie Levick: Thank you for picking this book out of your slush pile and believing in it. I'm forever indebted to you.

To my bad-ass readers Maureen, Ellen, Christina, Christie, Jeanie, Emma, Heidi, Shannon, Sara, Deanna, Jen, Kate, Todd, Kristyn, Nicki, Maria, Kelsey, Elise, Meghan, Billy, Krista, Gwen, Brandi, and Rhonda: Your thoughts and insights have been invaluable. This book would absolutely not be the same without you. To the Swoon Readers who championed my book, especially Kathy

Berla: You guys are everything. To the amazing authors I've met along the way: I'm so thankful for your advice and friendship.

To Stephanie Paras: Thank you for your creative brain and life-long friendship. To Christopher Barcelona: Thank you for being the person I could call on about the biggest news or smallest detail. To Mila Goodman, my go-to idea bouncer: I'm so lucky to have access to your brilliance. To Julia DeVillers, my Literary Fairy God-mother: Thank you for helping me navigate this world. To Jen Meredith: Thank you for your boundless encouragement, support, and friendship. To Hannah Hill: Thank you for believing in me. There's no friend I'd rather celebrate every single life milestone with than you.

To my teachers, especially Dr. Leahy, Dr. Laycock, and P. F. Kluge: Thank you for the incredible foundation. You turned a flicker of passion for writing into an inferno. To my Resource family: From brainstorming marketing ideas to beta reading my book, I always feel your support. To my friends: I wouldn't be the same person without you in my life. Let's stay friends until we're wrinkled and gray. To my family: Whether you provided me with detailed research (looking at you Uncle Terry and Brendan) or were there to celebrate good news, I'm forever grateful.

Katie, my constant supporter and friend. Thank you for reading a million versions of this book and for always cheering me on. Mom, thank you for being my biggest fan. You're forever the bright spot in my life. Dad, thank you for reading basically every single word I've ever written. From middle school papers to this novel, it's your opinion I always can't wait to hear.

And finally, to Michael. I say it often, but here it is in black-and-white: You are truly the best husband a girl could ever ask for. There's no one in the world I would rather spend my life with than you. Thank you for being the most supportive person in my life, for encouraging me to write this book, and for sitting by my side while I did. I love you.

FEELING BOOKISH?

Turn the page for some

 **EXTRAS**

REAGAN'S GO-BAG CHECKLIST

1) **Mimi:** I'd cry myself to sleep if I lost that doll. She was a gift for my first birthday and I carried her everywhere with me for years. I love her curly yarn hair, outie belly button, and adorable plastic face. (She still has pink crayon at the corner of her mouth from where I tried to draw on lips when I was three. I wanted her to look like my Barbie!)

2) **Great-grandmother's pearls:** I'm not really a pearl-wearing kind of girl, but these pearls are special. They've been passed down through the generations and were given to me on my sixteenth birthday. If I have a daughter one day, I'll pass them down to her just as my mother passed them down to me.

3) **Photos:** I have an envelope full of family photos and a few Polaroids of myself with Harper, Malika, and Luke. I can't take any digital photos that could end up on Instagram or Snapchat. But one night at Luke's, Harper broke out the Polaroid camera. Since I could take the evidence of my existence with me, I finally agreed to a few pictures. Really, though, I just wanted photos of those three. They are the friends I will always miss and want to remember.

4) **Letters:** Every Christmas, Dad puts a handwritten letter in my stocking. He's been doing it since I was a little girl. It's probably my favorite present and something I look forward to when I wake up on Christmas morning. I also have some really personal letters Mom wrote to me when she was out on missions. Their letters are my most prized possessions.

5) **Weapons:** At the bottom of every go-bag is a compartment for my weapons. Two loaded Glock 22 pistols with ammunition to spare, two knives, and a bullet-proof vest. We have to leave home sometimes

in a matter of minutes. It's important for us to always be armed and prepared.

6) Food: Girl's got to eat. I always keep a couple of snacks in my bag that will stay fresh for a while. Packaged peanut butter crackers, chocolate, and Skittles. I also have some dehydrated meals in case of emergency, but they're not my favorites.

7) Electronics: I have a Black Angel–issued tablet (although it doesn't give me the same classified level access as my parents) and a prepaid cell phone in my go-bag at all times. We have to always be connected in some way to CORE, especially when we are on the run or in hiding.

8) Clothes: We often leave with just the clothes on our backs, so I keep a pair of jeans, a T-shirt, a pair of socks, an extra pair of boots, underwear, a bra, and a sweatshirt inside my go-bag along with toothpaste and a toothbrush. There's nothing that makes me feel worse than spending days in the same clothes, and I can't fall asleep without that minty toothpaste taste in my mouth.

A COFFEE DATE

between author Kristen Orlando and her editor, Holly West

"Getting to Know You"

HW: Who's your OTP (One True Pairing)? Your favorite fictional couple?

KO: I'm going to embrace my inner nerd and say Mulder and Scully from *The X-Files*. I watched that show on DVD and it was their relationship that made me such a binge watcher. For so many seasons, you're just waiting for those two to realize they're in love with each other. Their chemistry is so intense and they balance each other out perfectly. I was so happy when they finally got together in the end. (But good move by the producers and writers for keeping them apart. It kept me watching!)

HW: The Black Angels are like real-life superheroes. If you were a superhero, what would your superpower be?

KO: I would give just about anything to be able to teleport. I would love to wake up and teleport to the south of France for really soft scrambled eggs and a croissant while overlooking the Mediterranean Sea and then maybe teleport to Florence for a walk around an art museum and some gelato and then to Spain for sangria and tapas. Notice all of my teleporting destinations are tied to food. Perhaps my superpower should just be a really fast metabolism.

HW: Reagan and her friends are very into music. What about you? What bands do you listen to? Is music part of your writing process?

KO: I absolutely love all kinds of music. Music has been a huge part of my life from day one. My grandmother was a Big Band singer in the forties, so some of my earliest (and favorite) childhood memories are sitting by the piano while she sang fantastic American standards like "A Sunday Kind of Love," "Fools Rush In," and "Moonlight Serenade." My father had a huge record collection, so Saturday afternoons as a kid were spent running around the living room and dancing to bands like Chicago, the Doobie Brothers, and Fleetwood Mac. He introduced me to James Taylor, Joni Mitchell, Cat Stevens, and Carole King, so I've got a soft spot for singer/songwriters. I also grew up playing the piano, so classical (especially classical piano) is one of my very favorite things to listen to and what I listen to the most when I write. It helps me relax and focus.

"The Swoon Reads Experience"

HW: How did you learn about Swoon Reads?

KO: I came across an article about Swoon Reads online a couple years ago. I thought it was an amazing idea and such a fresh approach to publishing. With traditional publishing, your book lands on the desk of one editor and they may read it or they may not. And it's only their opinion. With Swoon, I loved that real readers were having an impact on what was getting published and that multiple editors (including Jean Feiwel) were weighing in on the final books that were selected. I thought it was such an amazing, progressive idea. Sort of like an *American Idol* for writers!

HW: What made you decide to post your manuscript?

KO: After I had written the book, I remembered the Swoon Reads article and thought to myself, I'll just submit it and see what happens! If anything, I thought it would be an awesome way to get direct feedback from readers.

HW: What was your experience like on the site before you were chosen?

KO: Amazing! The Swoon readers are so nice and I've honestly become good friends with some of the people I've met through Swoon. Writing is sometimes a lonely craft so it's great to connect with other writers. When I was writing my book, I kept it such a secret because I didn't know if it'd ever get published. I felt lucky to meet other great writers who shared my passion. I'm grateful for the friendships I've made. It's a very caring, supportive community.

HW: What was it like getting the call saying that you were chosen?

KO: I was at work when the email came through saying Swoon Reads wanted to talk to me. My stomach was in KNOTS waiting for you guys to call me. I had no idea if it meant I was chosen or maybe you were calling to say "Hey, we liked it, you were close, but we're passing!" I was SO excited when I finally got to talk to you and Lauren and hear that I had been selected. I was sitting on the steps of a stairwell in my office on the verge of tears I was so happy. I'll never forget that call or that moment. It was truly the biggest dream of my life come true. My heart was just bursting!

"The Writing Life"

HW: When did you realize you wanted to be a writer?

KO: I always liked to read but it wasn't until high school that I realized how much I loved writing. I was planning on following in my father's footsteps and becoming a doctor. I even applied to college premed. As passionate as I was about writing, I was actually scared to be good at it because I knew it would take me off the path of becoming a doctor. Becoming a doctor, while strenuous, has a direct path: college, med school, internship, residency. Writing is such an undefinable path. My freshman year at Kenyon College, I was sitting in biology and thought to myself, "I don't even really like this. What am I doing here?" My heart wasn't in it. My heart was in writing and as scary as that path was, I knew I wanted to write for a living. So I took the leap, changed my major, and immersed myself in English literature and writing classes. I started out my career as a television news producer and then jumped to marketing and advertising. In both careers, I wrote every single day and that helped me become a much better writer. I'm very grateful for my roundabout path to writing a novel.

HW: Do you have any writing rituals?

KO: I like to be super comfortable when I write so I will always change into sweatpants and a T-shirt. (Really, I'll find any excuse to be in sweats. I'd live my life in PJs if it was socially acceptable.) I didn't write a single word of this book sitting at a desk, always on the couch or recliner or a comfy chair. I do my best writing somewhere quiet with a little classical or jazz playing in the background.

HW: What inspired you to write *You Don't Know My Name*?

KO: I came up with the idea in the shower of all places. I had rented the movie *Red*, which is about a group of retired CIA agents whose lives are being threatened by assassins. After watching it I thought, what would it be like to be the daughter of one of those super-secret CIA agents? What an interesting and dangerous life. And then I thought, oh wow . . . that's a book!! Before the end of my shower I had come up with half the plot and was so excited about it, I wrapped myself in and towel and ran down the hallway dripping wet to see what my husband thought of the idea. He loved it and encouraged me to write it.

HW: Do you ever get writer's block? How do you get back on track?

KO: Definitely. It's so frustrating to stare at a blank screen! Depending on what I'm writing, I'll sometimes listen to music that will get me into the mood of the chapter or watch movie or TV clips that convey the actions or emotions I'm trying to capture. I'll also crack open a book and read words from writers I admire. Their greatness inspires me to try to create something I can be proud of.

HW: What's the best writing advice you've ever heard?

KO: One of the best pieces of life advice I've ever gotten I apply to writing. My dad once told me, "Never be satisfied with success and never fear failure." It's the "never fear failure" part that has really stuck with me. When thinking about writing a book, there are so many roadblocks you could throw up: I'm not good enough, I'll never get it published, it's so hard to find an agent, I don't have time, etc. But his advice made me a close-your-eyes-and-jump kind of girl. I'd much rather try and fall flat on my face (and believe me I have . . . figuratively and literally—I'm quite clumsy) than never try at all. I'm so glad I took the chance to write this book. If you fear failure, you'll never know what you can accomplish.

YOU DON'T KNOW MY NAME

DISCUSSION QUESTIONS

1) How is Reagan MacMillan different from Reagan Elizabeth Hillis? What type of personality does Reagan try to project in front of her friends? Which one feels like the "real" Reagan to you?

2) Reagan suffers from "daymares" after Philadelphia. Do you think she should have spoken up about her problem? What stopped her from telling the truth?

3) One of the Black Angels' strictest rules is no social media. How would not being on social media impact your life?

4) Reagan feels pressure to follow the path that has been planned for her by her parents rather than following her heart. Can you relate to her struggle? How?

5) Reagan finally gives into her emotions and feelings for Luke. Was that selfish? Have there been times when you finally stopped listening to your head and listened to your heart?

6) Reagan decides to hurt Luke by kissing Oliver. Do you agree with the way Reagan pushed Luke away? Would it have been better if she just disappeared or would it have hurt him even worse?

7) The Black Angels' unofficial mantra is: "To whom much is given, much is expected." Do you think the life Reagan is given makes up for the danger she's put in?

8) Reagan tells her mother she's selfish for being both a Black Angel and a mother. Do you agree or disagree? Why?

9) Reagan breaks several layers of Black Angel protocol to get to Colombia to help save her parents. Do you understand why she broke the rules? Or was she out of line?

10) Do you want Reagan to choose a normal life or become a Black Angel? Why? If you were in Reagan's shoes, what life would you choose?

Becoming a Black Angel is the only way Reagan will be able
to exact revenge on her mother's merciless killer, Santino Torres.
But soon, her friend Luke joins her at the Black Angels training compound
and Reagan finds herself once again torn between the person
she was and the person she wants to be. . . .

KEEP READING FOR AN EXCERPT.

ONE

MY EYES FLIP OPEN AND MEET THE BLACK. THERE'S not a trace of pale light in this windowless room. The first two seconds are bliss. With my first conscious breath, I forget. But the next breath comes, tighter this time; that feeling of dread, a dark cloud, a shade deeper than this room, coils its way around my lungs. And I remember where I am. Why I'm here. What I've done.

I was a sound sleeper as a child. Mom said I wet my bed until the age of five, not because I didn't know how to use the bathroom, but because I slept so hard, even that urgent pulse in my bladder couldn't stir me awake. I haven't had a restful night of sleep since I was eight. Not since my parents sat me down over a scalding plate of chicken pot pie and told me what they really did for a living. Those long, dense stretches of shadowy sleep vaporized like the steam off my plate. Even as a kid, I think I was waiting for something bad to happen. I'd startle awake in the middle of the night, listening. Waiting. Watching. My fingers would search for the knife behind my headboard, and only until I felt its cool blade on my skin could I fall back asleep. The pluck and buzz of its steel was my screwed-up lullaby.

For the last six months, there's been no getting me back to sleep. Sam has tried with her tiny blue pills. I let them knock me out night after night because without them I'd never sleep. But once I'm awake, I'm up. There's no lulling me back into the misty gray of drug-induced rest.

I can hear Sam breathing somewhere in the darkness. I shift my weight, searching for her clock, and the military-style bunk bed creaks beneath me. The bright red digital numbers read 4:00 on the dot. It's the first time I've woken up on such a clean number. Last night it was 3:24. The night before: 4:51. The night before that: 5:42. I've been making mental notes of those times, memorizing the numbers, like they're going to mean something or decode some important secret. I know they won't. But locking in those numbers, tracking the time my body jolts me awake, feels like the only thing I've had control of since the fall.

My body slowly rises, my muscles rigid as I try not to make a sound. If Sam wakes up, she'll tell me I need more sleep before the Tribunal. She'll place another blue pill into my palm and stand over me while I choke it down. My feet leave the warm cocoon of blankets and find the icy, concrete floor. Goose bumps rise on my skin as my toes search for my slippers. My hands feel for the sweatshirt at the bottom of the bed, on loan from one of the Black Angel operatives. When the watchers transported me from the safe house yesterday, it was an unseasonably warm April day. Eighty degrees by noon. But several stories belowground, I've lost all sense of warmth. Of time, too.

I carefully pull on the door, cracking it just enough to slip my body through without letting too much hallway light spill into our cavernous, nearly empty dorm. The dorm is where all the female Black Angel trainees sleep when they're stationed at CORE. But their year in the Black Angel Qualifiers is nearly up and most have either been cut or are stationed all over the world, fighting for those last spots in the Black Angel Training Academy.

The sight of the empty hallway forces a cold and steady breath through my pursed lips. When I'm at CORE, all I get are questions in the form of words or looks. The concerned queries may be even worse than the debriefing questions from senior leaders, judgment and anger wrapped like barbed wire around every word. Those, I can handle. The "how are yous" I cannot. It's not even what they say or how they say it. It's the expectant body language that makes the tide of bile rise in my stomach. Head lowered and cocked to one side. Watery eyes. Lips creased into a sympathetic frown. A hand that carefully reaches for my shoulder. Most of the time I pull away. But if I'm feeling compassionate, I let them touch me. I remind myself they've lost her too.

My fingers brush alongside the cinder block walls in the tunnel beneath Langley. Thousands of the world's best spies track terrorists or intercept threats against the United States several stories above my head, having no idea this tunnel, these Black Angel situation rooms and training facilities even exist.

Six months ago, I never thought I'd see the inside of CORE. I was ready to turn my back on the Black Angels, escape into the warmth of a normal life. But now I'm back in the shadows, desperate to reclaim my place here. The people who once applied the most pressure to get me into the training academy are the ones pushing me out. It's been a long fall off the precarious pedestal they forced me upon. And I don't even know if I've hit bottom yet.

"What are you doing up?" a voice says from behind me. I turn around to see Sam mid-yawn, her hands fumbling through her sleep-matted blond hair.

"Can't sleep," I answer quietly. Sam walks toward me in plaid pajama bottoms and an oversized Georgetown sweatshirt.

"You really need your rest," Sam answers, looking toward the digital clock stationed at the end of the hallway. "You've got a long day ahead of you. I could give you half a—"

"No," I answer and shake my head slowly. "I'm fine. No more pills tonight."

Sam's eyes scan my face, her eyebrows raised, not believing me. The crescent gray moons that cradle my dark eyes give away my exhaustion. I lower my eyelids and dig my teeth into my sore, inflamed lips. I've been picking them again, an anxious tic my mother broke me of years ago. It's like my nerves know she's not here to gently grab my hand, pull it to my side. Without her, I've been pulling at long strips of dry skin until my lips are either completely smooth or red with metallic blood. Each tear is a risk with conflicting outcomes. There is no in between.

"Well, I guess we're both up for the day," Sam says, taking a seat on the steel bench outside one of the situation rooms. "Breakfast doesn't start for two hours. So come sit with me."

She pats the space next to her. I don't answer. Just stare at the cement floor, my legs pulling me toward her. I grasp the cold, smooth surface and lower myself down. The hallway's fluorescent lights' incessant buzzing burrows into my ear canals, sending a shiver down my body. I pull the collar of my borrowed sweatshirt toward my face and get a whiff of something floral. I breathe it in again, trying to decode the scent of a stranger. Lavender? Or maybe jasmine?

I wait for Sam to speak. She waits for me to do the same. My eyes stare forward at the white cinder block. I count the number of paint globs that hug the curve of each stone. One, two, three, four.

"They're going to tear me apart, aren't they?" I finally ask. In my peripheral vision, I can see Sam's face turn toward mine, but my eyes stare straight ahead, fixed on those tiny white globs.

Sam breathes in a heavy sigh. "I can't lie to you, Reagan. I can't tell you about the questions they asked me either. But my testimony yesterday was . . ."

"Brutal," I answer and suck in a painful breath. She doesn't need to answer. I know it was. I saw it all over her face when she hugged me hello in the dorm after I arrived. She smiled, her voice brimming with forced cheerfulness. But fear lingered in her two pools of blue and no matter how many times her eyes fluttered, she couldn't blink her worry for me away. "It's okay. I already know what will happen. I know they're going to question every single move I made. Pick apart every little choice until they can prove I got her killed."

"Don't say that, Reagan," Sam says and grabs for my wrist. "You did everything you could. You were willing to trade your life for hers. You have to fight to stay here or you're as good as gone. They want you out. You couldn't save her, but you can still save yourself."

"I know," I reply as an icy breath filters through my raw lips. Jagged pieces hit me all at once. That flash of light. That waterfall of blood. Mom's eyes, pleading and afraid. I put my free hand to my face and furiously shake my head, trying to erase the memory before I hear the echo of my own screams.

"But maybe they're right," I continue as the memory breaks apart. "Maybe if I had done one thing differently she'd still be alive. Maybe if I hadn't gotten in a fight with her, they'd have pulled me out of New Albany earlier and Torres would never have found them. Or maybe if I hadn't gone to Colombia at all or stayed on the truck or . . ."

"Stop," Sam says, her warm hands tightening around my freezing skin. "If you hadn't made those choices, they'd *both* be dead."

"Yeah, but maybe if I had let Laz go after her or shot Torres when I had the chance . . ."

"Reagan, no," Sam says, her gentle voice giving way to the beginnings of exasperation. "You can't do this to yourself. You can't or you'll go insane."

"Then I guess I'm insane," I say, my voice monotone. My breath becomes slower, shallower. Soon, the only sound I hear is the *tick, tick, tick* of Mom's favorite watch, which I've kept permanently on my wrist since Colombia; a present from her parents after medical school that she always kept in her go-bag.

Sam's fingers slowly slide off my wrist. She leans her back against the cold, cinder block walls and we settle into a heavy silence.

"I can't believe I'm even here," I say softly, searching up and down the deserted hallway.

"In this position or in this building?" she asks.

"Both, I guess. After all my training. After all the bullshit they've pumped into my head, trying to make me believe I'm special or something. The training camps and pep talks and money they've invested. I can't . . ."

A toxic mix of anger and sadness bubbles up my throat, stealing my voice. I face Sam; her kind eyes urge me to continue.

"I can't believe how fast they've turned on me. You should have seen the look on their faces when I said I still wanted into the academy. You'd have thought I told them I put my own gun to my mother's head."

After days of debriefing post-Colombia, Thomas Crane, my parents' main contact at CORE, and the other senior leaders were ready to hand me my new life, confined to a single manila envelope. New name, new passport, new driver's license, new cover story. Reagan Olson. Seventeen-year-old high school senior with a dead mother and government official father. They had secured a spot for me in a foreign boarding school. Said they'd get me into the University of Oxford or the Sorbonne, far out of the reach of Torres. Provide me with my own security detail. I told them that wouldn't be necessary. That I'd be attending the training academy with the new recruits this summer. With that, every eyebrow in the room rose in unison. Their mouths unhinged. I don't know if they were surprised I still wanted to be a Black Angel after everything that had happened or if they were just stunned by my nerve. I can only imagine what they're saying about me behind closed doors. The girl who breaks every rule, defies orders, gets her mother killed, and still thinks she belongs. Ballsy move, chick.

Thomas had put his hands in his pockets, his eyes fixed on the ground. Seconds ticked by. Perhaps he was waiting for me to say I was joking. How could I imagine I'd still be allowed in? After what I just did?

"That decision is no longer yours to make, Reagan," Thomas

finally said. "You have lost your automatic bid into the training academy. You'll have to plead your case before the Black Angel Tribunal and see if they'll even allow you into the Black Angel Qualifiers. If they let you in, you'll have to try out like everyone else."

And that was that. Only two spots in the training academy are offered to Black Angel children right out of high school, and the female spot that had been promised to me now belonged to someone else. And there was nothing I could do or say to get it back.

After my debriefing, I was shipped off to a farmhouse in rural Virginia. With Torres off the grid and promising revenge, I've spent the last several months cut off from the world, surrounded by security cameras and guards but no real people. Just online high school courses and Netflix to occupy the endless hours alone. Dad and Sam made the two-hour trip to check on me when they could. But my body still ached with loneliness for my mother, for my friends. Luke was whisked off the plane after we landed from South America and transported who knows where. I haven't been allowed to talk to him or Harper or Malika. We are ghosts to one another. Half memories and unanswered questions. It's hard to even think about them. But I'd do it all over again; I'd alienate myself from the world for twice the time for the chance to become a Black Angel. Because it's the only way I will find him. And kill him.

My fate now lies in the hands of five senior leaders. Five votes determine if I'll ever be able to snuff out the rage that flickers at my core. It's a slow-burning ember now, but its smoke has begun to fill my body, choke my lungs. This fire will soon engulf me and won't stop until I put a gun to the head of Santino Torres and watch his crimson blood pool from his brain.

Check out more books
chosen for publication
by readers like you.